Lost Days

Neive Denis

Book 12 in the Sonoma Whittington, Private Investigator, series

Copyright

First published in 2024
Copyright © Neive Denis 2024
All rights reserved.

Cataloguing-in-publication data
Creator: Denis, Neive, author

Cataloguing-in-Publication details are available from the National Library of Australia
www.trove.nla.gov.au

ISBN: 978-0-6489423-9-9 (paperback)
ISBN: 978-1-7635109-0-6 (digital)

Cover design: T A Marshall, Mackay, Australia

Disclaimer

This novel is a work of fiction. All characters and events are the product of the imagination of the author. While some of the characters might remind you of people you know, they are fictitious and any resemblance to anyone living or dead is purely coincidental. Although some locations also may seem real and familiar, most places referred to in this work constitute a collage of places the author has known and are fictitious. Any resemblance to an existing location is coincidental.

Chapter 1

"Oh, argh... my head....," I yelped as I tried to sit up. "How much did I drink? I don't remember a party."

I lay still, eyes firmly clamped shut, and trying to control my breathing – and my churning stomach. How long I remained there motionless and gritting my teeth remains a mystery because, within moments, I felt a wave of blackness descending again. While I don't know how long it was, I suspect it was sometime later before I became aware of myself again. Remembering my earlier attempt to sit up, I dismissed any thought of trying that a second time.

Without even twitching and eyelash, I remained as still as possible, only allowing my hands to feel what lay beneath them. It wasn't sheets or other bedclothes they discovered, and it took all my willpower to remain unmoving and not to spring up to explore further.

Whatever was under my hands – and presumably under me – felt damp and gravelly. How can this be, the little voice in my head demanded. Determined not to move and cause myself further pain, I ignored it, but that little voice was right. How could I be lying on damp gravel? Still not game to move, I forced open one eye – just a little – to squint at my surroundings.

Nothing. Nothing but thick, seemingly impenetrable blackness greeted me. I snapped that eye closed again and concentrated on keeping my pulse and breathing as normal as possible. After what felt like hours, but probably was no more than a minute or so, I tried another squint at my surroundings. This time, I kept it open and focused on the blackness around me until shapes began to emerge out of the darkness.

Buildings. I was almost sure they were the shapes of buildings (perhaps structures might be a better description) oozing into view. I closed my eye and waited a few moments before opening it again. This time, I felt braver and allowed my other eye to join its partner. It seemed to take ages for both eyes to be in sync and focus properly, but they did confirm structures of some sort surrounded me.

It was night. That much was clear, but what at first appeared an impenetrable darkness proved not to be the case. There was a moon, not much, but enough for me to distinguish shapes around me.

"Okay, it's night, and I appear to be lying on damp ground somewhere," I confirmed to the universe before continuing. "But where is 'here'? And how did I get here?" I carefully avoided asking, 'and how long ago?'.

The answer to that question might prove more than I could handle at this point of my exploration. One thing was clear. I did need answers. The other clear thing was that finding those answers was likely to involve a whole load of pain. I took a couple of deep breaths and then slowly, ever so slowly, rolled my head a little to the left. A sickening pain shot through me. I gritted my teeth and fought down the bile burnings my throat. Again, I lay there with my eyes closed for a few moments before embarking on the next big step.

That last manoeuvre brought the side of my face into contact with the gravel surface beneath me, but the pain that accompanied it dissipated more quickly than I expected. I opened my eyes and waited for the few seconds it took for them to focus again. So far, no immediate answers were forthcoming. Without moving my head, I allowed my eyes to roam freely within their field of vision. There wasn't much to see.

Not too far in front of me, my field of vision was cut short by something I couldn't immediately identify. I concentrated on my breathing while my eyes examined what was in front of them. At first, there was something strange – almost out of this

world – about it, but the recognition finally
managed to seep through the fog filling my head.

"It's corrugated iron. Yeah, corrugated iron," I advised the universe in a somewhat croaky voice.

Continued visual examination of the wall in front of me didn't produce anything more enlightening. Something about the iron suggested it was old. Maybe it was the patches of rust visible here and there across its surface. By looking down as hard as I could, I could almost see the bottom edge of the wall. A strip along the edge of the iron looked badly rusted and decayed.

What is this building? What is this place? How did I get here? Those questions were on a continuous loop running through my mind. It seems it didn't matter how many loops they did, they found no answers along the way. I knew what had to be done. Did I have the intestinal fortitude to do it? I'm no hero when it comes to pain, and I knew my quest for answers would be accompanied by a wealth of pain. Of that, I was sure… But I was equally sure it had to be done. Nevertheless, necessary as it may be, there was no point in making it any worse than it had to be.

"Sonny Whittington, you can do this," I snarled at myself. "You *have* to do it. So, get on with it."

A quick assessment of my situation indicated I wasn't lying quite on my side, but definitely leaning towards my left. Levering myself upright from my present position seemed impossible. There remained only one real alternative. Placing both my hands firmly on the ground, I eased myself up onto my left elbow. Everything began to swim before my eyes. My stomach became a roiling mass. I clamped my eyes closed, took a couple of deep breaths, and swallowed hard a few times. Then, feeling relatively in control again, I opened my eyes and took stock of what my efforts had produced.

My head still felt a bit dizzy. My eyes took a little while to refocus properly, but slowly shapes began to emerge around me. It was difficult to tell whether they were buildings or just structures housing equipment of some sort. The one thing that was clear was that they were old and not elaborate. Although I couldn't make out the finer details, I guessed the main cladding material was more of the same corrugated iron as I had discovered earlier.

It was obvious, even in my befuddled state, that this was some form of industrial site. What went on here was unclear. The one thing that did become clear to me as I visually examined my surroundings was that the place was old. And, along with being old, there was something else about it. Within a few moments, I realised what that something else was. The place looked abandoned. I felt a cold wave of fear run through me. One thing was certain. I didn't have the luxury of time to lie here on the wet ground contemplating my surroundings.

Gritting my teeth, I eased myself up into the sitting position and leaned back against that first corrugated iron wall I had discovered. The view from the upright position was no better and no more enlightening.

Turning my head a millimetre to expand my view resulted in a sharp pain. I waited for the pain to subside and my senses, such as they were, to return before investigating the source of the pain. Gingerly exploring the side of my head with my hand produced worrying results. I found a huge lump nestled in a clump of blood-matted hair and a substantial trail of dried, crusty blood running down the side of my face past my ear. I didn't need an expert to tell me this was a serious wound, but how had it happened? I had no memory of an accident or altercation that might have been the cause. What I did know, however, was that now, I really was concerned about my welfare.

"Where the hell am I?" I bellowed into the night. Nothing was forthcoming… not even an echo.

Chapter 2

After a few minutes of leaning against the rusting corrugated wall and having learnt nothing new, I needed to take a more radical approach to establishing my present location. The process of moving from a semi-reclined sitting position to being upright on two feet was not something I relished, but it had to happen. Without moving my body too much, I swept my arms out from my body across the ground as far as my arms could reach.

My right hand encountered a metal rod of some sort. By probing around it with my fingers, I guessed it might be about two centimetres in diameter. While I didn't know how long it might be, I figured that, if I could work it free of the soil it lay half buried in, it might prove handy in some way. After a bit of digging around it with my fingers and shaking it as best I could, the rod came free. Then, lying across my lap, I estimated it to be approximately 150 centimetres long.

"Ah, just what I needed," I told the universe… before getting on with the job of dragging my way upright.

By using it in much the same way as a hiker's pole, I pulled myself hand-over-hand up the upright pole until I stood beside it and held it in a white knuckle grip as I battled not to pass out again. But, at last, I was on my feet and, as soon as my head stopped spinning, I would investigate the site as best I could in the semi-darkness.

Leaning heavily on my metal pole, it didn't take long to confirm this had at one time been a mine site and, more importantly, that it had been long abandoned. I hobbled to what looked as though it might have been the site's admin building. A small, standalone, corrugated iron shack. Small windows set high in both its end walls, long ago, had the glass smashed out of them. At some time in the past, the top hinge on the heavy timber door had rusted through, allowing the door to hang at a crazy angle and slightly ajar. Its front corner rested on the ground, and over the years, dirt had piled up against the door. The only way to open that door would be to remove the dirt piled up against it. It wasn't a thought I entertained, as I knew there would be nothing of any help to me inside.

I hobbled over to what looked like a rusting drum of some sort and tested it for soundness. It seemed solid enough, so I perched my rear end on it and allowed the top half of my body to hang off my hiker's pole. As I glanced down at my feet, it registered that I was wearing only one shoe. It would explain why it had been so difficult to walk. Looking for the missing sneaker would be pointless. It was too dark to find it, and it might not be here anyway. I undid the laces and removed the remaining shoe. Now, it would make hobbling a bit easier.

From my new vantage point, I could see that the buildings had been laid out in a semicircle around some form of large, cleared space. It wasn't difficult to imagine a constant flow of trucks entering and leaving the area in front of me in a circular fashion through the cleared area. Snaking off into the distance from this forecourt was a track. It appeared to be the only way in or out of the site. Although I didn't know where it led, it had to go somewhere... And 'somewhere' was probably better than here.

As I made my way across the forecourt-type area, I confirmed my thoughts regarding vehicles turning in this space. More precisely, I confirmed a vehicle recently had done just that. Was it the chariot that brought me here? The thought that had been trying to have me acknowledge it suddenly hit home. It was the realisation that none of my vehicles were evident anywhere on this site and, if I didn't arrive in my own car, how else did I get here? There was nothing for it but to explore that track. My chances of someone finding me here in this abandoned place were about zero to none.

Walking was a little easier now I had shed both shoes, my head throbbed, and I found that every few metres, I was forced to stop and hang heavily on my pole as the world around me started to swim, and I again threatened to pass out. The shortest route between two points is a straight line. Once I was up off my rusting perch, I made a beeline straight for the entrance to that track.

It must be some time since this track saw any traffic. The surrounding scrub had spent that time slowly encroaching on the edges of the track to now reduce it to a narrow, rutted strip of dirt running off into the blackness of the night. The overarching branches and closeness of the scrub seem to exclude even the faintest hint of moonlight. Stumbling along in that darkness, I hadn't gone far when something made me stop and reassess my situation.

The surface of the track was strewn with branches and leaves that had done their damnedest to trip me as I trudged through them. I stopped to think about it and experienced a rare moment of rational thought. Was the vehicle that brought me here responsible for the debris now littering the track? I hurried back to the forecourt area to check the tyre tracks I had seen there before I entered the track.

Yep, just as I thought. The wheelbase of the vehicle that left those tyre marks was wider than the track. So, yes, it was likely that vehicle tore the branches from the scrub as it crashed its way along the rough track. Confirming the fact didn't help me much and didn't encourage me about my options at all. I had to accept the vehicle that left those tyre tracks and tore the branches from the trees was probably the same one that delivered me to this place. And, no other vehicle had been here for a long while before it. I felt myself returning to the hope that the track might lead me to something akin to, if not population, at least habitation.

There was nothing for it but to set off down the track again. A new worry accompanied me on my trek. I was thirsty and badly dehydrated. I needed water, but I hadn't seen even as much as a puddle to tempt me. Somewhere in the deep reaches of my befuddled brain, my self-preservation instinct kept telling me it hoped the track didn't go on for too long before breaking out into the open again.

My lank, damp hair clung to my scalp and face, and the crusty blood down the side of my face had absorbed the moisture and started to run and drip onto my shirt. How long had I been stumbling along the track? How much had I covered? It seemed like I'd been stumbling and tripping along for hours. I had no idea how far I'd travelled. On one of my rest pauses that were becoming more frequent and at shorter intervals, I looked along the track in desperation. Surely, it had to end soon, and I would break out of the scrub and into the open. Was it becoming lighter, or was it simply my eyes becoming more accustomed to the gloom? For a brief moment, I almost convinced myself more moonlight was penetrating the canopy above me. It wasn't as if I could see any light at the end of the track. I fought not to get my hopes up that it was becoming lighter around me.

At last, a lighter patch was evident further down the track ahead of me. Tears rolled down my cheeks as I tried to push myself forward towards it at an increased pace. I only succeeded in falling on my face again and had to endure once more the process of hauling myself to my feet with the aid of my pole. But minutes later, I had reached the end of the track and a fence that divided it from what appeared to be a sealed road.

A double wooden gate that once stood at the entrance to the track now lay crumpled like a stale biscuit on the ground at the start of the track. It didn't take me too much effort to work out that the gate had been rammed by a vehicle that then ran over the gate as it drove onto the property. There would have been no serious damage to its tyres. The gates' wood was so old and rotten that the vehicle's tyres had left it a mass of pulped fibres surrounded by several short pieces of rotten timber.

I picked my way around the remnants of the gate and out onto the wide grassy strip along the side of the sealed road. But I could go no further. My mouth and throat were so dry, I couldn't even produce spit. My tongue felt about three times its normal size and, some time ago, had glued itself to the roof of my mouth. I needed water, and I needed it now – before it became too late. While my head wound contributed to some extent to my light-headedness, I knew dehydration was also a major part of why I was constantly on the verge of passing out. I was becoming desperate and needed to sit down... before I fell down.

A few metres from where I stood, along the outside of the fence line, I spotted a couple of substantial-looking concrete plinths. Earlier in the history of this place, the plinths probably held significant signage relating to the property behind it. For the moment, however, the nearest plinth provided a welcome seat that wouldn't be too difficult to clamber off should the need arise, and I wouldn't injure myself too badly if I passed out and fell off it.

After a few moments perched on the plinth, a small part of the fog in my head cleared. My brain kicked into gear again. As I sat staring semi-trancelike at the bitumen road in front of me, a thought wormed its way to the forefront of my thinking: a sealed road ran from somewhere to somewhere else. Logically, there should be a 'somewhere else' at either end of that road in front of me. Logic also told me that at one end of the road might be a township or suburb. While, at the other end, there might be nothing more than farms and the occasional home. The little voice in my head was telling me either one would do. Just get off your backside and head along the road in one direction or the other. I chose to ignore it, believing I didn't even have the stamina to lift myself off the plinth, let alone wander along that road.

Slow though it was, clearer thinking returned. Perhaps there might be some evidence on the bitumen to suggest which way would be the better option, should I find the strength to continue. Heaving myself off the plinth with the aid of my pole, I staggered out onto the bitumen. Yes, there it was, a clue as to which way I should go.

The pulped rotten wood from the gate had lodged in the tyres of the vehicle as it drove off the mine site property. Then, as it drove along the sealed road, it left a barely discernible but clear trail of the gate's pulped timber. I felt a new determination surge through me as I stood on the edge of the bitumen, examining the evidence left by the vehicle.

No doubt existed in my mind. The vehicle that left those tracks was the same one that brought me and dumped me on the abandoned mine site. It's tracks indicated that, once it left the property, it headed towards my left along the sealed road. For wont of any better option, I would follow its lead. I stepped out onto the bitumen, turned to my left, and looked along the road for some clue as to my destination. Nothing helpful was visible. The road seemed to stretch on for some distance ahead of me before a slight curve hid anything further ahead from view.

Although I wouldn't allow myself to accept my end was near as I stumbled along the bitumen, tearing my jeans and grazing my knees, I knew I was in dire straits. How long I progressed in that manner is unknown, but it felt like days. Increasingly, I felt in danger of losing consciousness. I hadn't heard the vehicle approaching and wasn't aware of it until it beeped its horn at me. In trying to turn around to see what was happening, I fell over. Try as I might, I didn't have the strength to get up again.

When I opened my eyes, my view was filled with the brightness of a high-visibility work shirt. Strong hands and arms eased me up into a sitting position and held me there for a few moments, probably until I seemed stable enough not to require further assistance to sit there. The high-vis shirt came around and squatted in front of me. All I could see was the shirt. The wearer's face remained a blur. My attempt at speech failed.

I frantically gestured drinking, and hoped the request translated okay.

Suddenly, the shirt disappeared briefly before returning with a bottle of water. Despite the man's efforts to make me lower the bottle, I think I glugged down about half its contents before he succeeded in forcing me to stop.

"Take it easy there, Miss. You won't do yourself any good guzzling down too much in one go. You should just sip it for a while."

Granted, this bloke knew his stuff, and his advice was correct, but I was dying of thirst and knew what I needed. I tried to tell him so. Nothing but a faint croak came out. I snatched the bottle back up for another couple of swigs … before he wrestled it away from me.

"Have you been in an accident?" he asked, eyeing me up and down.

I shook my head and tried to speak. Only a croak emerged. I swallowed a couple of times and tried again.

"An accident of sorts, I suppose," I managed in response. "What time is it? Isn't it too early for you to be going to work? The sun hasn't come up yet."

"It's about 4.45AM, but yeah, I'm on my way to work. We're pretty busy at work, so we are running two shifts. I'm on the early shift that starts at six o'clock. Look, I do have to go, but can I give you a lift somewhere? Is there somewhere you want to go?"

"Where do you work?"

"The industrial area in Millhaven."

"Great. Millhaven is where I need to be if you wouldn't mind dropping me somewhere. I know I look a bit frightening, but I promise, I'm not toxic." And then I wondered about my last comment.

Was I toxic? What were they mining at that site, and could it have involved toxic materials of some sort? I decided that might be a question for another time and place. Right now, all I wanted to do was to get to Millhaven. Somehow, while I'd been wondering about my possible toxicity, the young lad had helped me up into the passenger's seat in his 4x4 ute.

About ten minutes later, he drove up onto Ben Richards' driveway and stopped.

"Do you have a key? I'll go and unlock the door for you."

A key…. Now, that would be handy, I thought as I ran my hand over all my pockets for the first time since regaining consciousness. I didn't expect to find a key or anything else for that matter, but I thought it worth a look. Having found nothing, I simply shook my head in response to his question.

"Ok-ay… Should I ring the bell or something? What do you want me to do? I can't just leave you here like this."

After a bit of a fumble, I managed to open my door. And then made the mistake of looking down. Everything started to swim before my eyes. I threw myself back into my seat and snapped my eyes closed. That's how I was when I heard a familiar voice.

"Good morning. Can I help you with something?" It demanded.

Ben Richards had arrived home from his morning run and hadn't expected to find a strange truck parked on his driveway. I tried again to open the door and met with the same result as before. Determined to get out of the truck, I was about to try the door again when it opened. My rescuer had run around and opened the door for me.

"Hang about. Don't try to do anything silly. Let me help you down." I swivelled round on my seat and swung my legs to the outside, ready to be helped out of the truck.

"I'll take it from here, thanks," that familiar voice of Ben Richards announced at the same time as I was being lifted off my seat and carried towards the house.

He sat me down on the front steps and then returned to talk to the driver. There was no question about it. Ben had taken command of the situation.

"Thanks for bringing her here. I'm curious to hear all about it, but let's start with your name, if you don't mind," Ben said.

"Gavin Frawley…."

"Frawley? Is that as in Frawley Farms?" Ben suggested.

"Yeah, that's my dad's operation. Look, I don't mean to be rude, but I don't know much about any of this. I just picked the lady up on the road on my way in to work." I saw Gavin (as I now knew his name to be) check his watch. "I can't help you, and I do have to go, or I will be late starting work this morning. My boss takes a bit of a dim view of that."

"Right, of course. I don't want to hold you up any longer, Gavin, but I would like to talk to you a bit more. What time do you finish work today?"

"I'm on the early shift, so we start at six o'clock, and I finish at two o'clock."

"Good… Please call at the police precinct after you finish work this afternoon. When you come in, ask for Ben Richards."

"What? I haven't done anything wrong. I didn't cause the state she is in. All I did was give her our lift to this address."

"No. No, Gavin, I wasn't suggesting you were in trouble. I just want to hear whatever you can tell me about what happened this morning. Will you come and see me this afternoon, please?"

The matter appeared resolved, and Gavin, looking a little more relieved than he was a few minutes ago, climbed back into his truck. As he drove off from Ben's place, he heard the siren becoming louder as it came in his direction.

Chapter 3

The last thing I remember was an ambulance coming along Ben's street. Then nothing. Nothing until I woke up in a hospital room and attached to all manner of technology, blinking and beeping continually.

How long I had been out to it was unclear, but a quick scan revealed I was now clean and dressed in a hospital gown. While I was assessing my current situation, a nurse came in and began fussing over my various machines and straightening my bedclothes – and generally being most officious. I queried the rail attached to one side of my bed and why my arm should be strapped to it.

"Stops the drip being pulled out or damaged if you start thrashing about," was her curt reply. And then she was gone without uttering another word.

After that, I suspect I lost another chunk of my life. This time, when I opened my eyes, a different nurse was fussing with the technology. This one was younger and quite attractive and, according to her badge, was called Sue. I suppose she might best be described as 'petite'. The previous version was older and (politely) best described as 'cuddly'.

"How does your head feel?" Sue asked as she fiddled with one of the machines.

"I don't know what you're giving me in the drip, but it has given me the mother of all hangovers."

"No, that's not our doing. You acquired the hangover you're complaining about all by yourself. We're just helping you to sleep it off. You will continue to feel groggy and will spend most of your time sleeping for the next little while… starting from now. I'll be back to check on you again later."

Yep, I preferred this version to the previous, more mature nurse. Nevertheless, she didn't score too highly on 'information sharing'. I made a mental note to interrogate her when next she came to check on me. I had a string of questions requiring answers. Top of the list was when I might expect to go home.

Apart from the fact I didn't like being in hospital, I had a business to run. I gave a satisfied nod to my empty room as I acknowledged my memory was unaffected. I had no trouble remembering I ran my own business. But there existed a little niggling doubt. One I was not prepared to accept or even acknowledge. *What exactly is my business?*

Was my self-congratulation about the state of my memory somewhat premature? It was a frightening thought, and it stayed with me until I slipped into oblivion again. If that young nurse, Sue, came to see me again, I was unaware of it, but on the next occasion I took any notice of my surroundings, yet another nurse was doing whatever they needed to do. Apart from a curt 'good morning', she wasn't interested in making conversation. That was okay because, of the two words she had uttered, one grabbed my attention and wouldn't let go: *morning!*

Her departure allowed me to devote my full attention to examining my surroundings. She was right. Judging by the pale sunlight starting to flood the outside world, it was morning, early morning. But, after her departure, the rest of my day was a blur of sleeping and waking until my body appeared to decide it had enough sleep and chose to stay awake for a while. By then, I judged it to be afternoon, but I had no idea of the actual time. I seemed to be left to my own devices for a while until a visitor arrived.

A young nurse I hadn't seen before pushed open my door and ushered in my visitor, giving him a stern warning as he came in that he could stay no more than ten minutes. The young man who entered was tentative and hesitant about being here. Although there was something familiar about him, it took me a few moments to realise who he was.

"Gavin…. It is Gavin, isn't it?" He smiled and nodded. "How nice of you to come. Take a seat. Now, tell me, did you get to work on time after I disrupted your morning?"

"Yes, thanks. I wasn't as early as I usually am, but I made it in plenty of time."

"I'm pleased you're here. I want to thank you for what you did for me. Words don't really express the gratitude I have but, simply put, you probably saved my life. I heard you explaining to Ben something about strange shift arrangements at your workplace, and I think I remember him asking you to come in to see him."

He was laughing so loud at my comment, it took him a moment or two to say anything, and was still chuckling as he explained.

"Yeah, it was pretty funny when I look back on it. The bloke said that after I finished work for the day, I should call in at the police precinct and ask for Ben Richards. Later, when we were all sitting around the table for morning tea, I was being ribbed about having slept in and barely making it to work on time. I explained that I had picked up an injured woman on the road on my way to work, had taken her to an address in Millhaven and, while I was dropping her off, the owner of the house came home. I told my workmates that the bloke had asked me to call at the police precinct after I finished work.'

The blokes all gave me hell then about what I had done and whether I'd be at work tomorrow or locked up. Anyway, in amongst all the yapping, I had mentioned that the bloke told me to call at the precinct and ask for Ben Richards. My supervisor suggested I leave a bit early to go to the police station. I laughed and told them I wouldn't be going to the police precinct. I told them I didn't know who the jerk was, but I know when I'm being played for a fool, and I certainly wasn't going to rock up to the police station and make a real fool of myself by asking for someone nobody had ever heard of."

"Oh dear, what did you end up doing?"

"Ah, yes… Well, my supervisor set me straight. He asked me if I knew who Ben Richards was, and of course, I had to say no. It was the truth. I didn't know who Ben Richards was. But my supervisor soon set me straight about who I'd been talking to that morning. So, I did as I was asked and fronted up to talk to Ben Richards."

"That's a relief. I'm pleased to hear you did go to talk to Ben. I assume the encounter wasn't too traumatic for you."

"No. No, he's a really nice bloke to talk to. I don't know what I expected, but it wasn't that. I was a bit sorry I couldn't help him more, but I really didn't know what had happened to you. All I could do was explain how I'd found you wandering up the road and took you to the address you gave me. Do you know Ben Richards well?"

"Ben is one of my best friends, and has been for the best part of two decades. Asking you to drop me at Ben's place was exactly the right thing to do … Except it has now landed me in hospital, and God knows how long I'm going to be kept here.

When you were talking to Ben, I think I remember there was some mention of your having a connection to Frawley Farms. Is that right?" Gavin nodded and looked a bit uncomfortable. "I don't mean to pry, but I suppose I'm surprised you work in town and not on the farms."

"Frawley Farms is my father's business. His property runs quite a long way down the other side of the road from where I found you. He always insisted I should do something with my life – get a trade or go to university – before deciding whether I wanted to work on the farms or not. I wanted to be a fitter and completed an apprenticeship but, along the way, I decided I wanted to be an engineer. So, I enrolled at university and did some of the subjects during the last year of my apprenticeship. Then, with cross credits for some of my apprenticeship stuff, it only took three years to complete my engineering degree.

So, I continue to work in town. After work, I help out on the farm until dinner time. Eventually, I will go back onto the farm full-time and will take over the whole show when dad decides to retire or at least take things a bit easier."

At that point, a nurse bustled in and told Gavin it was time for him to leave. I thanked him again as he bolted for the door. I was all set to tear a strip off the nurse for being rude to my visitor until I realised she was chuckling about Gavin's hasty departure.

"Nice looking young chap," Lisa (so her badge told me) said with a flick of her head in the direction of the fleeing Gavin. "Very nice manners, too. Your son, is he?" I blinked a couple of times at Lisa's question.

"Eh? No, just a friend. Uhmm, no, that's not right either. That young man is the knight in a high viz shirt and driving a shiny black truck who rescued me and probably saved my life."

"Like I said, he seemed a nice young lad. Now, let's talk about you. How are you feeling? How's your head feeling now?"

"The head is fine, but I am starving. What do I have to do to make some food appear?"

"Hmm, you are sounding a bit brighter. Your dinner for tonight will arrive soon, but you do have to choose your menu for tomorrow. I'll show you how to do that a bit later this evening. In the meantime, your afternoon tea should arrive about now."

Almost right on cue, a cup of tea and a dry biscuit arrived and were deposited on my table. I must've looked less than impressed about the fare on offer. When I gave Lisa an is-this-it questioning look, she burst out laughing but somehow managed to assure me things would be better tomorrow. Then she asked if I would prefer to be alone, or if I could stand some company for a while. As Lisa thought she was in for a quiet shift, she suggested she could be back later for a chat. I welcomed the idea as I hadn't been able to find anything resembling a remote for the small TV set mounted high on the wall opposite my bed. It had looked as though I was in for a long, boring evening.

Lisa returned about half an hour later. "How was your afternoon tea?" she chirped as she came in.

"I don't drink tea. I prefer coffee."

Her only response to my comment was a giggle. After checking all the machines yet again, she pulled a chair over beside the bed and flopped down onto it.

"You're starting to grizzle about things. That's probably a good sign. It suggests your recovery is going well."

"Does that mean I can go home? I have a business to run. It won't run itself while I am lying here doing nothing."

"No. I doubt you will be allowed home for another day or so. You suffered a serious head injury and were severely concussed and dehydrated when you arrived here. We need to be sure you won't end up back here because we discharged you too soon.

Anyway, it's that business you're so concerned about that I wanted to ask you about. What's it like being a private investigator? Until a few days ago, I didn't even know there was such a thing in Millhaven."

Private investigator… So that's what my business is. Ah ha, yeah, it's coming back to me now: Sonoma Whittington, Private Investigator. God, was I working on a case at the time? There could be a client out there somewhere wondering why I haven't reported back on my investigation's progress. What about appointments? Do I have other clients, or potential clients, trying to contact me while I'm lying here doing nothing?

So many questions flooded my thinking after Lisa's casual mention that I was a private investigator, including the really big one: *how long had I been lying here ignoring my clients?* I decided I wouldn't put that question to Lisa in case any apparent lack of memory might potentially extend my stay in this institution. It wasn't a problem anyway, as Lisa had taken control of the conversation.

"Yeah, I had never even thought about private investigators before my friend, Zali, mentioned you." Lisa looked a bit awkward and took a moment before continuing. "I know you can't discuss your clients or cases. I don't want to put you in a difficult position, but what did you think about Zali? Do you think you can help her?"

The little voice in my head asked, who the hell is Zali? I ignored it. I was too busy trying to piece together a picture of what my life involved to worry about a question that just did not compute. I'm sure the name Zali ran through my memory banks several times but came up empty.

Okay, so no memory of a Zali to be found anywhere. Perhaps that wasn't significant in itself. Maybe this Zali person hadn't come to see me as Lisa thinks, or maybe she made an appointment and will see me in the near future. Of course, there is another possibility. Maybe she did come to see me, but not as Zali. It wouldn't be the first time a potential client had used an assumed name, whether to avoid embarrassment or as a safety precaution. As I had no recollection of a young, female, potential client coming to my office in recent days, I needed more information about this friend of Lisa.

"Well, Lisa, you're correct about not being allowed to discuss my clients, but I don't recall your friend coming to see me. I assumed she was a young woman of about your age, but perhaps I got that wrong. Tell me about Zali. Have you known her long?"

"She has been my best friend since we first started school together. Although we spent a few years apart when we both went off in different directions to establish our careers, when we got back together again, it was as though we had never been apart. We were very close. Shared all our secrets. Argh, well, that's how it had been until recently."

"What had changed recently? Had something happened in either of your lives that impacted the friendship?"

"No, Sonny, we were still close. But, over the last few days, she seemed troubled. It was the first time she ever held anything back from me. I tried several times to find out what was troubling her, but she just brushed my questions aside. That was not like her, not like how WE were. Then, when she said she was going to see you, I knew something was really wrong – but she still wouldn't say what it was.

I don't suppose I will ever know now. Zali died later the day she was to see you."

"Hang on... Zali died the day she was to see me? Had she been ill? You said she seemed troubled over that last little while.

Might that have been because she found out she was seriously ill?"

"Zali was never ill. Although what you suggest is possible, I don't think that was the case. She was still doing everything she usually did, hadn't eased back in anyway – just seemed a bit troubled. That's probably why the accident happened. Her mind didn't seem to be focused on what she was doing much those days, and add a vehicle into that mix, and you have a deadly combination. Perhaps she just wasn't paying attention."

So it was a vehicle accident on the day she supposedly came to see me. That shouldn't be too hard to follow-up… if I ever get out of this place. Still, I need to know more about Zali.

"Describe your friend, Zali, to me. Give me a physical description first, please."

Lisa took a moment to answer. I observed her fight down her emotions before she spoke. The loss of her friend was still raw for Lisa, but she pulled herself together and set about describing the woman in question.

"How do you describe someone like Zali? I suppose the thing you would notice about her the first time you saw her would be that she was drop-dead gorgeous. A fabulous-looking brunette. Raven black hair, eyes as black as coal, flawless olive complexion, slim, and just under six foot tall – whatever that is in the new measurements. Zalika Standish had it all: looks, brains, personality, sporting prowess – and a wealthy family."

"Zalika…?

"That's the full name her father gave her, but she hated it. They used her full name all the time at school but, as soon as she left school, she never used it again. Only ever used Zali after that."

"What did she study at university, and what was her career after she graduated?" I didn't think my question was at all funny, but Lisa burst out laughing.

"Career! Zali didn't need a career. She didn't need to go to university. She only went there to defy her father. He was a bit old-world; thought daughters should remain at home and concentrate on developing into young ladies. Then, just before she graduated, her father became ill, quite ill. The upshot of that was that Zali came home to run the business while he recovered." Lisa was still having a bit of a chuckle about it when she finished speaking.

"I assume Zali's father did recover, and she would have then been free to resume her own life," I suggested.

"No… Well, yes, he did recover to some extent, but not fully. I thought he was just bunging it on to keep her at home and in the business, but she thought differently and felt she couldn't leave. I think she enjoyed running the business. That's what she was doing, with her father just looking over her shoulder all the time. But she got on with life and managed to maintain all those other things that were important to her, such as friendships and sport."

It was a relief when Lisa's pager summoned her to deal with another patient. It allowed me time to think about all she had told me and to work out how I was going to tell her I had no knowledge of her friend, Zali, having come to see me. I was still churning through Lisa's information when a knock on my door interrupted my thought processes. In hospital, everyone just barges into your room, but on this occasion, I had the option of allowing them in or not. I opted to bellow, "Come in."

Ben Richards strode in and promptly assumed the seat recently vacated by Lisa. "You're looking a bit brighter this evening, so I take it you're on the improve. I just wanted to see how you were going before I went to talk to a couple of my officers who are guarding a patient in another wing of the hospital. In fact, I might go and do that now and then come back and chat with you later. You don't have any big plans for this evening, I take it?"

Cheeky sod. Still, I was pleased he was here as I had a couple of things I wanted him to look into. I was in the process of making a mental list of those things I wanted to talk to Ben about later, when Lisa reappeared.

"Can't stay this time," she said by way of greeting. "I'm due to go off shift and have one other patient to see before I sign off. So, you will have a different nurse come to see you next time. Oh, look, your dinner has arrived."

A trolley rumbled its way into my room, and a tray was placed on my table... A tray containing mostly empty space. I tentatively lifted the cover of the solitary plate occupying the centre of the tray. Wrinkling my nose and looking accusingly at Lisa, I demanded, "What is this supposed to be?"

"It's soup... and that is all you are allowed to have tonight. It will prevent you from being hungry even if it doesn't do much else for you. I have to go. I'll look in on you tomorrow if I have time."

Then she was gone, and I was left staring at a bowl of the most unappetising-looking stuff that purported to be soup. Nevertheless, I was hungry, and it was better than nothing. It didn't taste any better than it looked, but I scraped the bowl clean before pushing the tray aside. I was still glaring at the offensive tray when Ben returned.

With a grunt, he planted his backside on the chair next to the bed. "This place is more like a maze every time I come here. They are constantly tacking bits and pieces on to it. Before long, they will need to hand out maps so you can find your way around the place." Then, almost as an afterthought, he asked, "How was dinner?"

"Don't ask, and I don't want to know what you planned to have either."

At that point, Lisa reappeared and apologised for her interruption. Ben sprang up off the chair and announced he'd wait outside.

"You have the most interesting visitors," Lisa chirped as she pushed the chair away from the bedside. "You must be special to warrant a visit from our top cop, Ben Richards. Do you know him well?" She was chatting aimlessly as she messed around with the various machines.

"Yep, Ben and I have been friends for the best part of two decades. What are you doing back here anyway, Lisa? I thought your shift had ended."

"Thanks to you, I'm now on overtime. Things have become very busy downstairs. My replacement and just about everybody else are fully occupied elsewhere. So, I've been asked to stay on for a bit. Now, tell me more about this friendship with our top cop."

"Uhmm, there's nothing more to tell."

"Just friendship…?" She asked.

"Yes… Just friendship and nothing more. Certainly nothing romantic. By the way, what are you doing?" I asked after watching her move from machine to machine.

"There, that's the last one. You're now unhooked from everything. Now, all I have to do is to remove this rail from the side of the bed and then read you the riot act about what you are not allowed to do."

An orderly appeared at that point and removed most of the bits and pieces Lisa had disconnected. As soon as he left, Lisa told me I could use the bathroom adjoining my room, but I was to limit my time out of bed until I was told otherwise. I demanded to know where the remote for the TV was hiding, and she produced it from on the shelf beside the TV. Then, after running her eyes over the room, she gave a satisfied nod and started for the door, pushing the last of the machines still in the room ahead of her.

Halfway to the door, she stopped and spoke to me over her shoulder. "I've got a day off tomorrow, so I might not see you again before they release you. Once you're back at work, I will come to see you. I still want to find out what I can about Zali."

Chapter 4

Then she was gone, and I felt both relieved and concerned. The relief was because she didn't ask me any more questions about Zali, but my concern was that she intended to question me about someone I didn't know – or couldn't remember. That latter possibility frightened me. Fortunately, I didn't have too long to dwell on it. A few minutes after Lisa left, Ben returned. I thought it a bit odd that it had taken him so long to come back into the room if he was only waiting outside for Lisa to leave.

"Okay, let's try again for a quiet conversation," he suggested as he pushed the chair back against my bedside. "It's good to see they finally set you free and removed the barricade from the side of the bed."

"Where did you go when you left here? You didn't wait outside, so what did you do?" I demanded.

"That's no way to welcome your visitors. Never mind, if you must know, I went to have a chat with the doctor I know. He's the one that's been looking after you since you were admitted."

"I hope you thought to ask him when they were going to discharge me. If there's not some move in that direction tomorrow, I will be discharging myself. I need to get back to my office."

"Hmm … I'm not sure about tomorrow, maybe the day after. Anyway, what's the rush to get back to your office? There is a sign on your office door telling people that you will be unavailable for a few days due to unforeseen circumstances. I think Emily might have put a similar message on your office phone. She said she couldn't find your mobile phone, so there might be a raft of calls backed up on that. Where is that phone, by the way? Do you have it?"

"Ben, I don't have anything. I don't have my phone. I appear to have lost my watch, and somewhere along the line, I lost one sneaker. I only discovered the missing sneaker when I found I was having trouble walking. So, I shed its mate as well to make it a bit easier to hobble along. Apart from the fact that everyone seems to believe I am Sonny Whittington, I have nothing to prove that's who I am. Are you in a hurry to leave, or could you stay for a while?"

"There's no hurry. I can stay as long as you like. What's bothering you – apart from the stuff you appear to have lost?"

"The stuff doesn't matter. My memory does. Ben, I'm frightened. I can't remember things, important things. Vague memories are plaguing me. Since talking to the nurse about her friend, I feel I should know this friend of hers, that there is something familiar about that Zali person. And the BIG one: there is something about the friend's death. It's as though I should know something but, when I try to focus on it, there is only a blank. I can't recall anything about it.

It is not just this Zali stuff. There are other things that I think I should know, but I don't know them and don't know why I think I should know about them. Ben, what else have I forgotten? How much of my memory have I lost?"

"Right, I can imagine how concerning that must be, but I was told it is to be expected."

"Nobody has bothered to tell me about it, so maybe you should share your superior knowledge on the matter." Ben took his time replying, and I knew he was considering how best to word whatever he was going to tell me. "Don't muck me about, Ben. I expect the truth from you – and the whole truth. As always, I need to know the whole story regardless of what it is."

"Okay, I wasn't going to sell you short. The doctor I spoke to, the one who's been looking after you, said memory loss was a part of your injuries. And, before you ask, yes, I quizzed him on what that really meant. He said each case was different. He couldn't define what yours would be like, as that would only become apparent over time after the incident. Apparently, memory loss is common with such severe head trauma. The loss can take many forms. It might involve nothing more than not remembering the incident that resulted in the injury. Sometimes, it can involve a longer period and extend from some time before the incident until some time afterwards.

He assured me that, apart from the memory of the actual incident, the memory loss is temporary and returns as the brain recovers from the trauma. So, what you are experiencing is fully in line with what the doctor expects."

"What are you not telling me? Ben, I can read you like a book. I know you're withholding something the doctor told you. So, spit it out. What's the rest of the story?"

"Ah, well, I tried, I suppose. But, okay, here's the rest of what he told me. In some cases, memory loss might not be so temporary. In such instances, some of the lost memory might return gradually as recovery progresses, while other bits that have been lost remain lost, more or less, permanently."

"Does he think my memory loss will prove temporary, or is it the more permanent kind?"

"Now you know why I didn't want to have this conversation. The short answer is: *nobody knows*. It appears that only time will determine the answer to that question. And, yes, I appreciate that is not what you wanted to hear. In the meantime, let's focus on what you might remember – with a bit of prompting – and what you don't and might be more difficult to recover."

Before I could answer, a message pinged in on his phone. After a quick read of it, Ben appeared to consider its contents for a moment before saying anything.

"I might just deal with that before we do anything else," he announced. "I'll be back in a minute."

True to his word, he wasn't gone for more than a minute or so. When he returned, he was a ball of business. Closing the door behind him, he turned off the room's lights on his way across to the chair beside my bed.

"Right, now let's get started. I want to try this the way we've used it in the past when chasing some elusive missing clue in a case. Where do you want to start?" He left no doubt he was in charge, but I wasn't in the mood for games.

"Maybe what has happened resulted from a series of events that are now too horrible to recall, and that might have concluded with my being dumped at that abandoned mine site."

"Well, even if we only confirm that to be the case, surely it will be worthwhile."

Not convinced, I argued against it, but Ben is a persuasive talker – especially when he is making sense.

"Ben, I have no idea. I haven't a clue about what I know, what I should know, or what I have forgotten. Maybe this isn't such a good idea, or maybe it's too soon." Ben persisted and wore me down. "Oh, hell, what have I got to lose? Probably only my sanity, but let's give it a go." I said and instantly regretted committing that thought to words.

"Nonsense," Ben snapped. "Come on, let's get started. Okay, I'll lead the way. Lie back, close your eyes and relax. No. I said to relax. You know this won't work if you're tense."

Of course, I knew it as well as he did. I just seemed to have trouble working out how to relax. While I struggled with it, Ben kept chatting in a quiet voice, and soon, the magic happened. I felt completely relaxed. His session began with the most basic of questions and then worked its way to somewhere else.

"Sonny, what do you do for a living?"

"Private investigator…."

"Do you work from home or have an office somewhere?"

"I can work from home, but I have an office in the city."

"Where in the city?" I quoted the street address. "Which building is it in?" I thought for a moment before explaining which building. "What do you remember about the last case you closed?" I took a moment to think about that one before answering.

"It was about a husband who supposedly was playing away. It turned out he wasn't. He had been diagnosed with a serious illness, didn't want to worry his wife about it, and was sneaking off to have treatment without telling her. All ended well when he received a clean bill of health and came clean to his wife about the whole thing."

That was easier than I expected. I wasn't aware that I had remembered all those details but, obviously, I had. But then the questions became difficult.

"Okay, you had wrapped up a case, did you have a new client – a new case – to be going on with?"

"Ye-es… I think … I had started a new case."

"What was this new case all about?"

"I… I… Uhmm, I don't remember. I don't remember, Ben."

"Relax. Just take a minute to relax again."

I know how to play this game. After a bit of an internal struggle, a minute or so later, I was ready to try again. Ben reiterated some of the stuff we already had covered before casually slipping his next question.

"Think back, Sonny. What is the last thing you remember before waking up at that abandoned mine site?"

"Uhmm… Dinner with you." That was easy, I thought and relaxed a little more.

"Give me details – a blow-by-blow report – of that evening," he asked quietly.

"Er … nothing exciting to report on that one," I told him, but he wanted details. "Right, it was barbequed steak, salad, and a beer, out on my back deck. Oh, that's right. You wanted an early night because you were on an early flight to Brisbane the next morning to attend some police conference or something. After the conference, you were going to catch up with your Ralston counterpart, Pete Messell. As you were booked to return on the late flight, we wouldn't be having dinner together the next night. I think that's all there is to tell you… ah, except you left my place soon after eight o'clock that evening."

"What happened after I went home?"

"Again, nothing very exciting to report. I spent maybe half an hour finishing the client's report on the case I'd just closed. Then, as I didn't have time during the day, I poured a glass of wine, put my feet, and read the paper before a shower and then bed by around ten o'clock."

"Anything interesting or different happen next morning? Again, a detailed report, please." Another question I thought was probably irrelevant and a waste of time, but I had agreed to play this game.

"Up at the usual time and left home at the usual time."

"Sonny, do you actually remember that, or was that response because you know that's what usually happens?"

"No… but that's what usually happens. I am on auto pilot in the mornings. Unless the power was off and I couldn't make coffee, or the roof fell in on me, I wouldn't remember anything in particular about it."

"Well, that doesn't answer my question. Please retrace your movements that morning for me. Start with leaving home, then tell me about the traffic, and finally arriving at your office."

"Nothing much to tell… Okay, okay, let me think… Right, I reversed out of the garage and swung the car around to head down the driveway. Hold on, something was different that morning. What the hell was it?" It wouldn't come to me, but I was sure something different had occurred.

In the same quiet voice he had been using, Ben told me to close my eyes and picture myself backing out of the garage. I nodded to signify I was back there, reversing out, ready to head down the driveway.

"Look around you. What can you see?" he asked.

"Aah, yes. At that hour of the morning, my neighbour is usually out in her backyard feeding her dog, Rusty, and filling his water container before the neighbour leaves for work. That morning, she waved to me, as she does every morning after I swing the car around to line it up with the driveway."

I sensed something was not right with that last statement and paused to revisit that morning's scene in my mind.

"Oh, no… not that morning! She wasn't in her backyard. Only Rusty was there that morning. I waited, wondering if something might be amiss with my neighbour and whether I should go over to enquire if everything was all right. Then, the neighbour's husband came out and started fussing with the dog's food and water. I assumed the woman might be away or ill, but there was no cause for concern, so I drove into work."

"Good. Now tell me about the morning's traffic."

God, Ben's questions are boring and irrelevant. I don't know what he hopes they might achieve, but I agreed to do this. So, I suppose I have to play along.

"The traffic; well, let's see. No, there was nothing unusual about the traffic. That's why I always leave so early. It always gives me a straightforward run into the city with minimal traffic around me."

"So you drove into the city; then what? Every detail, please."

"Drove into the parking area behind the building. There were no other vehicles there that morning. The pastry chef from the bakery on the ground floor starts early every morning, about five o'clock. His sports car is always parked there when I arrive, but it wasn't that day. I remember feeling concerned that I might have to forgo something freshly baked for morning tea that morning. Then, I went up to my office, using the stairs as usual. Nothing happened along the way."

"See yourself going up to your office. Tell me about it."

"Like I said, nothing happened. I went up the stairs and let myself into my office… Ah, no, that's not quite right. The office phone on my desk was ringing as I unlocked the door. It stopped as I stepped inside. The caller didn't leave a message.

Ben, is this stuff relevant? I mean, how does it help with the gaps in my memory?"

"You agreed to do this, so let's get on with it. I'll be the judge of whether it's achieving anything or not. We can argue about it later if you insist."

He was right, of course. I had agreed to do this, and from past experience, I am aware Ben knows what he is doing and always manages to get results. As I was becoming a bit restless, he suggested we take a break and resume the exercise at some later date. That didn't suit me at all. I wanted to know now how much I couldn't remember and, if I'm honest, I was banking on this question-and-answer charade maybe to bring some of it back. I told him I wanted to continue. After getting me to relax again, he paused for a few moments before asking his next question. It started a new line of questioning that almost knocked me off my perch.

"So, you had wrapped up your last case, and you thought you might have started a new case. Is that correct?"

"Uhmm… Yes, at least I think so."

There was a short pause. I didn't know whether Ben was unhappy with my response to his last question, or if he was trying to think of what his next question should be. But then he started again.

"Who is your new client?"

"Trina… Trina Blewett."

Jesus, where did that come from? Five minutes ago, I didn't know for sure if I had a new client, and now, here I am, giving him a strange name I didn't think I'd ever heard before. I was about to explain that the name might be a fiction that came from out of the fog in my mind and that I wasn't sure there was such a person. But, he fired off the next question at me.

"Describe her to me." I struggled with the question and shook my head. "Focus on her face, Sonny," Ben encouraged me. "Is she attractive?"

"A knockout. The name does not do justice to the face. Big dark eyes, wide cheek bones, lovely complexion. Uhmm, there's something else, but I don't know…. It's not about her looks … Or is it?" Then, a thought slamming in from left field almost stunned me.

"Christ, Ben, she was Zali. That woman, my new client, was Lisa's friend, Zali, who used a different name. From the description the nurse, Lisa, gave me, I'm almost certain it was her friend, Zali, who came to see me that morning. Why couldn't I remember her? She was such a stunning looking young woman. How could I not remember her?"

That was my new client I was talking about. My new client whose face was imprinted on some part of my memory. But, as I wrestled with the implications of that situation, something else tried to elbow its way into my thinking. Finally, it came through – almost – and it was my turn to go in search of answers.

"Ben, what do you know about an accident involving a vehicle that day?"

"Which day are we talking about? I'm unaware of a serious vehicle accident anywhere around the city recently."

"Argh, no, of course not. You wouldn't know about it. You weren't here that day. You were in Brisbane the day it supposedly happened. How come I thought of that but couldn't remember other important things? Or… Is that a memory of mine? Might it be no more than the suggestion of a vehicle accident having been planted in my mind by Lisa's mention of Zali's death in a vehicle accident that day?"

Silence shrouded the pair of us like a lead blanket. For me, there was a thought, a memory, trying to worm its way into my consciousness. Then, seemingly out of nowhere, it came through. I knew what it was that I couldn't remember … or maybe it was a memory I had suppressed because I didn't want to remember its details. But there it was being reenacted in my mind. I groaned. Ben flinched.

"What? What's happened? What have you remembered? Come on, talk to me, Sonny."

"Oh, God… Christ, Ben! I know what happened to Zali. I remember watching it happen. She didn't have an accident. *She was run down*… Run down in the street out in front of my office building. *I saw it happen.*"

I was hyperventilating and shaking. Ben leapt off his chair and rushed to hold me tight. He continued holding me tight until my breathing returned to as close to normal as possible. How long we remained like that, I don't know, but I suspect it was a few minutes. When Ben finally released me, I discovered tears had been streaming down my face and had created a large wet patch on his shirt.

After wiping my face on the sleeve of my gown, I reached out to test how wet the damp patch on his shirt actually was – very wet. I gave him a wry grin and suggested it was as well he had taken his uniform jacket off earlier, or I would be up for his drycleaning bill.

Our reclaiming-my-memory session came to an abrupt end when Ben's phone played its tune. He cursed, checked the caller ID, said he had to take it, and rushed out of my room. I was more than a little miffed about his departure. I know how important his job is, how his job owns his life, and how it was unreasonable to feel the way I did. Despite all that, I was angry that whatever had called him away was more important than my situation.

"God knows how long he will be away, or if he will come back at all," I grumbled to my empty room.

Although he was gone for only a few minutes, by the time he returned, I was in a foul mood and snapped and snarled at him.

"Well, I suppose now you're back, the question is, are we going to continue to try recovering my lost memories? Or have you only returned to say goodnight?"

"We definitely are not going to try finding any more of your lost memories, particularly if the exercise leaves you in such a foul mood. Anyway, that call wasn't work-related. It was the doctor I spoke to earlier, the one who's been looking after you. He had something of a postscript he wanted to add to the information he gave me earlier.

He now thinks that, although in your line of work, you've probably been a part of – or witnessed – numerous traumatic events, some of your memory loss now might be due to a self-preservation mechanism. He suggested that, in that lost segment of your memory, there could be some traumatic event that happened. It could be something you witnessed, but given your injuries, it's possible you might have been more directly involved in whatever it was." I was about to give him my thoughts on all that 'rubbish', but he cut me off and continued. "Don't interrupt. I haven't finished sharing all he told me.

It appears our memory retrieval exercise might not have been the wisest move. The doctor strongly suggested that forcing memories to return, and having you confront them, could make the situation worse – and possibly irreversible – in the long-term. So, you can be as cranky as you like, but we will not be continuing that session this evening."

"Sorry. I know we should heed the doctor's advice, but I need to get out of here. I need to get back to my world, to pick up where I left off, to deal with whatever has been happening while I've been lying here staring at these four walls and a tiny fuzzy TV. Did your friend, the doctor, mention when I might be discharged?"

"No, the matter never came up during our brief conversation. But then, I wouldn't expect him to tell me before he told you when you would be discharged."

"Right. Well, here is how it's going to be. If there is no indication that I will be released from this place sometime tomorrow, I will discharge myself. Regardless of what anyone thinks or says, I will be home in my own bed tomorrow night… And God help anyone who tries to interfere with that plan."

"Sonny, that's not really clever thinking. If the hospital is not prepared to discharge you yet, it's because they aren't sure serious problems won't still arise from your injuries. Please don't do anything silly. Whenever you are discharged, your world will still be there just as you left it."

Why does he always make sense when he tells me something I don't want to hear? I suppose I did accept that the doctors knew more about how to handle my condition than I did, but that wasn't helpful. Those vague memories plaguing me at the moment suggest they are important on a bigger stage than simply associated with my lost memory.

Another phone call had Ben announce, "Duty calls. I have to go. Talk to you soon." And then he was gone.

Chapter 5

Alone once more in my room with its insipid-coloured, unadorned walls and useless TV, I wasn't in the best of humour. But I also wasn't in the least bit tired or sleepy. I knew it meant I would be awake for hours to come. I had no doubt I would spend those hours trying to winkle more lost memories out of the dark, obscure reaches of my mind. Yep, I was in for a long, unsettled, sleepless night. Now, that can't be good for my recovery. At least, if I was home, I could find a decent program to watch on my large TV.

Whinging about my situation wasn't going to improve it, so I looked for something to do that might have more positive results. I remembered the menu for tomorrow's food. The nurse had shown me how to use the small computer screen attached to my bed to order my food, and I realised it was getting late and I still hadn't filled in my request.

"Well, I suppose that's something positive I could do, and it will probably ensure I am fed," I told the universe before pulling the computer screen on its arm down in front of me.

"Now, let's see. How does this work again?" A quick scan told me it was no more difficult than filling in a motel breakfast slip to order breakfast in your room. "Oh, now that is interesting – and a little more appealing," I told the universe.

The reason I hadn't submitted my menu earlier was the fact that there was nothing available to me. Well, nothing that sounded like real food or might be palatable in any way. But now, I'm being allowed real food and there is a wide selection on offer. I spent more time than necessary selecting my breakfast. Then, almost as an afterthought, I decided to order lunch as well.

"Just in case I do happen to be still here at lunchtime," I confided to my empty room.

Tomorrow's menus taken care of; I switched off my light and lay there, staring into the darkness and tossing and turning for what seemed like hours.

Morning eventually arrived and found me in a worse mood than yesterday. The trolley loaded with patients' breakfasts was my first visitor of the day. The woman in charge of it placed a tray on my table and cast her eyes over it.

"The first time you've used the computer to order your meals, is it?" I nodded. "We can always tell the first-timers. They never remember to order milk for their coffee. It's as well we sneak extra milk onto the trolley for just such situations." She grabbed a milk bottle and went to pour some into a small jug.

"I don't take milk in my coffee," I blurted out, "but thanks for paying such attention."

I suppose I might have sounded and looked a little smug. The woman didn't respond immediately and, instead, stood frowning at my tray.

"Am I to understand you don't need milk for your cereal as well?" she asked innocently.

"Eh? Yes, I have milk with my cereal."

"Well, it doesn't look as though you do. You didn't order any. Should I maybe fill this jug for you anyway?" she asked, a wicked grin spread across her face.

As I watched the food trolley depart, I admitted to myself it wasn't the best start to the day. The little voice in my head suggested I should try to manage the rest of my day a little better. The morning slipped by without offering anything to manage until soon after ten o'clock when a nurse arrived. She was another one I hadn't seen before, and wasn't interested in chatting. She carried out the usual checks without uttering more than a curt 'good morning'. I needed information and, so far this morning, this nurse was the only possible source to enter my room. I charged in looking for answers.

"Am I being discharged today?" I asked point-blank.

"No, not as far as I know."

"When am I to be discharged?

"Only a doctor can tell you that."

"And when am I likely to see one of those?" She looked confused, so I elaborated. "A doctor, I mean." She slammed her pen into her pocket and glared at me.

"Doctor is doing his rounds at the moment. He probably won't get around to seeing you until about lunchtime."

She then marched out of my room without further comment. Still not managing this day too well, I told myself after watching her disappear from view along the corridor. I didn't think I had said anything offensive. Maybe it was my lack of a deodorant….

A tall, skinny, middle-aged doctor appeared not much before midday. He looked a bit harassed. Seems his day is not going any better than mine … and I'm not about to improve it for him. He went through the motions of checking everything that had been done before attempting a weak smile and making the mistake of asking how I felt. I dredged up what I hoped was a convincing smile.

"I feel fine. The lump on my head is still there but has gone down quite a lot. My head has stopped throbbing and, apart from feeling half starved, I'm fine. So, when am I being released?"

"Ah, I doubt that'll be for a day or so yet. With injuries such as yours, we have to take every precaution. Sometimes, the full effect of them doesn't become apparent until a few days afterwards. We need you here in case that happens to you."

"No. No, that's not how it's going to be. If I am still here this afternoon, I will be discharging myself. So, one way or another, when you are doing your rounds this evening, I will not be here."

"Look, I know you think you feel fine, but you have a way to go yet. Your eyesight still hasn't returned to normal. We need to monitor that to be sure there is no serious underlying problem that is causing the situation."

"My eyesight is fine. What do you think is wrong with it?"

He shoved a chart of some sort in front of me and demanded, "Read this."

The heading posed no problems at all and I read it out to him. Beyond that, I could tell it was a chart of some sort with lots of columns that might have had handwriting in them. Try as I might, those columns and their contents would not become clear and remained fuzzy like looking through fog. I was about to try faking it by telling him I could see those columns, but I didn't know what any of it meant.

"If your eyesight were normal and as sharp as it should be, you would be able to tell me more about those columns. Accept it. Your eyesight hasn't returned to normal yet and it may take a few days for it to do so."

"Okay, but I can see well enough to get out of here… And that is exactly what I'm going to do straight after lunch." He did try to convince me otherwise, but eventually caved in under pressure.

"All right, we will discharge you this afternoon. But I can hear the meal trolley approaching. It is lunchtime. Why don't you have lunch and a little rest and then wait until about three o'clock before checking out?"

"As I'm not in the habit of having a rest after lunch, I don't feel inclined to do so today. I intend to be out of here by no later than two o'clock."

"Argh, I would prefer you rested until three o'clock, but I suppose two o'clock will do. I will advise people you will be checking out this afternoon. Now, is there anything else we should discuss before I leave?"

There was no doubt in my mind I already had upset the young doctor, but there was one other thing I needed to ask about.

"Yes, well, I could have a problem." My mention of 'problem' reignited his interest, so I continued. "I can hardly walk out of here wearing this gown. I need clothes. Where are the clothes I arrived in?"

"They should be in that little cupboard," he said, nodding towards a cupboard I previously hadn't even noticed.

He strode over to the cupboard and opened it. "Yes, there are clothes here. They look a bit the worse for wear, but they would be the clothes you arrived in. There's also a sports bag of some sort here." He unzipped it and scrabbled a hand through it. "More clothes and shoes. I think your dignity might be safe when you leave." Then he was gone to continue his rounds, and the meal trolley arrived in his place.

As soon as the meal trolley left, I scrambled out of bed and stumbled over to the hitherto unseen cupboard.

"A sports bag…! When… How did that get here?" I asked my empty room as I checked the bag's contents.

The doctor was right about me not having to worry about my dignity when I left. The bag contained a full set of clothes, a wet pack, and a pair of sneakers. Not for one minute did I think this was Ben's handiwork. It must've been Emily who packed the bag for me. Its contents were too well coordinated and thoughtful to be the work of a bloke.

My luncheon menu proved an excellent choice. By the time I had dispatched everything on the tray, I was feeling a little drowsy. Perhaps the doctor knew more than I did. The meal trolley arrived a few minutes later and collected my tray. Perhaps a short snooze might be such a bad idea. I was just starting to doze off when a doctor appeared again and, without any encouragement, launched into what he'd come to say.

"Everything is in place for your discharge this afternoon. I still strongly recommend you rest for a while before attempting to leave. There are a couple of things you need to be aware of and you need to adhere to after you leave this place. You must rest. Don't even think about going back to work yet or even trying to do housework. Just rest. The other important thing – and this is really important: you must not drive. Although you choose to think your eyesight is okay, it is not of a standard that allows you to drive. Do not attempt to drive until you can read a newspaper… And I don't mean just the headlines."

Okay, I had been given the rules of engagement. Now, it was time to get on with the show. While the doctor spoke to me, I had more or less decided that as soon as he left, I would get dressed and leave. It didn't quite happen that way. I decided to wait a couple of minutes to make sure he wasn't still around before I actioned my plan. That's when the plan went awry. I fell asleep. It was almost two o'clock when I opened my eyes again.

"Damn! Looks like he's won the battle anyway," I told the universe as I scrambled out of bed.

Minutes later I was dressed and downstairs going through the checkout procedure. That seemed to be unnecessarily complicated and time-consuming but, at last, I was no longer a patient and was using the free phone in the hotel lobby to call for a cab.

The cab arrived so soon after I hung up that I wondered whether it had been waiting in the hospital's car park. I gave the driver the address of my office in the city, and then quickly changed my mind and gave him the address of Millhaven's forensic laboratory. As we neared the address, I told the driver I needed to slip into the building to collect something and asked him to wait for me while I did so. The big question was where to find Emily at that hour of the afternoon. Finding her wasn't a problem.

She was coming along the corridor towards me as I rushed in through the front door. Emily Ibbotson is the forensic scientist in charge of Millhaven's forensics laboratory. We have been best friends for quite a few years, and she often – covertly – assists with some of my cases.

"Emily, can I borrow your key to my office, please? I've got nothing with me and, until I can get into my office to collect my bag, I can't get into my house either." I followed Emily into her office, and she handed me the key.

"Are you supposed to be out and about, Sonny? I had a feeling they'd be keeping you in for another day or two."

"Yes, I received an early release for good behaviour. Tell you about it later. My cab is waiting outside."

Back in the cab, I gave the driver the address of my office. He didn't seem at all pleased. As we neared the building, he voiced his concerns.

"I'll have to let you out some distance away from there. I haven't a hope in hell of finding a parking spot anywhere along that block where your building is situated."

"You don't need a parking spot. Go down the alley beside the building. There is a tenant's car park out the back that will give you plenty of room to turn around and come out again. Oh, and you'll have to wait a couple of minutes again. I have to go up to my office to get my bag before I can pay you." I was relieved to see my car still in the carpark and undamaged. Of late, the local teenaged darlings have been creating havoc at night in the city heart. It appears parked cars are irresistible targets.

It was nearly ten minutes later when I tackled the stairs up to my office for the second time. Life caught up with me about halfway up the stairs. "Should have taken it slower," I murmured as I clung to the railing for support, and to give my head a chance to stop spinning, before I tackled the rest of the stairs. Somehow, I made it to the top and, after several fumbles with the key, I again unlocked my office and raced in to collapse into one of the ancient lounge chairs in the front corner of my office.

This corner is referred to as my 'interview corner'. It contains two ancient lounge chairs and an equally ancient low coffee table. It's not the greatest looking space, but it is a more relaxed place to interview than at my desk. Now, having safely made it to one of the lounge chairs, I slid down in the chair and put my feet up on the coffee table. I had been there for some time before the phone on my desk dragged me back to reality. I stumbled as quickly as I could to answer it.

"What the hell are you doing in your office?" Ben's voice bellowed out of the handpiece at me. "You were told to go home and rest."

So much for patient confidentiality, I thought as I fought back the response I wanted to deliver.

"I would love to go home. And that will be the next thing I do after I collect my bag. Then, I will have a key and will be able to let myself into my home. I wasn't planning on staying...." I didn't have a chance to finish what I was going to say before he cut me off.

"Sit down, put your feet up, and stay there until I arrive. I'll be there in a few minutes."

My attempt at convincing him he didn't need to come to my office fell on deaf ears.

"As soon as I pick up my bag, I will be going home. So, there is no point in your rushing around to my office. I won't be here."

"How do you think you're going home? You are not to drive for at least another week. Stay where you are. That's not a suggestion or a request, Sonny. I mean it. If you attempt to drive away from your building, you will be unfit to drive, and I will have one of my traffic patrol officers pick you up."

Sometimes, it pays to know when you are beaten, but I had a cab waiting downstairs. Going down the stairs wasn't nearly as exhausting as going up them. I needed to be back in my office when Ben arrived. Without wasting any time on niceties, I paid the driver and then tackled those stairs again, this time at a more realistic rate of ascent. I returned to my lounge chair and put my feet up on the coffee table again. I was dozing there when Ben arrived. He seemed in a hurry.

"Come on, pick up your stuff and let's get you home." I scrambled out of my chair and rushed to my desk.

After stuffing all manner of things that I thought I might need into my oversized tote bag, I paused to consider if there was anything else I should take.

"Don't take any work stuff home. You're supposed to rest, not work. If you've got everything, let's go."

It seemed wise to comply, so I ran up the white flag and started for the door without a murmur. When about halfway across the room, I remembered something else and dashed back to my desk for it.

"What else could you possibly need?" Ben demanded. I waved my phone at him in response. "I didn't think it was here. Emily couldn't find it when she looked for it to put an out-of-office message on it." I shrugged and let it go at that. A much bigger argument loomed once we hit the carpark downstairs.

Ben held me by the arm and deliberately slowed the rate of our descent of the stairs. I braced myself as we stepped out into the carpark area and…. Oh, Ben's car was not there.

"Did you walk from your office to here?" I demanded.

"Yes. Sometimes, it is quicker to walk than drive and, besides, I don't need my vehicle. Please see if you can find your car fob thing in that bag of yours and unlock your car for us."

"If you're planning on driving me home, how do you plan to get back into the city to collect your vehicle?"

"Don't worry about the plan or me. Just get in the car, please, so we can be on our way. No. In the passenger's seat, thanks."

Riding in the passenger's seat in my own car was a new experience. Everything looked a bit different from that side of the vehicle, but the drive home was without mishap or further argument. And, of course, Ben insisted on accompanying me inside and making sure I was safe, before once more reading me the riot act about resting and not working.

As he made moves to leave, he repeated his 'rest not work' mantra. "What are your plans for the remainder of the afternoon?"

"Uhmm… no plans really, that is, not after I make myself a coffee. Shall I make you one too?"

At that point, a patrol car pulled up out front to collect Ben, and I was soon standing at the door watching him disappear down the driveway. I didn't feel in the least interested in coffee. Mentioning it had been nothing more than putting on a bold front about how ordinary and normal I felt. In reality, I felt shattered. I was sinking fast and needed a rest. As I threw myself on my bed, I told myself an hour's rest would be all I needed.

So much for an hour's rest. It was long gone five o'clock when I prised my eyelids apart and then spent the next few moments wondering where the hell I was. Once functioning normally again, I went for a shower and to wash my hair. The latter operation being somewhat tricky, thanks to my recent injury. As I wandered out to the kitchen, the process had breathed new life into me – and I kept wandering through the kitchen and into my office. But now I did need coffee and went to make one while my computer booted up. Instant would do. I had neither the time nor the patience to be fiddling with the coffee machine today.

"Crikey," I yelped. "Has the world gone mad?"

My setup allows me to access emails, messages and files from both my city office and my home office. The flood of emails and messages that flowed through to me was unbelievable. How could everything become so busy in the space of just 24 hours? I decided to check my calendar to see if that might shed some light on the volume of emails and messages.

There it was. An entry for 10:10 on Monday morning for Trina Blewett, who arrived without an appointment. I gazed at the entry in my calendar for a few moments as I tried to recall her visit. I could picture her face and I now knew the time and day she came to my office, but details of her visit eluded me. Why had she come? What did we talk about? What was worrying her sufficiently to warrant talking to a private investigator?

While I churned my memory banks for even the slightest clue, the little voice in my head kept reminding me to check the time. It was right, of course. I should check the time. Ben was likely to arrive soon and it would not do to have him find me working here in my office. I glanced at my wrist to check the time.

"Damn! That was my favourite watch. Now, for the next little while, I suppose I'll have to wear my other one."

The one I had lost was the older of the two I owned, but its black body and black sports-style strap made it more suited to 'work wear' than its newer rose gold counterpart with the pinkish-coloured strap. I pulled open the top drawer of my desk and reached in for my remaining watch. Then I remembered the time was on the far right end of the task bar at the bottom of my computer screen. I squinted at it, but my currently sub-par eyesight rendered it nothing more than a fuzzy blur. I had thrust my hand into the drawer at the same time as I tried to read the screen. I spun around to look in the drawer and found my hand resting on the magnifying glass I kept there. Grabbing the magnifier, I held it up to the screen.

"6.45…," I yelped. "Jesus, Ben will be here at any moment. I need to shut everything down and be out of here now." I checked the time again. Perhaps I had misread it.

No, it said 6.45. As I reached for the mouse to close down the computer, my eyes strayed to the day and date shown below the time.

"What the…. That can't be right. Something has happened to this machine while I was away. Where's my watch?"

I scrabbled around in the drawer, located my second watch and checked its version of the day and date.

"That can't be right. What is happening here?" I demanded of the universe as I shut down my computer. For a moment, I sat at my desk, too stunned to move.

Chapter 6

Still somewhat dazed, I switched off the light in my office on my way past as I rushed to my loungeroom and collapsed in a chair.

"How can today be Friday?" I asked my silent house. "What happened to Tuesday, Wednesday and Thursday?"

I sat, zombie-like, staring at the floor in front of me as I tried to compile a list of everything I knew about this past week.

"Right," I murmured. "Today supposedly is Friday: I left hospital, picked up a key from Emily, went to my office, and Ben brought me home. Yeah, that's about all that happened today."

Thursday was a little more tricky to recall, but I did remember Ben had visited me in hospital that evening, and a nurse unhooked me from all of the gadgetry. She also showed me how to use their online system to order food for the next day, and I did that after Ben left in the evening. So far, so good, I told myself.

Wednesday was more of a challenge. I could remember several other things had happened, but slotting them into the correct day proved difficult. After tossing them around in my mind for a while, I decided that it was Wednesday afternoon when the young lad, Gavin, came to see me. Was that the day Lisa chatted to me about her friend Zali? After a few moments, I decided that, yes, Lisa spoke to me on Wednesday – a couple of times, I think. While remembering those two events was useful, I couldn't remember much else about Wednesday.

"Never mind, leave it for now," I told myself. "Move on and see what else you can remember."

A quick check on the time told me it was gone seven o'clock. Ben was running late… If he intended to come back at all. Yes, of course, Ben was coming back. He had an overnight bag in my spare bedroom. Well, come on, what else can I remember before he arrives?

Tuesday… Tuesday… "What the hell happened on Tuesday? I can't remember Tuesday." My voice had become increasingly louder as the realisation that I could not recall anything about Tuesday hit me like a thunderbolt.

Logic returned, and a little voice in my head told me to leave Tuesday alone and go back to Monday. Okay, well, Monday was when Trina Blewett came to see me. If it were a standard first interview, it would have taken the best part of an hour. That's where I drew a blank. I could not remember anything about the interview. Maybe it will come to me later after I've sorted out the rest of the day.

So, Monday, eh? Something else must've happened to fill in the day, but a search of my memory banks came up empty. I itched to go back to look at my online calendar. I knew there was nothing there after the entry for Trina Blewett, but what happened in the preceding days might provide a clue. Frustrating though it was, that would have to wait until tomorrow. A car had just pulled up out front. Ben had arrived and let himself in.

"What's happening? Are you all right?" he demanded by way of a greeting. "Sonny, talk to me."

"I'm fine. What are you fussing about?"

"You were sitting there looking stunned, as though you had seen a ghost or something."

Another car arrived. Emily. Her arrival brought that conversation to an end. I scrambled out of my chair, relieved her of the bag of food from one of our favourite takeaway places, and took it through to the kitchen. Emily followed me through with containers of gelato and fruit salad. It was agreed we should get straight down to the business of eating dinner. The meal was notable for the absence of wine. No one brought wine, and none of mine was opened. So, after we finished the main meal, we took our bowls of gelato and fruit salad through to the lounge room with nothing more than mugs of coffee to accompany them.

"Just because I can't have alcohol while I'm on antibiotics, there is no need for you to abstain. Open a bottle of wine or help yourself to glasses of port if you prefer." They both claimed to be happy as they were.

Contrary to my best efforts, Ben insisted on returning to the conversation he'd started when he walked through the door this evening. After a bit of none too gentle coaxing, I decided to share my concerns.

"I suppose I was stunned. I had thought today was Wednesday. So, it came as a shock to discover it was Friday. It sent me into something of a tailspin as I tried to work out what had happened on those days between when I saw Trina Blewett – or Zali, if you prefer – and today. Today wasn't a problem, and I more or less sorted out what happened yesterday, which I learned was Thursday." I paused for a moment to sort out what to say next.

"Keep going," Ben insisted. "We'll discuss everything in detail after you've finished."

"Well, there isn't much else to tell. My memory banks produced only two things for Wednesday. Gavin, who found me and brought me into town, came to see me in the afternoon after he finished work. It was a short visit of not much consequence, but it gave me an opportunity to thank him before the nurse bustled him out when his time was up. The only other thing I remember about Wednesday is chatting to Lisa. I think she might have visited a couple of times. Yeah, twice, I think, and it was during our second chat that she told me about her best friend, Zali, whom she believed had come to see me."

"Don't stop. You're doing well. Keep going," Emily encouraged me.

"Well, the rest of it can be summed up in about two sentences. I have nothing for Monday apart from the visit by Trina Blewett, and Tuesday just doesn't exist in my memory banks. Although I remember those couple of events on Wednesday, the rest of the day is a blank.

I know everyone is going to tell me that's all part of the concussion and the head trauma, and that I have to give myself time to recover before I worry about memory loss."

"If you know that's the advice you are going to be given, we won't waste our breath saying it," Ben said with a chuckle before continuing.

"I'm not surprised you can't remember Tuesday. When you were admitted to hospital, they put you into some sort of induced coma to assist your recovery. That would have taken care of Tuesday and, as they were just bringing you out of that coma on Wednesday, it's not surprising there are gaps in your memory of that day."

"But what about Monday?" I demanded. "Something must've happened at some time on Monday, even if the only thing that happened was that I was attacked and dumped at an abandoned mine site. Did that happen during the day or at night? If it happened that night, what else happened between when Trina Blewett left my office and I was attacked?"

Emily and Ben exchanged a look, and I saw Ben give Emily just the hint of a nod. I was about to demand to know what was going on when Emily sprang up off her chair and went over and turned off the lounge room lights. We were not in darkness. The kitchen lights were still on and flooded the lounge room with a soft glow. I felt a little uncomfortable. I wasn't sure where this was heading, but I didn't have long to wait to find out.

"Thanks, Emily," Ben said and cleared his throat before continuing. "Sonny, as you said, we could tell you that what you're experiencing is consistent with your injuries – but we won't bother. Instead, we are going to explore those memory banks of yours to see if we can discover anything relevant that might be hiding there."

"Don't you think that might be a waste of time and energy? If I can't dredge up anything out of the fog currently surrounding my brain, why do you two 'outsiders' think you can do better?"

"We don't think we can do better," Emily said quietly. "But we do think we might be able to help you to retrieve a bit more from your memory banks." I shrugged and told them to do their damnedest, as I was sure the missing bits had gone down a black hole somewhere.

Once Ben was convinced all three of us were satisfactorily relaxed, he began what amounted to, in general terms, a casual chat about the things I had remembered. Then, after a short while, he took the 'chat' into more serious territory.

"Let's go back to that Monday. Close your eyes, Sonny, and let your mind drift back to that Monday. Obviously, you went into your office in the city, because that's where Trina Blewett came to see you. Did you have any other appointments that day?"

"My calendar doesn't show any."

Ben nodded and then changed tack. "You had just wrapped up one case. Were you working on another one?" I shook my head. "Okay, so you didn't have an investigation to go on with, but you went into your city office anyway on Monday. Why? Why did you go into your office in the city if you had nothing to do there?"

"Uhmm… I did have to go in that morning… I had to finish off something." The other two sat silent while I churned through my memory banks. "Ah, yes… The case I wrapped up; I had to finish the paperwork for the case."

"You had to finish writing the client's report on the investigation?" Ben asked.

"No-o, not the report. No, I had finished the report the night before, after you went home early because you were going to Brisbane the next day. It was something to do with the final invoice that I had to do." I mentally walked myself through the memories of that Sunday night as they emerged from the dark recesses of my memory.

"You could have done that at home, just as you did with the report. Why did you have to go into your city office the next day to do it?" Ben probed again.

"Something…. Yes, that's what it was. I couldn't finish the final invoice because I thought I was missing a piece of information. I felt I had missed something, so I went to my city office the next morning to check. It took me a while, but I found I had overlooked four hours of surveillance one night. Then, I finalised the invoice and sent it and the report off to the client."

"If you went into the city at your normal time, you would have been in your office by just after eight o'clock. What time did Trina Blewett come to see you?" Ben asked.

"A little after ten o'clock…."

"You had been in your office for a couple of hours by then. What else did you do after you sent off the client's documentation?" Emily asked quietly.

"Nothing…. Ah, yes, I remember now. I did all the usual admin stuff first. There were a few enquiries that required brochures and other information to be sent. It was after that when I started checking my billable hours to finalise the invoice and it took me a while to find what I had missed. After I sent everything off to that client, I made a coffee and had drunk about half of it when Trina arrived."

"Had someone recommended you to her, or had she just found you in the phone book?" Ben was back in charge of the questions again.

Eventually, I shook my head and shrugged. It didn't matter how hard I tried, I couldn't find an answer for him. He made sympathetic noises, told me it wasn't important, and to relax and not worry about it. After a few moments, he asked his next question.

"What had she come to see you about?"

Again, I drew a blank and, in the end, just shook my head in response. Then, it was Emily's turn again.

"Was she just making general enquiries about what you do, or did you conduct a typical case preliminary interview with her?" I sat totally confused and stared at Emily. She reworded her question. "Did she stay long? Maybe about an hour while she outlined what the problem she wanted investigated was?"

At first, no answer emerged from the soup of my addled brain. Ben brought question time to an end.

"I think that's enough for now. You've done well to recover that much, Sonny. Tomorrow's another day. Maybe you'll remember more then, or maybe we will have to wait until next week. Who knows? However long it takes doesn't matter."

Emily scrambled out of her chair and announced she was going to make another coffee. Ben followed her example, but he was going to pour himself a port and asked if anyone else would like one. Emily said she would have one with him. They both disappeared into the kitchen, leaving me alone with my churning mind.

It wasn't long after that Emily went home and Ben announced he would have a shower and then call it a night. That left me sitting in the lounge room alone and still trying to resurrect lost areas of my memory. Last thing before going to bed, Ben came out to once more deliver his message about 'resting' and urged me to go to bed.

While my inclination was to sneak back into my office the moment I thought Ben was asleep, I knew it would be futile and would only result in my incurring the wrath of my houseguest. So, instead, I dragged myself off for a shower and went to bed. Sleep was a long time coming. When it did, it wasn't restful. After dozing in fits and starts and tossing and turning for what felt like more than half the night, Morpheus finally took hold of me.

When I managed to untangle my eyelashes on Saturday morning, I had overslept my usual wake-up time by quite a bit. Still half asleep, I wandered out to the kitchen, half expecting Ben to be there. He wasn't. Evidence indicated he had an early breakfast and then went somewhere. I held the hope he had gone home for something, or into his office to work for a while. I decided to allow myself a leisurely breakfast before absconding to my home office to make the best of his absence. It wasn't to be.

Before I was halfway through breakfast, Ben returned and strode in, brandishing the weekend papers.

"Thought we might find these useful on a lazy weekend. Oh, I forgot. Your eyesight… Never mind. You should at least be able to read the headlines. If all else fails, perhaps I could read a few articles to you." That was never going to happen, and I said so.

Bugger. It looked as though Ben planned to dig himself in here for the weekend. Within an instant, I knew that was likely to result in an argument before the weekend was over. I wanted – needed – to spend time in my office. Although I'm not allowed to drive into the city, I can do everything I want to here at home … if I'm just allowed to spend time in my office. To confirm my suspicions about Ben's plans for the weekend, I asked what was on his agenda for the next two days.

"Nothing. We are still snowed under with cases, but it's all petty stuff and nothing needing my attention. So, I plan to have a lazy weekend right here, keeping you company while you have a restful couple of days."

Shit! That was not what I wanted to hear. How am I to get rid of my watchdog so I can do the things I need to do? I suppose I could pray for a major crime wave to hit Millhaven sometime today, except the Big Man Upstairs doesn't appear in the mood to grant me any favours lately.

Ben took one of the papers and sprawled out on the couch on the back deck. With few other options open to me, I grabbed the other paper and put my feet up in the lounge room to sulk for a while. I was well and truly into a really good sulk when a stray thought slammed in from out of nowhere. I sprang bolt upright in my chair.

"What about Lisa?" I whispered to the room before devoting a couple of minutes to thinking about the nurse and the information she had given me about Zali.

How much did Lisa really know about her best friend, Zalika Standish? Did she have more insight into whatever supposedly was troubling her mate than she indicated? The more I thought about it, the more convinced I became that was the case. The only problem was, I had no evidence to support my suspicion.

I knew Ben would pounce on that fact the moment I mentioned my current thinking about Lisa to him. After worrying the idea to death for a few minutes, I decided to risk running it past Ben. But, my approach needed to be subtle, even devious maybe, if he wasn't to dismiss the suggestion out of hand.

While devising my 'devious plan' for Ben, something else occurred to me and raised an interesting question. A question to which I didn't have an answer. Who was the nurse, Lisa? Maybe I should contact her to set up a meeting. The only problem was, to implement my approach, I needed to know her surname and how to obtain that might be tricky. After a little more thought, I came up with an approach that just might work.

Picking up my phone on the way, I snuck into my bedroom and called the number from my contacts list, all the while hoping Ben was sound asleep and wouldn't burst in on me while I was on the call.

A receptionist of some sort answered. I launched into my hastily prepared spiel. She apologised for not being able to help me with the information I wanted and said she was putting me through to the main nurses' station, where someone else might be able to help. I was losing confidence as I listened to the phone at the nurses' station ringing without being answered. Then, a friendly, mature voice asked if she could help me.

"Well, frankly, I'm not sure that you can… and I'm sure this call is going to sound really strange." She encouraged me to give it a shot and told me she was well-practised at dealing with strange calls.

"Okay. Well, while I was a recent patient in the hospital, one of the nurses was particularly helpful and kind. I would like to drop a card in at the hospital for her to say thank you. My problem is that I only know her first name from her badge, and I think I at least need to include her surname on the envelope. Is there any way you might give me her surname without breaching confidentiality rules or whatever?"

She hesitated for a moment before answering. "Uhmm… It might be possible. What was this nurse's name?"

"According to her badge, her name was Lisa."

"Give me a moment while I check for you."

After what I considered an abnormally long time, the nurse came back on the line. I had a bad feeling starting to develop.

"Excuse me, Miss, can you tell me how long ago you were a patient here?"

"I was released yesterday after spending the week as an in-patient." More bad feelings rushed in to join the first lot.

"If you wouldn't mind, describe Lisa for me, please."

Yep, bad feelings are piling up now. I gave her an amateur's attempt at a physical description, dotted throughout with regular insertions of 'I think'.

"When did you last see or speak to Lisa," she asked in a guarded sort of way.

"Uhmm… last Wednesday, I think." The instant I said it, I knew that was wrong. It probably was Thursday, but I was still confused about the days.

"Look, I'm sorry, Miss. I don't mean to be difficult, but I can't help you. I've checked our records for both our nurses and contractors currently working in the hospital. There isn't a Lisa amongst them."

"No one working at the hospital at the moment is called Lisa?" I asked to confirm I had understood her correctly.

"That's right, Miss. We don't have anyone called Lisa working here now. We did have a nurse named Lisa who worked here for a couple of years, but she left to go overseas a bit over six months ago."

After thanking her for her trouble, and having drawn a blank at finding Lisa by myself, it was time to enlist the aid of someone with a bit more clout. I returned my attention to the district's top cop, Ben Richards, currently snoozing on my back deck, and revived my plan for how to approach the conversation I wanted to have with him,

'Subtle', I reminded myself as I strolled out onto the back deck. The newspaper was lying across Ben's chest as he dozed.

I pulled a chair out from the table. Its scraping across the floor achieved the desired effect of waking him.

"I've been thinking, Ben…."

"That's always a worry, but go on, tell me about it."

"Remember Lisa, the nurse who was Zali's best friend? It would be good to talk to her again. I was still a bit groggy when she told me about Zali. Now I'm wondering if I might have missed something, maybe nothing more than a subtle nuance of something. Anyway, I feel I need to know more about Zali, who looked like becoming my new client. Lisa said she would contact me after I was discharged, but maybe she has moved on since then, and Zali's death isn't so raw anymore.

Do you think I should try to contact her? How would I do that anyway? I don't even know that nurse's full name."

"Don't worry about it just yet. I put in a request to the hospital's authorities for information on the nurse you mentioned. Nothing has come through yet, but I really wasn't expecting anything until Monday at the earliest. What else do you think this Lisa might have to tell you?"

"It's possible there won't be anything useful in terms of the investigation, but I would like to get a feel for my new client. More of Zali's background information might help me remember why she came to see me. I know I'm probably clutching at straws. But, Ben, they're the only straws I have, and something tells me that getting to know my client better will be a worthwhile exercise in terms of recovering my memory."

Ben nodded to indicate he knew where I was coming from and then checked his watch. "It's almost lunchtime. I could go out to fetch something for lunch, or we could go for a drive to the marina and grab a bite at a bistro or restaurant there. What would be your preference?"

While a drive to the marina and being out of the house for a while had a certain appeal, sending Ben out on his own to find something for lunch had a much higher appeal rating. Although he wouldn't be gone long on his foraging expedition, it would allow me a few precious moments in my office while he wasn't here. Decision made… I blamed feeling a bit weary for my preference to have lunch at home. A few minutes later, Ben drove off in search of food.

Chapter 7

As soon as I saw his vehicle disappearing down the driveway, I bolted into my office and booted up my computer.

"Right… now I'm here, what am I going to do?" I asked my empty office.

I hadn't thought it through and didn't have a plan, but I knew I had to capitalise on whatever time he'd given me. As soon as my computer was right to go I went straight to my calendar. Nothing had changed overnight. There was still only one entry for last Monday: Trina Blewett. As expected, when I worked backwards through the calendar, there were no entries over the previous weekend. Okay, Friday is my last hope, I told myself as I brought up Friday's page. A bit happened on Friday last week. I had a final meeting with my then client prior to wrapping up that investigation. Two potential clients had made appointments and took away with them all of my information documentation. A couple of phone enquiries also came in. One of those I immediately deemed a waste of time, but my entry regarding the other one now held my attention.

Why would that entry be dragging me to it like iron filings to a magnet? My entry suggested it was nothing more than another enquiry phone call. The only thing that stood out about it was that I had noted my offer to send out relevant information to the caller and that she had rejected the offer. But, it was my final comment in the entry that held my attention. The caller said she would make an appointment early next week to come to see me personally. Frustratingly, I hadn't recorded the caller's name anywhere.

Was the caller Trina Blewett? That assumption would be a bit of a long shot and, if it was, why had she then turned up without an appointment? Somewhere in the fog filling my head,

I heard the distant tinkle of a little bell. A little voice in my head kept repeating the name Trina Blewett on some sort of continuous loop.

"Yes, I know that's the bloody name she gave me, and no, I'm not sure it was her real name." I quickly checked around my office to make sure no one had snuck in and heard me having a chat with myself.

With a bit of effort, I visualised the young woman sitting talking to me. It reinforced my earlier thought that the name she gave me didn't suit that gorgeous looking young woman. Still, I don't suppose parents, when they are naming their child, have any idea what that child might look like in the future. Her parents certainly did this child of theirs a disservice. But, what if Trina Blewett was her real name? If that were the case, she should appear somewhere in official records. My first thought was a local phone book. After all, what young woman doesn't have a phone these days? Then it occurred to me. She might well have a phone, but its number might not be publicly listed anywhere.

The only other place I thought might be worth a quick look was a local electoral roll. Trina certainly was old enough to vote and, as she lived in Millhaven, she had to appear on at least one of the federal, state or local electoral rolls, and probably on all three of them.

As I expected, there was no listing for Blewett in the online phonebook for this region. So, I took a deep breath and embarked on the mammoth task ahead of me. Which electoral roll should I start with? As far as I knew, Blewett wasn't a common name locally, so maybe the smallest, the local government electoral roll, was the place to start.

It took me no more than a minute to confirm Blewett wasn't a common local name. There were no entries for the surname on the local government roll. After a few moments of thought, I persuaded myself that Trina might be registered at a former address somewhere in this state. She wasn't. I wasn't too inclined to search the huge federal electoral roll, so I opted to sit back and give the matter further thought before rushing forward.

A bit slow off the mark, Old Girl, I told myself after staring at my desktop for a minute or two. While I was checking the rolls and the phone book, I should also have looked for entries for Zali. The easiest option remained to take another look at those records I already had checked for Blewett. Not surprisingly, perhaps, Zali did not appear in the phone book, but the Standish name was on the local government electoral roll. I assumed, perhaps a little carelessly, that the name also would appear on the state electoral roll, so I didn't bother to check.

Having found two mentions of the Standish surname, I now had created another problem to ponder. The people attached to those Standish surnames I had located did not include Zali, or any name that might suggest one of them was her, and neither of them was located anywhere close to Millhaven. When I have one-of-those-days, I make a good job of it. Today, I was batting three strikes. Were all the names I had come up with nothing more than figments of my damaged mind?

"Face it. You've hit a brick wall," I muttered to myself. Perhaps Ben and all the experts were right. My recovery still had a way to go before I was up to the task I had given myself. I dropped my head onto my arms on the desk and prepared to give the matter some thought. My phone playing its tune put paid to that. I checked the caller ID: Ben.

"How hungry are you? I thought I might call at the precinct to check on something before I head back. Is that okay with you? It shouldn't take me anymore than ten minutes or so," he told me.

"Take as long as you need. I'm not in danger of succumbing to starvation any time soon," I assured Ben.

Okay, that gives me another few minutes before he returns. How best can I use the time? Emails… perhaps, if I check my emails, not just for anything new, but those from the recent past. I grabbed my phone to move it out of the way before I started on my emails, but a sudden thought made me check how much charge was left on my phone.

"Whoa, that can't be right. How can that be?" I yelped. "I can lose four days of my life but, during that time, my phone remained fully charged." I checked the charge level again just to confirm that it remained almost fully charged. The bit of charge used only occurred after I collected the phone from my office late yesterday. That brought something else to mind. When he visited me in hospital, he told me Emily had looked for my phone in my office to give it to him to bring to me in hospital, but she couldn't find it.

No, of course. Emily couldn't find it. Some time ago, I installed a small, narrow shelf high up along one side of the well under the desk in my city office. With the aid of a small power board, I was able to charge my phone without having it cluttering the desk. That's where it was when I collected it yesterday. Obviously, Emily doesn't know about my charging station. The picture I conjured up of Emily going through my office trying to find my phone gave me the giggles... Until another thought slammed in from left field.

It had nothing to do with my phone, but it had brought something much more important to mind. It was then I heard Ben coming up the driveway. I grabbed my bag, threw my phone into it, and raced out to meet him, closing my front door behind me. He had his car door open and was about to climb out. I slammed his door closed as I raced around and scrambled into the passenger seat.

"I need to go to my office, Ben. Right now. Don't argue, please."

"What happened? Talk to me, Sonny. What's going on?'

"Just drive, Ben... Please. I'll explain on the way."

In truth, I didn't explain the urgency of needing to go to my office, but he responded to my actions, and I don't think he worried too much about speed limits all the way into the city. By the time we were in the car park behind my building, I had my keys out of my bag and firmly in my hand. As soon as we pulled up, I dived out of the car and sprinted for the backdoor of the building. Ben sprinted after me and grabbed me by the arm. I heard him arm the car's security system before he spoke to me.

"Right; now you can calmly unlock the door, and we will go inside. There will be no rushing about, just a calm entry after you unlock that door."

He let go of my arm as I fumbled with the keys. Then, with the door unlocked, I dived inside and quickly keyed in the security code to prevent the alarm sounding. I dashed for the stairs, but Ben again caught me by the arm.

"No. No, there will be no rushing about. We will calmly and sedately climb those stairs together."

To ensure we did climb them together, he didn't let go of my arm until we were at the top of the stairs and I was ready to unlock my office door. After yet more fumbling with keys, the door was open and I raced to my interview corner and pushed one chair out of the way. Grunting, I reached down behind the other chair before coming up again brandishing my prize above my head. In attempting to regain my feet, I stumbled and fell into the chair beside me. Laughing, I looked up at Ben. His face told me he couldn't see the funny side of anything at that point in time.

"Oh, for goodness sake, Ben, this is going to help me fill in some of the gaps," I snarled as I waved my digital recorder at him. "I've got to play the last recording."

He reached over and swiped the recorder out of my hand and shoved it in his pocket, before reaching down and helping haul me to my feet.

"Ye-es, we do need to listen to the last recording on that machine, but not right now. I have our lunch downstairs in my car. We are going to go back to your place to sit down and have a quiet, leisurely lunch. Then, it might – might – be time to listen to whatever you've recorded on that machine. Now, come on. Let's go home."

"I'll need to take the charging cable," I said a little petulantly, and he gestured to me to retrieve it from where it was plugged in behind the lounge chair.

Our drive home from the city was in silence. I was too angry to speak. I'm sure Ben was aware of that and chose to ignore me. Not a word was exchanged until we were inside and dealing with lunch. Strangely enough, lunch did take longer than I thought I would allow it to. It was due largely, I suspect, to the fact that I had spent the whole time trying to recall what we might hear on that recording when we finally played it. At last we had stacked our plates in the dishwasher. We took our coffees into my office.

Within moments, the recorder was plugged in, the start of the file found, and I pressed PLAY.

"What's happening?" Ben demanded. "Is that how the entire recording will be?"

Unintelligible babble came from my recorder in Morse code-like fits and starts. Not one word of it was clear enough to be understood. Ben continued to ask what was wrong with my recorder and whether it would become better as it progressed. I ignored him as I tried to figure out why the machine hadn't functioned properly. Slowly, my mind cut through its fog and took me back to last Monday morning. Without realising what I was doing, as my mind retraced those events, I murmured a running commentary.

"My first task of the day was to send the report and invoice to my previous client, then I took care of all the usual admin stuff... A few enquiries… Sent off information… Going to make a coffee but stopped when someone rang the doorbell... Thought it might be previous client come to pay her invoice or argue about something on it… Switched the recorder on behind the chair on my way to answer the door… not my previous client… Someone I hadn't seen before standing there… Looked unsure about being there.

The commentary paused for a moment while I coaxed more of the story out of the fog and before haltingly beginning again. The woman was unsure, nervous, and not suited to a chat in my interview corner. I ushered her to a seat at my desk and tried easing her into explaining why she was there. So we could converse on a more friendly note, I introduced myself as Sonny and asked for her name: Trina Blewett. She seemed more intent on apologising for coming without an appointment than telling me why she had come.

After a minute or so, she began to speak a little more freely but continued to hedge around why she was there. Finally, she asked what I did, what kinds of cases I took on… Gave her copies of my documentation that explained my services… Suggested she not study them in detail now, but tell me about her problem instead, so I could tell her whether it fitted with my operations.

She continued to appear uncertain and uncomfortable. I wondered whether she might be concerned about the fees I charged, so I made a show of rattling around in my desk drawer as I told her I was looking for another document (fees schedule) to give her."

At that point, my running commentary stalled. I slapped my hand down hard on my desk, causing Ben to flinch.

"Don't stop there," I snarled. "What happened next?"

"What has happened?" Ben asked cautiously from the other side of my desk. He then set about prompting my memory. "You were going to give her a copy of your schedule of fees and made a show of digging a copy out of a file in your desk drawer. Why put on a show? Why not just give her a copy to take away with her?"

I replayed Ben's summation in my mind. Something was trying to emerge from the fog but couldn't quite break through. I ran his words through my mind again as I stared fixedly at the blank whiteboard on the wall opposite me.

"Yes! Yes, something else happened," I yelped. "What else? What did I do?" I growled. A moment later, my commentary resumed.

"The fuss I made of finding a fees schedule was to cover something else I did at the same time. I had the drawer pulled out as far as it would go and… *And I dropped something on the floor… No, I didn't… I pretended I had dropped something.* It was meant to cover what I really did…"

"Ben, I know what I did," I shrieked at him. "It was a ruse to cover the fact that I reached under my desk and grabbed my phone off the little shelf where it was plugged in and charging. I switched the phone on to record the interview with Trina Blewett."

"You recorded the interview on your phone?" he asked. I smirked and nodded. "Well, I don't imagine that is going to be any better than the stuff your recorder had to offer. After all, your phone was *under* your desk, not *on* it, where it might pick up everything clearly."

"No, Ben, that's not the case. I don't know why it works as well as it does, but I've recorded conversations that way a few times before."

"So, in this Blewett woman's case, what prompted you to record the interview when the conversation had been going on for some time already?"

"That's something I'm not clear about either. Perhaps it was Trina's demeanour. The woman remained unsettled – nervous – the whole time she was in my office. The interview didn't start smoothly and didn't improve as it progressed. I suppose, I suspected, or hoped, a bombshell might be forthcoming somewhere along the line and that, perhaps, she just needed to feel sure about me before she properly opened up. Unless the recording indicates otherwise, that never happened. I don't think she ever relaxed or told me exactly why she had come to see me.

I know there's more than that hiding somewhere in my head, but I can't grab hold of it to drag it out into the open."

"Maybe we should take a break, have a coffee, and come back to it fresh again later," Ben suggested, but it was the last thing I wanted to do.

"Look, Ben, I don't know whether I'll be able to dredge up anything else out of the murky blackness of my memory, but I know there is more there. I also know – at least, I'm fairly sure – that by the time she left, Trina Blewett was not an actual client. Now, whether that means she was going to go and think about it a bit more, or if she had decided against hiring me, I don't know. But I am fairly sure she was not a new client when she left my office."

"Well, as you seem so sure your phone will have recorded all that was discussed, maybe we should listen to it. Perhaps listening to the recording will help you recall any visual or other observations you noted during the interview."

While I couldn't argue with Ben's suggestion that it might be the best next step, it wasn't what I wanted to do. I wanted to remember the rest of what happened, and all of the finer details, for myself without the aid of an audio prompt. I was about to try explaining that situation to him when his phone chirped for attention. After checking the caller ID, he went out onto the back deck to take the call.

He returned after only a couple of minutes, but the grave look on his face suggested a serious work-related incident had occurred. He confirmed my suspicions as soon as he walked into my office.

"Sorry, Sonny, duty calls. I don't know when I'll be back, but try to rest this afternoon, please. I'll give you a call when I know what's happening. Don't do anything while I'm gone, just rest" And then he was gone.

"Rest… Who did Ben think he was kidding?" I asked the universe.

At last, maybe the gods have decided to smile on me and, with Ben called away, I would have the rest of the afternoon to do whatever I wanted to do. As I made a coffee before going back into my office, I sifted through everything I had managed to dredge up about that visit by Trina Blewett. I knew there was more that happened or was said before she left my office. I was determined to remember it without the aid of the recording.

There was something I could do with the recording, even if I didn't want to listen to it. I could ask my phone to produce a transcript and save the transcript file in the 'My Files' app on the phone. It took me a little while to remember how to do it but, at last, it seemed to be happening okay. So, I shoved the phone to one side, put my feet up on the desk, and stared off into the distance. At first, all that happened was that the stuff we already retrieved came to the fore and dominated my thought processes. I had finished my coffee by the time I started on new ground.

It wasn't much, but it was progress. I remembered the woman had become increasingly reticent as we progressed until there was a long pause. Perhaps it was as long as three minutes. I began feeling uneasy and wondered about Blewett's mental stability. Was she about to snap, and what might be the outcome if she did? Before the pause occurred, I had asked her a question about what might be troubling her and why she thought she needed a private investigator.

Initially, I thought that pause occurred because she was considering her answer and, perhaps, how much she should tell me at that time. I remained silent while I waited for her answer. But as the pause stretched on, and I became uneasy about it, I sought to remedy the situation. I remembered how I tried to prompt her to say something.

Trina, is the reason you came here so embarrassing you're having difficulty trying to discuss it with me? Whatever it is, I promise you I probably have dealt with worse. You also need to know that whatever you discuss with me is completely confidential. Client confidentiality, such as you might find in the legal world, applies here as well. So, rest assured, whatever you tell me remains here and goes no further. The only time that might change is if, in the course of my investigation, something illegal or a threat to life is discovered.

The spiel I eventually delivered was not unique or even unusual. I had often found it necessary to use the same words to reassure other potential clients. It generally was effective enough to make them relax and let us get on with things, but I remembered that wasn't so in Blewett's case. I recalled she remained on edge, and there were further long pauses in the so-called interview until she finally left my office. The big question then was, had she elected to become a client or not?

I pondered the question for some time before I thought I had found the answer. It wasn't so much that I remembered something said or done, it was more a feeling I developed as I thought about the question. That feeling suggested Trina Blewett had left my office without officially becoming a new client.

Think, Sonny, think. Why do I feel that's what happened? I allowed my mind to revisit the latter part of the interview. It consisted of more pauses than words. I told myself to picture Blewett sitting at my desk. What was she doing, or what did she say to make me think she was leaving? I closed my eyes, relaxed my neck and my shoulders, and slowed my breathing. After sitting like that for a few moments, a video from my memory banks started to play.

Blewett suddenly sat upright on her chair, picked up her bag from the floor beside her chair and plonked it on her lap. She gathered up the documentation I had given her at the start of the interview and shoved it in her bag. Then, Trina was on her feet. With no more than a curt thank you, she was heading to the door… And then she was gone.

Well, so that's what happened. At least, I now know Trina did not officially become a client and, by the time she left my office, I still had no idea why she had come to see me or what might have been troubling her.

Chapter 8

I swung my feet off the desk and reached for the daybook that was open on the desk beside me. I needed to note those memories of the last part of the interview that had now come to me. So I didn't forget them, I scribbled as quickly as possible into the daybook with the intention of typing them up as part of a larger file note at some time in the future.

Having recovered another major missing chunk of my memory, I should be feeling somewhat elated. Why was that not the case? I pondered that question for a moment or two without finding a definitive answer. Yes, I was thrilled and pleased with myself today for having dragged so much back from the brink, but I expected to feel more excited about it. Although I had no idea what it might be, maybe there was more to the story that I had yet to remember. I decided to sit back and have another try at dredging up a bit more, but I soon found that, with no idea of what I was looking for, nothing further emerged.

"Okay, let's not waste any more time. What else can I do while Ben is not here?" No answers were forthcoming from the universe or anywhere else, so I turned my attention to my phone.

After checking that it had created a new document in My Files, my next step was to WiFi the document to my printer. That done and my phone connected to my computer, I set about trying to remember how to download a copy of the transcript file onto my computer. Eventually, probably due more to something like 'muscle memory' than anything on my part, success was achieved. Then, yet another question confronted me. Should I continue to refrain from reading the transcript and continue to work on dredging stuff out of my memory, or should I take the easy route and just read the bloody thing? I was saved from making the hard decision by Ben's return.

As he came in the front door, the aroma of food wafted through the house and into my office. It prompted me to check the time.

"God, where did the afternoon go? It's almost seven o'clock and dinnertime," I muttered as I sprang off my chair and rushed out to meet Ben in the kitchen.

"Emily will be here in a minute," he announced, "but neither of us will be able to stay after dinner. Very unpleasant scene downtown requires attention."

From experience, I knew it was pointless to ask questions. If Ben wanted me to know what had happened 'downtown', he would have told me about it. The fact that Emily was also working on the investigation suggested there might be bodies involved. Emily arrived a few minutes later and we sat down to a variety of Chinese takeaway dishes. It was a subdued meal. Ben and Emily were obviously still processing whatever they had encountered at the crime scene they were investigating and, if I'm honest, I was feeling drained after this afternoon's memory reclamation exercise.

They took a bit of convincing but, after I assured them I was capable of clearing away and stacking the dishwasher, the other two left to return to their crime scene. Feeling a bit mentally exhausted, I decided not to go back into my office this evening, opting instead to channel-surf until I found something to watch on TV. An ancient movie was the only thing vaguely interesting on offer on a Saturday night program overloaded with almost every form of sport. Still, it was a movie I hadn't seen before. So, with no idea when Ben might return, or if he would return at all that night, I made myself comfortable and sat back to watch.

It seems the movie was not as entertaining as I first thought it might be. I was sound asleep in my chair and some sci-fi show was flashing bright colours across the screen when Ben shook me awake in the wee hours of Sunday morning.

"You didn't have to wait up," he admonished me. "For goodness sake, go to bed and have a decent night's sleep."

Zombie-like, I followed his instructions and headed for my bedroom. When halfway there, I remembered I hadn't showered before I sat down to watch TV. I tried to detour to the bathroom, but found my way blocked by the man-mountain of Ben Richards sternly pointing towards my bedroom. I tried explaining the situation, but he was having none of it. Grabbing me by the arm, he bustled me along to my bedroom door. Resistance was futile.

"The bathroom will still be there in the morning. You can have a shower then," he hissed at me. "Now go to bed. Besides, I want to have a shower now before I drop into bed."

Both of us slept late next morning, but Ben was halfway through his breakfast by the time I finally surfaced.

"The bathroom is free now if you still want to have that shower," he quipped as I came into the kitchen. "As soon as I finish breakfast, I'm going to my office, so I probably won't see you again until sometime later this morning."

I turned the shower fully on and stood there, letting the needle-like spray work its miracle. By the time I stepped out of the shower, I was pink all over, my extremities were as shrivelled as prunes and, for the first time in a week, I felt fully alive. As Ben had indicated, he was gone when I next ventured into the kitchen. Dawdling over breakfast and a second mug of coffee helped fill in a little time, but what else to do to fill in the rest of my day was a mystery to me as I sat with my second coffee on the back deck. Slowly rational thought returned and brought with it the memory of yesterday's recovery of some of my lost memory.

"Why am I still sitting out here doing nothing except drinking coffee?" I asked the Willy Wagtail that sat scolding me from the deck's railing.

He was right to give me a mouthful. I should be back in my office by now, seeing how much more I could winkle out of the remaining fog in my head. Minutes later, I was settled in my office and confronting my next problem: where to start?

A review. Yeah, start with a review of everything recovered to date. Apart from confirming its reliability, it also would highlight the remaining gaps in my memory. I knew this approach had been prompted in part by a lingering feeling that there was more to the Trina Blewett story and that whatever was still missing, was important. Maybe it was nothing more than a legacy of yesterday's mental gymnastics, but my thought processes this morning were slow and soggy as I tried to pull together everything I had established so far.

An additional hindrance to moving forward was a vague, half-formed notion that kept rolling around in the far reaches of my mind. It persisted in hovering just out of reach. In the end, I decided to abandon my original plan for this morning and, instead, try clearing my mind to allow the annoying thought to come forward. Easier said than done, I discovered. Although it took a while, more of it started to come through and gave rise to a strange feeling.

It was about the nurse, Lisa. The feeling suggested I had missed something – something important – about her. There was nothing for it but to revisit my conversations with Lisa. I slumped down in my chair, put my feet up on the desk, closed my eyes, and allowed my mind free rein. Almost instantly, an image of Lisa filled my mind. So, having made the connection, I willed it to dredge up my memory of our first conversation. After worrying that memory to death for a bit, I accepted there was nothing useful to be gained from exploring it further.

That first conversation was after Gavin had come to see me. After he left, she asked if he were my son and I had to explain he was only my knight in shining armour who had rescued me after finding me wandering along a road in the middle of nowhere. Lisa hadn't pushed me for details of my rescue, or how I had come to be wandering along that road. Was there something significant in that? Although I pondered it for every possible angle, I couldn't find anything concerning in any of that conversation.

I allowed my mind to drift on to my next conversation with Lisa. That second conversation was the big one. Thanks to her comments, I discovered I was a private investigator. That was big, but of more significance was her telling me about her best friend, Zali, coming to see me on the day she died. No one called Zali existed in my memory banks – such as they were at the time – but the physical description she gave of Zali, later triggered a recollection of a client fitting the description.

Revisiting that conversation took a while and the process was a bit unsettling, just as it had been at the time. Why was it unsettling? Was it nothing more than Zali's death on the same day as she came to see me? After giving it some thought, I decided that was not the case. No, there was something else about Lisa's discussion of her best friend that was a bit off somehow. Lisa would still have felt raw from the loss of her friend only a couple of days previously, so it would have been upsetting to talk about it.

Upsetting?.... Of course, Lisa would have been upset so soon after the incident. Was she upset? Nurses have to deal with all sorts of difficult and sometimes tragic situations in the course of their work. Maybe Lisa, as a nurse, had learned to compartmentalise her emotions and was coping with her loss better than perhaps others might. Who was I kidding? A couple of times during that conversation, Lisa had looked awkward – or unsure, perhaps – but she had never once looked upset.

Was that an amazing display of professional self-control, or was it something else? An apparent complete lack of grief, perhaps? She did not appear upset at any time while discussing her late friend.

"Well, what do I make of that?" I asked my empty office.

Ben arrived home while I was still pondering the question of Lisa's behaviour. He wasted no time in taking me to task about being in my office and didn't mince his words while he was about it. From experience, I know it's pointless to try to interrupt such scenes, so I sat silent until he had finished. Then, I exploded and told him in no uncertain terms that I was sick of being babysat and treated like an invalid. Having vented my spleen, I was happy to move on to sharing my recent discovery with him.

After explaining my assessment of Lisa's discussion of her friend, I expected Ben to ridicule my outcomes. He didn't… but he did question almost every aspect of that conversation with Lisa and my assessment of it.

"People do deal with grief in different ways. You would have discovered that in the course of your investigations. How convinced are you that Lisa wasn't trying to hold it in so as to appear professional?"

"Fairly convinced. I did consider such a situation, but it didn't quite fit with her behaviour. It was an observational thing, as well as perhaps a reaction on an emotional level – I sensed perhaps that there was no grief involved in her story."

"Did you have any other conversations with Lisa that you might use as a yardstick for comparison of her behaviour?"

"Uhmm… I had three conversations with Lisa – no, there were four. But, no, I didn't detect any change in her demeanour across all those conversations."

Of course, he wanted details of those conversations, so I listed them for him: after Gavin's visit, to tell me about Zali, after Ben's visit, and when she unhooked me from all the machines. He remained deep in thought after I finished speaking. I sat patiently and waited for the Third Degree I knew would follow. But, contrary to what I expected, his questions were focused and not as extensive.

Ben's focus was on what Lisa had asked about Gavin, and then, not unexpectedly, I suppose, he was particularly interested in everything said in relation to himself. Dealing with the question about Gavin was easy. There wasn't much to tell. But, when it came to what had been said about Ben, I had to dig into my memory not only for what was said but also for any nuances, or what might not have been said but was there between the lines. Was my being quizzed about Ben more than a passing interest might generate? It was a question that would hound me long after I'd explained Lisa's interest in him.

"Lisa didn't ask about you as such. It seemed to me at the time that her interest was in the nature of our relationship. I shut it down quickly by simply saying we had been friends for a long time. I didn't expand on that or give her anything else that might come back to bite us."

"Was there anything else, no matter how insignificant, about any of your conversations with the nurse?"

"No, not really. With the benefit of hindsight, the only other thing of interest was Lisa's statement that she would be coming to see me after I was released."

"Coming to see you for what reason? Was it to be a social call to see how you were going or for some other reason?"

"We hadn't become friends, so she wouldn't be coming to check on my health. No, she claimed she wanted to know more about Zali, although I ready had explained about client confidentiality. If I'm honest, at the time, I doubted she would come to see me, so I didn't take much notice of it. Now, although I still don't think I'll see her again, I'm a little more unsettled by the possibility of a visit."

I stopped myself from saying more just in time to prevent my mentioning that my concerns about Lisa had mainly developed after I discovered the hospital did not have a nurse named Lisa working there. While Ben appeared to be considering all I had said about Lisa so far, I thought of a further comment that might prove useful.

"More information about Lisa, or at least her surname, would be good. I know you asked the hospital for her details, Ben, but I'm now becoming anxious to see what their response might be."

He nodded as he pulled a notebook out of his pocket and scribbled something in it. "I will be contacting them again tomorrow to chase up the information I asked for. I'm surprised Lisa was interested in the nature of our relationship, especially when you had explained we'd known each other for years. Another thing has just occurred to me. Did you give that nurse anything?"

"Anything like what?" The question perplexed me. What could I give her?

"Argh, I don't know… anything… information… addresses… business card… anything at all that could come back in some way to bite you."

"Of course not. Anyway, along with my phone, watch, and one shoe, I also didn't have any business cards on me at the time. You know as well as I do that I don't give out personal details such as my addresses. I suppose, if Lisa was keen to find my address, she could look at my admittance record. But we both know that would only give her the bogus address of the one-time police safe house."

"Right… Anyway, I suppose she could find your city office's address without too much trouble."

"That's not likely. That address is not listed anywhere. My phone number is all that is available out there. People have to call for an appointment to see me and are given the address then. The only other way people I don't know can find my address is via word of mouth from my other current or previous clients. I know it doesn't make good business sense for potential clients not to be able to locate me but, because I spend so much time out of my office, it is the best way for it to be."

It seemed as though I had settled any nervous twitches Ben had, and the topic of Lisa and what I had or had not said to her was left in abeyance. Still, I had a sneaking suspicion it would return in the not too distant future, possibly as soon as the hospital spoke to Ben about the information on Lisa he wanted. Ben's phone ended the conversation when it demanded his attention. While he went out onto the back deck to deal with it, I had plenty of time to think. The matter of what I had said to Lisa regarding my relationship with Ben continued to occupy my mind.

I replayed in my mind what immediately went through my mind when Lisa questioned my relationship with Ben. I remembered well the response that immediately came to mind:

There's not much to tell. We met here in Millhaven very early in our careers and went from being friends to something more. We were about to take a big step and make it a permanent partnership when both of our careers scuttled that plan. Ben was transferred on promotion to somewhere else in the state, and I was transferred to Ralston. I met someone else, was married, and soon after widowed. Ben moved around all over the state as he climbed the rankings ladder for the next few years, until a couple of years ago when we both ended up back here in Millhaven. Our friendship was as strong as ever, but that's all that remained.

For once, my brain kicked into gear before my mouth did, and that response I almost delivered remained unspoken. While that was the true history of our relationship, Lisa didn't need to know any of it. Now, I was glad and relieved the fog in my head had cleared a little just in time to prevent my revealing too much to the nurse. I breathed a silent sigh of relief.

His phone call ended, Ben returned from the back deck with a dark look plastered across his face. I suspected he would soon go out again, and it wasn't long before he announced he was needed back at work. I made him a quick sandwich for lunch as he freshened up, and soon, he and his sandwich were on their way to the police precinct. Although I knew he was likely to be away for some time, I wasn't in a hurry to return to my office, instead opting to make myself a sandwich and take it and a long glass of iced tea out onto the back deck for a leisurely lunch.

Then, I made the mistake of stretching out on the couch out there. "Just for half an hour's rest," I told the universe. It was almost five o'clock when I returned to the land of the living… and my phone was ringing. Ben.

"The way things are going here, I doubt I'll be back there before seven o'clock. Emily will be joining us for dinner, but both of us probably will need to come back to work straight after dinner. What would you like me to pick up for dinner?"

"Don't worry about takeaways tonight. I feel like something homemade, so I'll cook something. See you whenever you manage to make it back here for dinner."

Sometimes I do the most ridiculous things. What was I going to cook for dinner, and how was I going to have it ready by seven o'clock? A quick check of my freezer produced two packs of lamb shanks. Each pack contained two shanks, so there would be one extra for later. The time constraints meant I had to partially thaw them as quickly as possible before starting their real cooking process. A few minutes on medium-low in the microwave did the trick. Then, as the shanks browned, I prepared the vegetables. With the sauce flavoured and thickened, I slammed a lid on the pot and shoved it in the oven. It was 5.30, and the others would be back around seven o'clock. The shanks really need two hours of slow braising to tenderise properly, but I'd just have to risk it tonight. With bread rolls thawing and ready to go in the oven with the lamb for the last few minutes of its cooking time, dinner was under control.

Rushing about to make dinner, had shaken off the remnants of sleep. I felt re-energised. Moments later, I was back in my office and wondering what else I might explore before the others arrived. At last, I deemed I was at an appropriate juncture now to look at the transcript of my phone's recording of my interview with Trina Blewett. I centred a printout on the desk in front of me and began to read.

By halfway through the document, I was reassured and thrilled that the details of that interview I had recalled over the last little while were so accurate. Having read to the end of the printout, I went back to read the last quarter of the transcript again.

Yes, that's where it started. That was the start of Trina's becoming…. Becoming what?... upset?… withdrawn?… agitated?... There was a marked change in her behaviour. It was as though she was struggling to hold something back, trying not to speak at all anymore, and none of my prompts reversed that situation. Then, there it was, the end of the interview. It was an abrupt end that left me with no clues about the reason for her visit. I read the last line of the transcript again:

Trina, what's happened? Tell me why you came to see me. How can I help you?

That was the end of the transcript and the end of the interview. I had a vivid recollection of how it ended, but I decided to compare my memory with the actual recording, as opposed to just reading the words on the page. After a few moments of faffing about with my phone, I played the last couple of minutes of the recording. There it was, the last bit just as I remembered it – and a clear visual record of it returned as I listened to the recording.

Trina Blewett pushed her chair back from my desk, hoisted her bag over her shoulder, turned, and strode out of my office as I called after her. My words seemed to make no impression. She didn't hesitate as she continued out the door and disappeared.

Listening to it, made me relive those moments and, again, it left me sitting stunned just as it did on that fateful morning.

Chapter 9

Despite an early night, I was decidedly below par this morning. Not surprising, I suppose, given I had spent half the night reliving Trina Blewett's visit to my office. But, here I was a week later, and I still had no clues as to what prompted her visit. Somehow, I had managed to convince myself the clues must have been there. After spending so much time last night reviewing that interview, I found nothing. In the cold light of this Monday morning a week later, I wondered if I was losing my touch … had lost my touch, even before my head injury.

Last night, Ben had come in after I had gone to bed. I hadn't heard him get up this morning, but he had left for work by the time I made it out to the kitchen. It wasn't surprising that Trina Blewett's interview kept me company through breakfast. Two questions kept nagging me. Had I lost my touch, or was there something in it, but because I was so preoccupied with getting away to my beach place for a few days, I had missed it?

"What the….?" I shrieked. "Going to my beach place, where had that come from?"

"Christ, how much more of my memory have I lost? Would I ever remember some of that stuff?" I murmured as I thought aloud.

Beach place…? Beach place?… Slowly, a small clear patch opened in the fog that still blocked my memories. Recall seeped through. No clients had booked appointments for last week… None all week…? Probably, I decided. It was a rare but ideal opportunity for a few days of doing nothing at my beach place.

"Yes. Yes, I remember now. That's what happened," I chirped as more of the fog shifted and further memory slipped through to the front.

I hadn't planned to go to my city office that day or that week. I intended to finalise everything for my last client and send it out over the weekend. Then, come Monday morning, I would head up the highway and go across the bay to the island where I have a beach house. But things didn't go to plan. I had to check something before I could send everything out to my client, so I went into my city office first thing last Monday morning. It was a coincidence – or just plain bad luck – that I was in that office last Monday when Trina Blewett chose to see me without an appointment.

Okay, I went to the office, and Trina Blewett came and went. What happened after she left and I woke up at that abandoned mine site sometime on Monday night? It would be handy if I knew how long I might have been lying there after I'd been dumped. I let my mind wander back over my sketchy memories of regaining consciousness there. What was I wearing – apart from only one sneaker? I checked the sports bag I had brought home from the hospital. The battered clothes I wore when admitted to hospital remained in the bag. I had left hospital wearing the fresh clothes Emily had sent in the sports bag.

Fit now only for the rag bag, the clothes in the bag told their own story. They were the clothes I had worn to work last Monday morning, minus the footwear, of course. So, what can I assume from that? One obvious conclusion was that I hadn't been home and changed before it happened. What else?

"Come on, Sonny, think," I growled. "You planned to go to the beach. What else would you have done to prepare for that?" I folded my arms on the kitchen table and dropped my head onto them.

After about a minute of willing more recall to emerge from the fog, a moment of logical thought occurred. I would have needed to visit the supermarket to purchase a week's supplies to take to the beach with me. Had I bought groceries?

"Oh, God, have groceries been sitting out there in my car in the garage for the last week?"

Bounding out of the kitchen, I raced around, opened the garage, and stood there sniffing. No unpleasant odours drifted out to meet me. Filled with trepidation, and shallow breathing,

I eased into the garage and along the side of my car. Nothing unpleasant assailed my nostrils. I worked my way around the car, peering in every window as I went. No sign of groceries left mouldering away in the vehicle. After breathing a sigh of relief and relaxing a little, I went back into my office to think about the situation.

Perhaps I had bought groceries and then put the perishables in the fridge after Ben drove me home from my office in my car. A check on the fridge scratched that as a possibility. There was no sign of any extras having been added to the fridge. So, it was back to focusing on my office and more thinking.

Rational thought suggested that, as I had no other appointments last Monday, I would have followed a fairly routine program for the rest of the day in preparation for an early departure for the island on Tuesday morning. I thought about how that might have played out after Trina Blewett left my office shortly before lunchtime: go downstairs and find something for lunch; scribble out a shopping list while having lunch; attend to any last minute admin chores; leave the office, and go to the supermarket to buy groceries before going home to pack the car ready for the morning.

Yes, that's the way the rest of the afternoon would have played out. My satisfied smile soon disappeared when I remembered one critical flaw in my thinking. If I had followed that plan, why was my car still parked behind my office building when I was released from hospital?

Okay, logic says that if my car was still there on Friday, it had probably been parked there since I arrived at my office last Monday morning. That surely indicated I had not gone to the supermarket last Monday afternoon. What did I do for the rest of the day? Maybe someone else came in without an appointment, and I stayed until my normal close of business time. No, that didn't cut it either. There was still the matter of my car remaining parked behind my office.

For lack of further possibilities to explore, I finally had to confront reality. It had taken me a while to accept that whatever happened to me, happened in the vicinity of that office building, and that I had never left the building before being abducted. I felt a chill run through me. Why? What had happened to precipitate my abduction? If no one else had come to see me after Blewett left my office last Monday, why would I be attacked later that afternoon? It made no sense, unless…. Unless the whole incident somehow hinged on that interview with Trina Blewett.

While it only took me a few moments to accept that probability, it didn't address the question of why it had happened. Blewett had told me nothing, not even why she had come to see me, and she certainly didn't point the finger at anyone for whatever was troubling her.

Somehow, that line of thinking took me full circle back to Lisa, the nurse and self-proclaimed best friend of Blewett… No, that's not correct. Lisa claimed to be the best friend of Zalika Standish. The somewhat tenuous connection between Blewett and Zali was my doing. Had I put two and two together to come up with five? It was starting to feel very much like that's what happened.

The possibility that I had made a connection that had sent me chasing a rabbit down the wrong burrow added to my concern about possibly losing my touch. It didn't matter how many times I ran it through my mind, Lisa's physical description of her friend, Zali, fitted Trina Blewett to perfection. There was always a chance that it was nothing more than my mind playing tricks. Maybe if Lisa had a photo of Zali, it would prove, one way or the other, if that was who came to see me last Monday.

Oh, yeah… And that might be possible if nurse Lisa even existed. How else can I prove whether Trina was Zali? While I pondered that, another aspect of the puzzle came back to me. The nurse had claimed her friend, Zali, had died last Monday as a result of some incident involving a vehicle. Ben knew nothing about it when I asked him a few days ago, but I think it might be worth a follow-up. Details of the accident might at least shed some light on a part of this story.

As I didn't know when next I would see Ben, my level of frustration continued to rise to almost self-destruct level. It was a week since my abduction but, despite the bits and pieces of my memory I had managed to recover, I still didn't really know anything. Everything I thought I knew to date was based on hearsay or assumptions. I had no definite evidence to substantiate any of it. I needed to nail some of it down. If I could confirm some of what I already think I know, it might be possible to move forward, not only with my investigation, but also with the recovery of more of my lost memory.

"There must be something else I can do from here," I snarled at the universe. "If only I could see what either Trina or Zali looked like, I would at least know if I was on the right track or not." I slammed my fist down on my desk and took a couple of deep breaths before inspiration intervened to save the day. "Security camera!" I yelped.

Why had it taken me so long to think about it? Probably because my installation of a security camera some months ago had slipped my mind. Another bit of my lost memory, perhaps…? A security camera strategically placed some distance along the corridor from my office doorway captured images of all foot traffic to and past my door. My unexpected visitor last Monday morning should be on that day's footage – and therein lay my next challenge.

Apart from immediately after its installation to check it was operating appropriately, since then, there had been no reason to check the footage recorded by the camera. Of course, the camera came with the usual owner's instruction manual, but that was safely filed away in my city office. Who reads manuals anyway, until something goes wrong? But now, I wasn't at all confident I could remember how to access the camera's recordings without reference to its manual.

"What the hell? Give it a go," I growled. "After all, what can you wreck that can't be fixed later?" If only I felt so confident about it.

Ben arrived as I was about to 'give it a go'. After one false start, I was already in the process of logging into the camera's files and didn't want to abandon things to talk to Ben in case it did something to damage a file or something else equally unwelcome. It wasn't a problem. He knew where I would be and was soon standing beside my desk, demanding to know what I thought I was doing.

"What I think I'm doing is trying to find even a skerrick of evidence to confirm at least one 'fact' that we think we know. Anyway, why have you rushed back here at this hour of the morning? I didn't expect to see you until at least lunchtime at the earliest."

"Do you feel up to going for a drive?"

"Yeah; anything to get out of here. Where are we going? And, more to the point, will I regret having agreed to go with you?"

"Uhmm… I don't think so, but there is something I need you to look at. Grab your bag or whatever you think you need, and let's go."

"Are you taking me somewhere nice, or just taking me parking?" I asked sarcastically in a little girl's voice.

"Parking? What are you on about, Sonny? Why would I be taking you parking?" I didn't respond, but I remembered there was a time when it wouldn't have been such a silly question.

"Well, I thought it would be handy to know where you were taking me."

"Didn't I say…? We're going to the hospital to…."

"I have no need to go back to the hospital, Ben Richards, so you can turn around and take me home again."

He heaved a theatrical sigh of resignation. "I knew today would be one of those days when you just know you should have stayed in bed. We are going to the hospital to try to find out something about that nurse called Lisa you keep talking about. I told you I asked for all her personal details. Well, I spoke to the hospital first thing this morning and…."

"And you discovered there ain't no such nurse…?"

"How did you find that out, and when?"

"It's what I do, remember. I'm an investigator. At least, that's what I've come to believe I am, but maybe that's another assumption requiring confirmation."

For the remainder of the short trip to the hospital, I explained how I had tried to find out Lisa's surname, only to end up being told there wasn't a nurse named Lisa.

Despite not knowing the reason we had rushed to the hospital, I felt a frisson of excitement running up and down my spine as we made our way to the hospital director's office. I wasn't formally introduced, but Ben called him Terry, so I followed his example. Moments after entering Terry's office, I discovered the hospital also had some strategically installed CCTV cameras, including one covering the corridor outside my former room.

"Your request seemed straightforward when I received it, Ben, but after spending much of the week searching for the information you needed and coming up empty, I thought of the camera on that floor. Bearing in mind that we don't have anyone employed called Lisa, I thought that you might be able to identify the person if she appeared on the recording."

Without wasting any time, he rolled the recording through to Wednesday of last week. All three of us sat glued to the screen as images of traffic along the corridor scrolled across the screen.

"There! Take it back a bit," I yelped. "Yeah, that's her. That's the nurse wearing the name badge that identified her as Lisa."

"Let's have a look at you, lady," Terry murmured as he fiddled to enlarge the image centred on the screen. "Still think it's the same woman?" he asked.

"Yep, that's the one. Can you enlarge it just a little more?"

After fiddling for a moment, he gave up and made a phone call. Almost immediately, a young man with thick glasses and a beard in need of a good dose of fertiliser appeared. Terry spoke to the latest arrival without bothering to introduce him.

"Justin, is there any chance we could enlarge the image on the screen a little more?"

After a few clicks on the keyboard, Justin had enlarged the image. Terry, like me, wasn't happy with the result, and he voiced his disappointment.

"Thanks, Justin, but it really hasn't given us what we wanted."

"What do you want me to try to improve for you?"

"Enlarging the image has made it a little more blurry than before. I think we hoped that, by enlarging the image, we might be able to read the woman's name badge."

"No problems…," Justin said as he attacked the keyboard once more. "How's that? I might be able to get a l-i-t-t-l-e more for you, but it won't be much."

"That's fine, thanks, Justin," I said as I leaned closer to the screen and peered at the name badge in the image. "See what you think, Ben. It does say Lisa, doesn't it?"

"It sure does," Ben and Terry responded in unison before Terry added more.

"All we need to do now is find someone who can shed light on who that person really is. I'll make a couple of calls. I can think of at least two people who should know."

Moments later, a woman, who I recognised as the nurse in charge of the nurses' station on my floor, knocked on Terry's door and came in. About a minute later, another woman I had never met joined us. Terry asked them both to study the image on the screen and say if they recognised the person.

"She's not one of my nurses, so she must be on one of the other wards. But that image does look like it is of the corridor on my floor. Sorry, Terry. I've had a few staff changes come through my station recently, including contractors, but I don't think I've seen that one before."

"Me too, Terry, I have to echo that comment," the older woman (Connie, who I discovered later was the Director of Nursing) said. "While I don't recognise her, there is something vaguely familiar about her."

"Hmm, Connie, do you remember that spot of trouble we had? When was it? Probably about two years ago now," Cheryl, the head nurse on my floor, asked.

"Oh, yes, that's it," Connie gasped. "Thanks, Cheryl. You are right. I think that's who it is. Terry, is she working back here again?" Anger tinged Connie's words.

Then, both nurses had their memories tested when Terry asked for the name of the person they were suggesting it was. It took a couple of minutes of to-and-fro between the two nurses before they finally agreed on the name of the person in the image.

"I'll check my files when I'm back in my office, but I'm sure that's who it is," Connie told Terry. "But, Terry, what is she doing working here in this hospital without my knowledge of it?"

An internal administrative matter appeared set to be discussed at some length by Connie and Terry, and Ben and I had no place in that. Ben thanked the hospital staff, and we were on our way to the door when Ben stopped.

"Before we leave, could I just ask one question about the person you think is on the screen?" Terry gestured for Ben to go ahead. "You mentioned a spot of trouble associated with the nurse in question," he said, looking at Cheryl. "What was the nature of that trouble?"

"Light-fingered," Connie answered economically before expanding her response. "Quite a few patients had valuables go missing. The resultant investigation found she was the culprit. She was dismissed. I believe that, after she returned some of the items and made restitution for others, none of the victims laid charges, so she wasn't prosecuted."

"I see. Thanks for that. Oh, just one other thing; I don't suppose she was ever known as Lisa while she was employed here?" Ben asked and saw all three hospital staff shake their heads in reply.

Ben headed for the door, trailing me in his wake until a thought stopped me in my tracks.

"Excuse me, ladies, but if her name wasn't Lisa, what was it?" I demanded.

There was a moment's hesitation during which Connie glanced at Terry and received an almost imperceptible nod in response.

"Greta Lomax…. Her name was Greta Lomax. At least, that's the name she was employed here under," Connie replied.

Without exchanging a single word, Ben and I made our way out to his car. The silence continued for a few moments after we were strapped in, and before I managed to shatter it.

"Well, it might not be the result we wanted, and it might not get us anywhere with our investigation into my incident, but it eases my mind a bit. The woman was real, and she was calling herself Lisa – for whatever reason. She wasn't a figment of my imagination."

"Is that some form of relief for you?" Ben asked quietly. "I never once doubted there was a nurse named Lisa involved. After all, I met her when I came to see you."

"Right, I had forgotten about that. Still, having established she wasn't who she claimed to be does raise another question. How much credence can we give her story about her 'best friend', Zali?"

"Yep, we have a long way to go before we start to make sense of any of this," Ben agreed. "What's your next move, Sonny? I've given up on trying to get you to rest."

"Having discovered all was not as it seemed to be with the nurse, I now want to focus on the Trina Blewett/Zali Standish situation."

Ben drew his eyebrows together in confusion and shook his head, giving me a clear indication he didn't understand what I meant. I tried to explain.

"The strange meeting I had with Trina Blewett might have been no more than just that, a meeting with Trina Blewett. If it hadn't been for Lisa's physical description of someone who so closely resembled Trina Blewett, I would never have linked the person I spoke with to Lisa's so-called friend, Zalika Standish. Did those two names belong to the same person, or did the person I spoke to have no connection whatsoever to someone called

Zali? I don't think I can move forward with my investigation until I've answered that question."

"Hmm… Yes, I see your point, but I'm not sure how you're going to do that. Unless we locate that nurse who fed you the line about her best mate, it won't be easy to establish anything beyond what we know now. Locating that nurse seems like no easy task to me. So, I will be interested to hear what your next move is going to be."

Before I had a chance to suggest what I might do next, we had pulled up in front of my house. Ben said he had to get back to work and probably wouldn't return until this evening. It suited me that our conversation had ended when it did. I wasn't sure I wanted to share my next moves with Ben at this stage, perhaps not until after I'd proved they were worth the effort. But, after I had a bite to eat for lunch, I knew what I was going to do, and I almost gave myself indigestion by bolting down my sandwich in order to rush back to my office. Before Ben dragged me off to the hospital this morning, I had made a start on what I was going to do next.

I admit I have no complaint about being interrupted earlier, as it resulted in a most productive visit to the hospital. Now, using much the same technique again, I was going to attempt to revisit other faces. Within moments of finishing lunch, I was a quaking mass of excitement mixed with nervousness as I again attempted to log in to my CCTV camera files. The machine didn't blow up; no files were damaged (or so it appeared). To my relief, all that happened after a few moments was that a new screen asking for a date range appeared.

"I'm in!" I told my empty office as I typed in the relevant dates.

Chapter 10

I pressed PLAY and watched the footage start scrolling across the screen. Yep, that looks about right, I told myself as I watched myself arrive at my office last Monday morning. After I disappeared into my office, images of an empty corridor slipped past at snail's pace. I knew it was possible to increase the speed, but I wasn't sure how to do it and didn't want to risk damaging the recording by fiddling with it. While nothing was happening on the screen, I took the opportunity to drag over a notebook and open it at a new page before fossicking in my drawer for a pen. Now all set to note details of anything interesting that had been recorded, I looked back at the screen.

"What the….? Whoa, whoa, go back," I yelped, and then held my breath as I tried what I hoped would rewind the recording.

Of course, I went back past the bit I wanted to watch and had to make it play up to the interesting bit again. This time, I risked slowing playback down to a mere crawl. And then, there it was. The image I had caught a brief glimpse of before I rewound the recording. Feeling more confident about how to run the program, I advanced the images frame-by-frame.

"Yes. Yep. YES!" I shrieked. There she was, my Monday morning unexpected visitor.

"Let's have a good look at you. Yeah, I still think you are a good fit for the physical description of Zali that the Lisa-imposter gave me." I gave the universe a running commentary as I noted the time from the ribbon below the image for when the woman first appeared… and before attempting to set an index marker on the recording. I tried printing a copy of the image on the screen and felt chuffed when I saw the printer spit out a reasonable copy of it.

Perhaps because I was so engrossed in the image on the screen, or because I had been yapping so loudly to an empty office, I wasn't aware I had company until someone knocked on the wall beside my office doorway.

"Emily! What are you doing here at this hour of the day? Is everything all right? Has something happened to Ben?" I had to wait until she stopped laughing before I received answers.

"Everything is fine. I was supposed to be having today off but then something came up at work just before lunch. Once I had dealt with that, I decided I was suffering withdrawal symptoms and needed to deal with them. So, here I am dealing with not having spent more than a few minutes with you since you were released from hospital. Well, now I'm here, I want to know everything about anything that's happened. Start talking."

"It won't take me long to bring you up to speed. Nothing has been happening. No, that's not quite right. Have you spoken to Ben since lunchtime?"

"No, I haven't seen him since we worked a crime scene last night. Why? What happened this morning?"

Explaining about our visit to the hospital this morning and its outcome took longer than expected. Although I thought I had covered it reasonably well, Emily had a heap of questions. A few minutes later, we were sitting on my back deck with coffee, and Emily and I were having our best conversation in over a week. Apart from discussing what we knew – or thought we knew – I gave her an earful about my frustration at not having any real evidence to work with.

"You seemed a bit excited when I arrived. So excited, you didn't hear me arrive. What were you working on, and what had you discovered?"

"Don't laugh, but I have expanded my technical know-how to include accessing recordings from the CCTV camera I had installed at my city office. And… Oh, now that is something I should talk to you about. If you've finished your coffee, let's go back to my office."

After making several photocopies of the printout of the image from the camera footage, I gave a copy to Emily. After glancing at it, she looked perplexed. While Emily continued to study the copy, I launched into what I hoped was a not too convoluted version of the story behind the image.

"That is an image of a woman who arrived at my office without an appointment at 10:10 last Monday morning. I believe later that day, a young woman was killed in some incident involving a motor vehicle. Do you remember an accident like that last Monday?"

"Uhmm… Yes, there was an incident here in the city. In fact, it occurred in the street outside your office and, from memory, it happened around lunchtime – maybe just after lunch."

"Is it routine for the forensic team to be called in for a simple motor vehicle accident?"

"No, but, as I recall off the top of my head, there wasn't anything routine about it. Give me a moment to think about it." After a few moments' silence, she continued. "It's been a helluva few days and I'm not sure I have the details of this case straight in my head. If it's important, we could go to my office now and have a look at the case file."

"I'm not allowed to drive yet," I said.

"You don't need to drive. We are taking my car. Come on, grab whatever you need and let's go."

I grabbed another copy of the image, picked up my bag, and sprinted after Emily out to her car. About ten minutes later, I was perched on a stool on the opposite side of her desk, watching her rifle through a filing cabinet to find the right file.

"What have you found?" I demanded a touch too sharply after Emily had sat staring at something in a folder longer than I considered necessary.

"Eh? Ah, well now, before I answer that, I need to ask you how your intestinal fortitude is these days."

"For God's sake, Emily. What are you on about? And what have you found in that file that is so fascinating you can't take your eyes off it? I doubt whatever it is will shock me. I've probably had just about as much exposure to crime scene images as you've had."

Emily shrugged and handed me two sheets of paper facedown. I took one in each hand, flipped them both over at the same time… and gasped.

Looking back at me from each sheet was an image of my last Monday morning's visitor. One was much as you might expect from a CCTV camera some distance further along the corridor but still exceptionally clear. It was the printout of the image from my CCTV camera I gave Emily earlier, while the other was a photo of a young woman, very dead and sprawled on the road outside my office.

"Christ," I said in disbelief, "they are both of the same person, my potential new client, Trina Blewett. Or, maybe that should be Zali Standish, depending on whose story you want to believe. What name do you have her registered under?"

After an uncomfortable moment, she sighed. "She's a Jane Doe… there was nothing to identify her, and we've been so busy since then, I haven't had time to pursue it. I had expected confirmation of her identity to come through from Ben, but there's been nothing from him. Tell me more about the woman's possible name confusion."

I recounted the story given to me by Greta Lomax when she posed as nurse Lisa. "It wasn't long after I spoke to your Jane Doe that I lost the chunk of my life that I'm still trying to recover. So, I'm still trying to confirm her real name. Emily, tell me about the accident – or incident, if you would prefer – that led to this," I asked as I waved the photo from the crime scene at her.

"It's all a bit sketchy. Obviously, it was in the city heart, so there were people on the street at the time. But everything seems to have happened so quickly, nobody actually saw how it happened; didn't see what led to her being hit by the vehicle."

"And, of course, the vehicle didn't hang around afterwards, and nobody noted its registration number."

"That about sums it up. It was a hit and run, and the police have had no success tracking down the vehicle. There's always so much traffic on that street. It's almost impossible to believe a vehicle could hit someone and then completely disappear in the blink of an eye, but that appears to be what happened.

Are you all right, Sonny? You look a bit shaken. Maybe I shouldn't have shown you the file photo."

"No, no, it's not the photo. It's something else… half a memory that's trying to come back to me. It has something to do with that hit and run. I don't mean it's because the victim had just been to see me. What was the exact time of the accident?"

"About 1.00PM, according to my file records, but that would be the time I was called, and it might have been a bit after the accident actually happened."

"If I remember correctly, Trina would have left my office by a bit after eleven o'clock. That then begs the question of where she had been during the intervening one to two-hour period after leaving my office."

As I spoke, I was aware of a thought – a memory perhaps – trying to come through to me. Don't fight it, I told myself. Give it time and free rein to come through. Maybe sharing it with Emily will help.

"For some reason, I think I saw Trina again after she left my office, but I can't work out why I think that or how and where I might have seen her. Something is suggesting I knew she went to the bakery."

"The bakery? Sonny, what makes you think she had been to the bakery? Was it something Trina said or did before she left your office?"

"No… at least I don't think so, but I can't be sure. I need to think about it a bit more. Maybe going back to my office might help jog my memory."

"Okay, that might trigger some further recollection. Come on, grab your bag and let's go."

It felt a bit weird being back in my office and knowing I had to do something, without knowing what that something was. I felt twitchy and restless. Emily sensed there was a problem and took charge.

"Sonny, sit down at your desk and try to relax while I make us coffee. Don't try to think about anything specific. Just sit and let your mind roam back to that Monday morning and your meeting with Trina. We'll talk more after I make us coffee."

A few minutes later, Emily was sitting opposite me at my desk and we were both sipping coffee. We sat in silence like that for what seemed like a long time, but it probably was no more than a minute or two before Emily made her next suggestion.

"Take me back to that Monday morning and your interview with Trina. What was her manner like? What sort of vibes did you get from talking to her?"

"Dunno… That's foggy territory you're asking me to explore, but I have the feeling it wasn't a good interview. Don't ask me what I mean by that comment, because I don't know."

"Right… Sit back and relax. Close your eyes if it helps, but let your mind find its way back to that interview on Monday morning."

With that, Emily bounded up off her chair and switched off the main office lights. It left the only sources of illumination in the office, the myriad of LEDs associated with the various devices and light coming in through the windows. Then she was back sitting opposite me again – and maintaining a firm hand on proceedings.

"Now, relax, Sonny, and talk me through that interview from the moment Trina entered your office."

Easier said than done, I discovered as I struggled for a while to get into the flow of things. But, a few minutes later, I had given Emily a fairly succinct account of my interview with Trina Blewett and how it ended. Then, I was forced to pause for a few moments until I had clear recall of what happened after the interview. Emily suggested it might help my recall if I went and physically walked through it to re-enact what happened. Her suggestion made sense, so I went and stood at my door and began what amounted to a running commentary as I retraced my actions that morning.

"After seeing Trina out… well, really, she just about bolted out of here… I closed my office door again and went to make the coffee I was about to make earlier when Trina interrupted me by arriving without an appointment. I made the coffee and was thinking about what to have for lunch as I took the coffee back to my desk. On my way, I detoured over to look out that window at the street below."

"Was there a prompt of some sort, something that drew you to the window?"

"No, I was just wandering around while thinking about what to have for lunch." Emily nodded and gestured for me to carry on. "I put my coffee down on the windowsill and looked out. I wasn't looking at anything in particular. Then, something grabbed my attention.

It was Trina Blewett… She walked out from under the awning to stand at the edge of the pavement. That's what it was! That's what caught my eye and made me think she had been to the bakery. Trina had been to Justin's bakery and held one of Justin's garishly coloured bags in her hand."

Complete recall of Trina standing there at the edge of the pavement with her expensive-looking handbag over her shoulder and the bakery bag in her hand brought my commentary to a halt. Seeing that image in my mind seemed to elevate my pulse rate as well as take my voice away. I swallowed hard, and tried to relax again as Emily encouraged me to do. After a moment, I nodded and was about to begin my commentary again when something made me freeze. Another image flashed to the forefront of my mind.

"Then it happened!" I yelped. "I saw it happen. Someone – a man – slammed into her back, sending Trina flying out onto the road. The bag of cakes flew out of her hand as she fell and sprawled out on the road." I felt myself shaking and couldn't go on.

After a few moments, Emily asked quietly, "What happened next?"

"Argh, it's a bit hard to describe. It all happened so fast. A car seemed to be waiting. I know that sounds ridiculous. How could a car be paused and apparently waiting in the middle of traffic on a busy street? But that's how it looked to me in that split second between when Trina hit the tarmac and when the car moved forward. No. No, wait… that part of the story is not quite right."

I paused again to refocus on the events as they unfolded in my mind. I knew how important accurate recall was. It only took a few heartbeats for the sequence of events to clarify, and I could begin my updated version of the car's involvement.

"That car actually raced forward as Trina was flying through the air. It sort of slammed into her while she was still in the air. It bounced her further along before she hit the bitumen." By the time I finished recounting the incident, I was shaking and hyperventilating.

"Stop! Stop there, Sonny," Emily demanded. "Take a moment to settle. Come and sit down again." She watched me like a hawk watching its prey until she was satisfied that I was sufficiently calm to continue before asking her next question.

"What, if anything, do you remember about that car? Any details at all could be important."

"Not much…."

Closing my eyes, I took a deep breath and began searching my memory banks for anything about that car. Sporadic glimpses of the car and its actions returned. I began a hesitant recital of its description as images of it emerged from my memory banks.

"It was one of those big 4x4 utilities with an enormous bullbar on the front. The sort of protection 'roo shooters and people who work stock – people from the bush – often have fitted to the front of their vehicles. What else can I tell you? Uhmm….

Oh, hang on. It was a dark blue colour… and it had a bar across the roof, a light bar of some sort with a huge spotlight-looking thing mounted in the centre of the bar."

"You are doing great," Emily confirmed, "but relax for a moment and see if anything else comes back to you."

She was not as good at this as Ben, but she was getting results. Bits and pieces that I was not sure I wanted to remember from that Monday were coming back to me. Emily allowed me a brief pause before continuing.

"What happened to the vehicle after it hit the woman?" she asked. I was about to tell her I didn't remember anything more, but she continued her questioning.

"Did it stop to check what had happened?" I shook my head. "Did it even slow down or hesitate for a moment?"

My reply caught in my throat. The words emerged as nothing more than a croak. After clearing my throat, I tried again.

"No. If anything, it kept going flat-out. Traffic was flowing well along the street at the time, but the vehicle was being driven dangerously. It was weaving its way through the traffic at high speed. I heard the brakes of other vehicles screech as their drivers took evasive measures to avoid collisions. The blue utility just kept going flat-out, almost as if its driver believed no one would take him on if he didn't slow down."

"Sounds like he might have been right about that. Were you able to track it? Did you see where it went?" Emily's excitement came through in her rapid-fire questions.

After a moment's thought, I guessed my answer would disappoint her. "No. As I watched it along the street, I saw it hit the lights at the intersection at just the right time to sail straight through. It was about then that my brain kicked into gear and refocused on Trina lying out there on the road. I raced out of my office to go to her.

Huh… that's probably how it happened. I must have automatically pulled my door closed behind me, and it locked."

Emily nodded her understanding before firing her next question. "Did any of the other people on the street rush to help Trina?"

The memory was difficult to recall and it took me a moment before I could verbalise it.

"It was as though everything and everyone – including me – stood still for a few moments. Then, I saw a couple of pedestrians running toward her. I suppose their reaction was what got me moving, and I rushed out to go to her."

Our question-and-answer session seemed to be working well for both of us. Bits of my lost memory, although some of them painful, were returning, and Emily was collecting information she needed, but progress was halted by loud pounding on my office door.

"Do you have any appointments booked for today?" Emily hissed at me. I shook my head. "Right, I'll get rid of them."

She raced to the door and threw it open... only to be confronted by Ben standing there with a set jaw and a look on his face as black as hell.

"Your staff told me you had Sonny with you when you left your office. They thought you might be heading here to Sonny's office," he snarled at Emily as he pushed past her.

Then, it was my turn to be barked at by Ben in Millhaven-Top-Cop-mode, and he wasn't too interested in asking questions about what we were doing or why. Ben in this mood is not a pretty sight and can be quite intimidating for some. I have been on the receiving end before today and have learned how to manage it.

"You are not supposed to be working... Supposed to be home resting. I thought you had more sense than this. But, no. I leave you alone for a few hours and you come straight here to your office. You don't even bother to hide what you are doing by working covertly in your home office."

Ben paused to draw breath... and probably to refill his spleen for the next outburst. My way of dealing with such incidents is to say nothing until he has said all he has to say – and then I pin his ears back with a few home truths. Emily doesn't have that technique yet. When he paused, Emily cut in before he could begin again.

"Shut up, Ben Richards. Don't come in here chucking your weight around. Just shut up and listen. No! Do not say another word until I say you may."

A moment later, the office was filled with the sound of a recording playing on Emily's phone. She had recorded our whole session. Everything I had remembered and told her. It worked. Ben backed down and, in a more civil voice, suggested Emily stop the tape and restart it once we were all sitting more comfortably with coffees. His suggestion met with unanimous support. While Ben and I attended to the coffees, Emily volunteered to run down to the bakery for something to have with them.

With a spare chair dragged over so Ben didn't have to continue perching on a corner of my desk, we had a few sips of coffee and a mouthful or two of lamington before Ben told Emily to rewind and restart the recording.

Our memory-recovery session had taken longer than I thought. The length of the recording surprised me, and sitting through it made me more than a little uncomfortable, but there was an upside to listening to it. The recording awoke something else in the back of my mind, and it was now knocking to be let out. If only I could coax it from that dark place where it resides now....

When the recording ended, Ben cleared his throat. "Emily, is it possible for you to send me either that recording or a transcript of it?" he asked quietly. "Now we know what we are looking for, we might be able to pick up something on the traffic cameras that will give us at least a clue as to who owned the vehicle."

"Sonny, are you all right?" Emily murmured. "Has this been too much for you?"

"Eh? No. There's another memory, or more images ... or something ... trying to come back to me, but I can't seem to grab hold of it. Maybe if I leave it alone for a while, later, I might manage to recall whatever it is. Take me home again, please, Emily. I think I need to give this memory time to percolate through to the surface before I try sharing it with anyone."

Emily dropped me at home. She needed to check something at work but would return for dinner tonight. It was late and not worth doing anything in my home office, so I took myself for a long, leisurely shower before watching dusk become night from my back deck.

A few minutes after Emily returned at seven o'clock, Ben arrived armed with takeaway roast dinners for three. An early night for me ensued after both Ben and Emily returned to their respective offices to devote some attention to the contents of Emily's recording of our session this afternoon.

Chapter 11

Although I would never have admitted it at the time, my session with Emily this afternoon left me feeling drained. While a part of me felt I should try to recover more of those memories lurking in the back of my mind, wisdom told me to leave it alone. For a change, I decided to listen to wisdom and was in bed by nine o'clock. Ben was still occupying my spare bedroom, but I didn't hear him come in after I went to bed.

This morning didn't see any vast improvement in my outlook on life, and I still felt flat from yesterday's 'memory recovery' session. When I finally scrambled out of bed, I spent a long time over breakfast to avoid leaping into the day. With no real purpose in mind (after all, how long can you spend over toast and coffee), I finally stirred myself and wandered into my home office.

One monumental question pushed all else from my mind. What could I do to bring to the surface that elusive something lurking way back in the darkest reaches of my damaged mind? I instinctively knew it was important… An important element in my understanding of what had happened for me to end up dumped for dead at that abandoned mine site.

It was a useless battle. I couldn't settle and was unable to focus my thoughts enough to achieve anything. In desperation, I dashed off a text to Emily asking for a copy of her recording of yesterday's session. Then, I frittered away the rest of the morning, waiting for the recording to arrive. Emily does have more to do than deal with requests from me, and it was lunchtime before the recording arrived. Despite having nothing to show for a wasted morning, I decided to postpone listening to the recording until after lunch. I justified it by telling myself there was no point in starting on the recording only to have to stop again for lunch.

Not having spoken to Ben before he left for work this morning, I had no idea what his movements were likely to be today. Having decided there was no point in waiting to see if Ben would come home for lunch when he might have no intention of doing so, I made myself lunch and dined alone on my back deck. The resident Willy Wagtail perched on the railing and gave me a mouthful about intruding in his territory during the day. It was cool and restful – despite the bird – out on the deck. I was becoming drowsy. Maybe a snooze wouldn't be a bad idea....

With the lure of sleep successfully overcome, I was on my way back to my office and Emily's recording when Ben arrived home for lunch. The recording would have to wait a bit longer. I didn't want to be subjected to another round of Ben laying down the law about my need for rest and that I must not work for a while yet.

"Sorry, Ben. I didn't know if you would be back for lunch, so I've already eaten. I'm going to lie down for a while, and maybe read for a bit, if my eyes say open long enough." He appeared happy about it, so I disappeared into my bedroom without having to face a barrage of questions or advice.

As soon as I heard Ben drive off, I bolted for my office to listen to Emily's recording… again and again. Listening to the entire recording twice did nothing but leave me feeling frustrated and cranky. I had come tantalisingly close to retrieving a memory buried so deeply and stubbornly that it refused to come through to the surface. While so much caffeine can't be aiding my recovery, I gave up on the recording and headed for the kitchen and another coffee.

Emily arrived carrying a bag of salads just as the coffee machine started doing its thing. Her arrival made me realise how late it was and how I have a rule about not drinking coffee after five o'clock. Regardless, we both indulged in another dose of caffeine anyway. As we sat sipping coffee, Emily said Ben was planning an early dinner this evening. She thought he would arrive around six o'clock and will be bringing steaks to barbeque.

When Ben arrived with the steaks, we all relocated to my back deck to sit and chat while the barbeque heated up and Ben was ready to start cooking. I insisted Emily and Ben entertain themselves outside while I went to gather the salads and everything else we needed to eat out on the deck. As I loaded everything onto a traymobile ready to wheel it out, an interesting fact about our conversations so far tonight occurred to me. The conversation had been about everything except Emily's recording yesterday and my recovered fragments of memory. The other, and probably the most notable, aspect of those conversations was that there had been no questions about whether I had remembered anything else about the events of that Monday.

In a bid to clearly identify 'Trina' and gather possible information on what happened and who was involved, I had no doubts both Ben and Emily spent much of today working with the memories I recovered yesterday. The fact that they weren't talking about any of it just added to my crankiness and frustration.

At about eight o'clock, Emily announced she had to leave to check on something at work. I hoped Ben would follow her example and also opt for an early night. I felt decidedly antisocial, and I definitely didn't want the company of supposed friends who insisted on treating me like a fool. I waited for Ben to announce he was going to bed, but he obviously had other ideas, and it didn't work out that way.

Although I thought I had maintained a good pretence all evening of being normal, apparently, I am not a good actor and didn't pull it off. As soon as Emily left after dinner, Ben quizzed me on my behaviour.

"Are you all right, Sonny? You seem withdrawn tonight. Is there something bothering you – something on your mind – or are you feeling unwell? I am concerned that yesterday's experiences might not have been in your best interest and might have set back your recovery."

"What? No, I feel fine. Oh, all right, I do have something on my mind, but it is not something that will impact my recovery. Come through to the office with me, and I'll tell you about it and show you what triggered it."

After bringing up the footage from my CCTV camera again, I fast-forwarded through to the images of Trina leaving my office.

"Notice her demeanour. She appears to be rushing, or upset, or something. During her time with me, she was tense and hesitant but, in these images, that situation seems to have worsened."

We watched Trina start down the stairs, then pause and start to come back up again before finally racing down the stairs and out of sight.

"Ben, just keep watching as I slow the recording down and let it run on until the next image appears." Images of an empty corridor seem to crawl across the screen for a long time before another image of interest filled the screen.

"That's you," Ben chirped. "That's you racing out of your office, presumably on your way down to check on what happened to Trina."

I explained how the camera only captures images along the corridor and isn't angled to capture any activity on the stairs. For the brief period it took, we watched as the images showed me starting down the stairs and continued to the last shot of me, which showed just the top of my head.

"Sonny, stop the recording. Forget about the fact that we can't see what happens as you run down the stairs or what happened after that."

How can he not be interested in what happened after I ran down the stairs? I wondered about it but kept it to myself. He seemed more interested in discussing my CCTV camera, its make and model, and who had installed it for me. I knew I was becoming even more cranky and frustrated than I had been earlier in the night. The camera wasn't important at this point.

What was important to me was what happened after the camera footage of me came to an end. In desperation, I tried to bring the conversation back to what was important, but Ben seemed intent on talking about everything else other than what happened after I ran down the stairs.

At last, he paused almost mid-sentence. I thought he had detected my rising anger and was about to return to discussing the topic that was important to me. I was wrong. He changed the topic but not to the one I wanted to discuss.

"Do me a favour. Describe the area – that small area – at the bottom of those stairs," he asked.

"You know what it looks like. You've come to my office so often, you are as familiar with that area as I am. Why do you want me to tell you about it?"

"Humour me. I need you to describe it in detail for me so I can picture it clearly in my mind."

When Ben uses that tone of voice and is so insistent, it is wise not to argue. I launched into a description of what amounts to a small vestibule area at the bottom of the stairs.

"It features an industrial bin against the wall opposite the staircase, and there is a door on either side of the area. The one on the left and almost at the bottom of the stairs leads out through the shops to the street. If you turn right at the bottom of the stairs, you go past the lift to the rear door of the building that opens out onto the tenant's car park. Is that sufficient description for you?"

"Uhmm… What? Oh, yes, that will do – for now – thanks," he said in a distracted way. I thought we would now refocus on the main issue, but again, I was wrong. Ben launched off in a different direction that, while perhaps tangentially associated with what happened to Trina, was not where I wanted to go.

"What would you have done if, instead of Trina, it was a stranger who had been knocked down and was lying out there on the street? Would you have raced down to see what you could do for that person, as you did with Trina?"

His questions sounded almost as if he was thinking aloud. I knew I had to answer them and, while I had a whole mouth full of venom I wanted to spit at him, I swallowed hard to steady my voice before I replied.

"No, I would not have raced down to investigate what had happened or to check on the victim's condition. I probably would have remained at the window and just reached for my phone to call the police or an ambulance. Would you mind telling me what that's got to do with anything? And how it might help me in any way recover more of my lost memory?"

Ben either didn't notice how cranky I was or chose to ignore it. Although he then continued by questioning me about how I might react to a different scenario, it was still not something I wanted to discuss.

"Suppose it had been a close friend – someone like me or Emily – who had been knocked down out there on the street. How would you have reacted?"

"My reaction would have been much the same as it was for Trina. I would have raced down to the street to see what I could do for my friend, and I probably would have grabbed my phone on the way out so I could call the police or an ambulance. Ben, where is this going? What has this got to do with my situation?" He ignored me and, again changing the scenario, continued questioning me.

"This time, I want you to think about someone somewhere between a stranger and a close friend. Perhaps it might be just an acquaintance. What would you have done?"

"Probably much the same as I did in Trina's case. I would have grabbed my phone and raced down to see what I could do."

"Right... I see. In such a scenario, might a client be considered an acquaintance?"

"Yes, of course. I would be acquainted with the person, and perhaps even on a quite personal level, depending on the nature of the situation I was hired to investigate. It would have nothing to do with being concerned about whether they would still be around to pay my bill. I think that it would be nothing more than a normal reaction to my concern for somebody I knew – although only professionally."

"Think back to that incident on the street outside your office and what your reaction might have been if it was an acquaintance or a client who was involved. Is that reaction you described likely to be the way you behaved when it was Trina lying out there on the bitumen, even though you had spoken to her only once prior to the incident?"

"I suppose it's possible that's what I did. Yes, I assume that is what I did. But I don't want to make assumptions, Ben. I want to know exactly what happened after I raced down those stairs to go to Trina."

"Okay, let's find out. Bring up that image of you rushing out of your office… Yes, that's it. Pause the recording to freeze that image on the screen. Now, relax and let your mind explore what's on the screen. Don't think objectively. Just look at it." Then, I heard his chair scrape back.

As soon as he stood up and turned off the lights in my office, I knew what would come next. It's a method we have used a few times in the past when I've been stuck while trying to sort out a case. With the only light in my office now coming in from the kitchen, as Ben rubbed my neck and shoulders, he lowered his voice to nothing more than a purr.

"Sit back and relax. Close your eyes and take a few deep breaths – slow and easy. Good. Now, bring the image you have on the screen to the forefront of your mind. Don't open your eyes, just think about it. Think about that morning and your interview with Trina. How did that go?"

"Not one of my better interviews," I murmured, sounding as though I was half asleep as Ben kept rubbing my neck and shoulders.

"Think about your actions after you realised it was Trina lying out there on the road. What did you do?"

"Ben, this is a waste of time. I can't remember anything after racing out of my office. I'm not even sure I remembered that, or if the images from the CCTV suggested that's what happened, and now I'm convinced I remember doing it."

It's as though I haven't spoken. Ben just ignores what I've said and keeps urging me to relax and let my mind roam free. "Don't fight it. Keep your eyes closed. Take a few more deep breaths. Relax and feel my hands on your shoulders and up your neck." After a few moments, he begins leading me through that episode again.

"Now, you are upset and concerned about what has happened to Trina. You must go to her to see if there's anything you can do for her. You race out of your office and start down the stairs. Talk me through that."

"For a moment, I'm frozen to the spot, unable to move. Then I am racing to the door. I rush out when it has opened barely wide enough for me to fit through. I hear the door slam closed again behind me, but I have already started down the stairs, and the door is of no concern."

"Tell me about rushing down those stairs to the ground floor," Ben purred.

"I was hyperventilating and taking the stairs two at a time, and almost losing my balance. I don't want to end up rolling down the stairs. I slow down a little to land on every step on the rest of the way down. Then, I bounce off the last step to land on the floor at the bottom of the staircase."

"Did you meet anyone on the stairs? See anyone else going down or coming up?"

"No, but I wouldn't expect to see anyone. Other than people coming to my office, it's rare for anyone else to use those stairs. And, people who have never been there before tend to use the lift, but only on their first visit, and then never again."

"Right… You've made it safely down the stairs to reach that small, vestibule-like area. You need to go out to the street. You need to go to Trina. There are two doors leading outside. What do you do as you bounce off that bottom step?"

"As soon as I hit the floor, without hesitation, I spin to my left… take the two or three strides to the door that leads out through the shops to the street."

"So, you go to the left door that leads directly out onto the street?"

"Yes, I race through that door and along between the shops to the street."

"Then what happens? Describe what you see as you race out to the street."

In that instant, I felt myself become tense – almost rigid – and my breathing became shallow and rapid.

He repeats the question, "Sonny, what do you see out there on the street?"

Something is wrong. I'm struggling with something trying to emerge from the depths of my mind. I don't answer Ben, not for a few moments as I wrestle with whatever is stirring up my mind. Then it comes through.

"No. No-o, that's not right," I murmur and then become quiet for a few moments before yelping, "No, that's not right. I think there was something wrong with that door." I felt myself becoming more agitated with each shallow, rapid breath.

Not a sound came from Ben as I struggled to assess and deal with this new revelation. Swallowing hard to steady myself, I resumed my commentary. But, regardless of my efforts, when I next spoke, my speech was rasping and rapid.

"Something is wrong. The door won't open. It must be locked. I push and shove against it. Nothing happens. I charge at it and ram it with my foot… and then again. This time, I loosen it a little, but it doesn't open. I ram it again. Nothing happens. It won't budge any further."

Ben chants slowly and quietly, "Relax, relax… concentrate on your breathing. Breathe deep and slowly. Let everything become quiet again."

It takes me what seems like quite a while to regain that restful state so necessary for this process to succeed. Ben senses the time is right and continues the session.

"So, the door to the left of the stairs isn't locked?"

"No, it isn't locked. It's more like something on the other side of the door is preventing its opening. I stare at the door in disbelief. I don't know how this can be happening."

"Okay, you establish that the door won't open. What do you do? Do you go back upstairs?"

"What? No. I need to assess the situation out there on the street. I don't go back upstairs."

"Well, what did you do?"

After a moment to think about it, I tell him, "No. I definitely don't go back up to my office. I give up on the door. I spin around and race across past the lift to the other door, the one opening out to the tenants' carpark behind the building."

"You race across the vestibule, past the stairs and the lift, and across to the other door. Do you notice anything different about the vestibule as you do so? Is there anything there that shouldn't be there, or is there anything missing from that area?"

"There is nothing there, nothing in the vestibule at all. There isn't supposed to be anything there. The only thing that is ever there is an industrial bin against the wall opposite the staircase. And that bin… And … And that bin isn't there. There is nothing at all in the vestibule apart from me. The bin is missing."

"Might it have been put outside for some reason?"

"The only time it goes outside is when the janitor puts it out for collection. He takes it out and parks it next to the back door ready for the truck to pick up."

"Right, might he have put it outside today?"

"No-o, I don't think… No. Today is Monday. Collection day is Wednesday."

I confirmed there wasn't anything else unusual about the vestibule, and Ben resumed his questioning.

"Nothing about the vestibule caught your eye or made you stop, so you continued to the back door. Is that door locked, too? Do you have a key?"

"To open it, a code needs to be keyed in on a pad beside the door. A key code is needed to go out through that door. There is no key required."

"Do you key in some sort of code, or do you give up and go back to your office?"

"As I've told you, I did not go back to my office. So, yes, I key in my code to open the door. When I hear the door unlock, I push the door open and rush outside."

"Is the carpark where you want to be?"

"No… Well, yes. When the other door doesn't open, the only other way out to the street is out the back door to the carpark and across to the alley."

"What do you see in the carpark, apart from vehicles? Is there anyone around? Is the missing industrial bin out there?"

"Nothing catches my attention. I'm just focused on racing to the street and going to Trina."

"As you race down the alley, what do you see? Is the traffic still flowing past along the street?"

"Yes… No-o… Uhmm, I don't think so. Well, it wouldn't be, would it, not with Trina lying out there on the road."

"So, you notice the traffic is stopped. What types of vehicles can you see in front of you as you run down the alley?"

This line of questioning has me feeling agitated. Why should it? It only takes me a moment to work it out before I give him an answer.

"That's not right. I can't see any traffic. I can't see anyone walking along the pavement past the entrance to the alley. Ben, I don't remember anything about the alley at that time. I don't have any memory of running along it and out to the street."

Questioning was suspended yet again for a brief period while Ben tried encouraging me to relax. Then, as he told me later, when he thought I was sufficiently relaxed, and against his better judgement, he decided to try again.

"Sonny, cast your mind back to that point when you raced out the door and into the carpark. What do you see?"

"Nothing…."

"Okay; what do you do next? You are outside the building now. Walk me through what you are doing."

"Argh… I don't really know. Let me think. Oh, yeah, that's right. I race out the door and turn to run along to the corner of the building to reach the alley."

Silence, heavy and stifling except for the sound of my distressed breathing, enveloped us. A few heartbeats later, reality delivered a powerful blow.

"I can't see it," I croak. "I can't see anything outside the building. There is nothing after I step out the door into the carpark and turn to run to the alley."

"That is great," Ben almost shouted. "Now, slow down and stop thinking about what happened. Stop thinking about what happened in the carpark and everything else to do with trying to reach Trina out there on the street."

"What? No, I want to know what happened. Why can't I remember?"

"We know what happened next… Well, I do anyway… and you will too if you stop trying to recall stuff that didn't happen. You were clobbered the moment you raced out through that back door. A vehicle probably was waiting in the carpark to cart you away."

"But why? Why would they be waiting for me? If it wasn't a case of mistaken identity, why would anyone think I would race out through that door at that precise time of that day?"

"Because they had engineered for you to use that door."

Chapter 12

Finding out the truth about those missing hours was not only a shock, it was devastating. Instead of the revelation easing my tension, I was hyperventilating. My mind was racing in all directions at warp speed. If Ben was right…. Of course, Ben was right. He didn't need to fill in the 'bottom line' for me. Even my befuddled mind had managed to work out what happened to me had been a targeted hit. But by whom and why?

While it seemed almost implausible, I instinctively knew it was linked somehow to Trina's visit to my office that fateful morning. And that begs that same question: *but why?* Without a doubt, I knew that question would haunt me until I knew its answer. That posed another question: how to find that answer?

Ben had taken a break from trying to quieten me down and had disappeared into my kitchen. He was right, of course. I would be in for a sleepless night tonight – and maybe for other nights to come. I stood up and was about to go in search of him when he wandered back into my office carrying two glasses of port.

"While I know going alcohol-free will probably aid your recovery, I think we both need a little something after tonight's adventure. It's up to you whether you drink it or not," Ben said as he set one of the glasses down on my desk in front of me.

"It would be a shame to waste it now it has been poured," I replied as I raised the glass in salute.

We abandoned my office in favour of the lounge room but didn't bother turning on the lights in that part of the house. Enough light came through from the kitchen and the various LEDs on appliances to create a calming ambience. We sipped in silence for a minute or so before I felt compelled to voice a thought rattling around in my mind.

"You probably will come up with a whole raft of objections to what I'm about to say, but I'm going to say it anyway.

Tonight, we found the answer to one question for me, but other questions remain unanswered. I believe I need to be in my city office to search for those answers. I want to be in my city office tomorrow."

"That's not going to happen. You were told your best recovery chance was with two weeks of rest. You haven't had two weeks off work yet. Anyway, there's no way I will take you to your office tomorrow."

"Okay, that's fine, and it is the response I expected from you. But, let me spell it out for you, Ben. If you don't take me into the city tomorrow, I will drive myself to my office. And, before you start laying down the law about my not being allowed to drive, let me assure you I am completely okay to drive."

"Because of your concussion, it is safer if you do not attempt to drive for at least two weeks."

"To hell with all that nonsense. I am fine to drive and, to put your mind at ease, I am not experiencing any symptoms of concussions. So, one way or another, I will be at my city office tomorrow."

Although he carefully sidestepped the issue by changing the topic, I knew we would revisit it… and probably before the night was over.

"Why do you need to go into the city? What can you do in that office that you can't do here? I thought that was the reason you went to the trouble and expense of replicating your office here so you can work from home if you need to."

"Perhaps it isn't about the work I want to do there. I have this weird idea that being there might help trigger further recall."

"Recall of what?"

"I don't know. Maybe I've overlooked something or thought it wasn't significant at the time. Maybe being alone and quiet in that environment again will trigger a memory, even a vibe of some sort, that might prove useful. Ben, I'm not going to argue about this. I will be going into my city office tomorrow."

"Do you think you might be able to be out of bed early enough to come in with me when I go to work?"

"Definitely… and I suppose I can always get a cab home when I'm done." My last comment probably wasn't necessary, but I felt I needed to reacquaint him with my independent and obstinate side.

He heaved a theatrical sigh of resignation and threw his hands up in the air. It was a good sign. I knew I had won that battle, although I wasn't sure of the exact outcome. If Ben ran true to form, I knew it also would open up more useful dialogue. It took a few moments, but it did happen.

"Right… Well, perhaps we should develop a bit of a plan of what you might look at while you are there. Do you already have some ideas?"

"Not really, but I do intend to scrutinise my CCTV recordings. I'm not sure that will produce anything worthwhile, but it will deal with something that has been rattling around in the back of my mind. After that, I thought I might try visualising my whole interview with Trina. It might seem weird, but I intend to sit at my desk, visualise Trina sitting opposite me, and try to relive that interview."

To my relief, Ben didn't as much as snigger at my plan, so I pushed my luck a bit further. "Has what we discovered tonight given you any thoughts on how your investigation might proceed?" I asked. "I don't mean in regard to what happened to me, but about Trina – her real identity and why she ended up dead."

"A couple of things that might be worth following up have occurred to me. They might go nowhere, but at least we will be able to cross them off the list. I guess that, for both Emilly and me, our main focus will be on confirming Trina's identity, whatever it might be. If we manage to achieve that, who knows what else it might reveal about this case?"

Ben's pounding on my door had me out of bed early this morning and on my way into the city even earlier than I usually manage.

As he dropped me at the rear of my office building, he was adamant he needed to know the moment anything untoward or concerning happened. It was a relief to finally flop down behind my desk, alone and in familiar surroundings.

Adhering to routine, first, I checked messages and emails and found nothing requiring attention – probably due to my message that I would not be back in my office for another week. That done, I could sit back, close my eyes, and relax as I tried to revisit Trina's time in this office. At first, there was nothing. I was beginning to think coming into the office today was a harebrained idea that would prove a waste of time.

Amid those thoughts came the suggestion that coffee might help. I was about to go and wake up the coffee machine when I remembered I had recorded my interview with Trina. It's not something I do on a regular basis, but I think, because I was planning on being away for the following few days, having it recorded for my return made sense at the time. After settling back in my chair and locating the recording, I started it playing. Although I had a transcript of the recording, I wanted to hear it, to relive it.

The first run-through of the recording produced nothing new and certainly no new clues as to what was going on in Trina's life. Resisting the temptation to make a coffee, I dug out the transcript. Then as the recording played again, I followed along on the transcript. By the end of the recording, my antennae were twitching. There was something there, but I couldn't quite put my finger on it. Nothing more than a hint of something in passing. But the reason for her visit remained as big a mystery as it had been since she left my office that morning.

So engrossed in rummaging through my brain for ideas on what else to try, I was startled when my phone played its tune. My first reaction was to ignore it. After all, as far as the rest of the world is concerned, I am not working yet, and I am not here. Then I realised would-be clients wouldn't have my mobile number, so I glanced at the caller ID: Emily.

"Where are you, and what are you doing today?" she demanded when I finally responded.

"In my city office today."

"What, are you back at work already?"

My explanation of the situation was succinct and resulted in Emily telling me she would be up to see me in a few minutes. It seems that, after leaving my place last night, she called at the lab to check on something and was still there at three o'clock this morning. After a few hours sleep, she came into the lab again to check there were no problems before taking the rest of the day off. About twenty minutes later, she used her key to let herself into my office.

"I hope you haven't had coffee yet," she announced as she came in. "I'm desperately in need of a caffeine fix." I agreed it felt like time for coffee.

On my way to the coffee machine in my kitchenette, pounding on my door stopped me in my tracks. Emily started towards the door before turning and raising her eyebrows in question at me. I shook my head to indicate she should ignore it. That's when Ben's voice boomed through from outside.

"Sonny, if you are all right in there, open this bloody door… Otherwise, I will assume you are not all right and will have to break in." I heaved a sigh and signalled to Emily to let him in.

Aware of the dressing down I probably was about to receive, I jumped in first.

"Has something happened? I wasn't expecting to see you back here so soon this morning. Now you're here, I suppose you won't say no to joining us in a coffee." He agreed a coffee would go down well.

"I'll slip down to the bakery for something to have with it," Emily quickly volunteered and headed for the door.

"Coward…," I muttered as she rushed past me. Then, I turned my attention again to Ben. "Please tell me something exciting has happened, Ben. Has your investigation uncovered something about Trina?"

"Uhmm… The short answer might be yes… and no. Perhaps we should wait until Emily returns before we get down to business."

Emily returned carrying a box of cakes and with something else clutched in her hand. After setting the cakes down on the bench, she waved at me the thing she had been hiding in her other hand.

"My watch! Where did you find that? Is it all right?"

"Well, it is flat, but it looks okay. It's a bit grubby looking and might need a wipe over, but apart from that, it looks fine."

Ben repeated the other part of my question. "Where did you find it?"

"I didn't find it. It was given to me. Justin at the bakery saw me being served and came out and asked if I was going upstairs to see you. When I said I was, he went out the back and fetched the watch. He said he found it over a week ago on the ground in the carpark and thought it looked like the one you wore. He has been waiting for you to come into the shop to ask you about it."

Stunned, I turned the watch over in my hand to examine it. There was no obvious damage. So, after cleaning it with a damp cloth, it was being charged. After we all stopped commenting on how good luck sometimes comes when you are least expecting it, I got on with making the coffee while Emily grabbed small plates from the cupboard for our cakes. Ben's contribution to the exercise was to study the collection of cakes and decide which one to select.

With coffee and cake in hand, as we adjourned to the ancient lounge chairs in my interview corner, I detoured past my desk to check on my watch. It showed two percent charged.

"The phone appears to be charging okay," I told the others. "I must go down to the bakery and thank Justin before I go home. It was astute of him to recognise it as my watch."

"Maybe you should have a chat with Justin, too, Ben," Emily said as she wheeled over the chair from behind my desk to join us in my interview corner. "Justin said he came up here to return the watch when he was leaving work the day he found it. Of course, no one was here. But he did encounter a bloke out there in the corridor. He wasn't someone Justin recognised. At first, Justin assumed the man was someone coming to see you, Sonny, but later, he was not so sure. He said the bloke looked a bit 'shifty' and didn't seem too pleased to encounter Justin up here."

"Justin came up here… How come I didn't know about it? Ooh, of course, I haven't checked the CCTV footage beyond where it recorded me running from my office."

"Perhaps we should do that when we finish our coffee," Ben suggested. "It should not only have captured images of Justin up here, it should have recorded anyone else roaming around out there in the corridor over the last week or so."

My stomach tightened when I realised the implication contained in Ben's words. Emily had picked up on it as well and was looking intently at Ben.

"Before we look at that CCTV footage, I think I might take a wander along that corridor out there."

"What do you expect to find?" I demanded.

"Nothing, I hope… but it won't hurt to check."

Somehow, my appetite for coffee and cake had deserted me. I ended up burning my mouth as I gulped down my still too hot coffee in my rush to return to my desk to check the camera footage. Ben insisted I wait until after he had patrolled the corridor before I ran the footage. My argument fell on deaf ears, so my frustration mounted until he returned.

"Right… Let's have a look at what the camera can tell us," Ben said on his return to my office.

"Did you find anything out of the ordinary out there?" I demanded.

"Let's just look at the footage. We can talk later." I know when I'm beaten.

I logged into the camera app, sent the footage to my big screen so all three of us could see it, and then fast-forwarded the recording through to the end of the week before the incident occurred on the following Monday morning. That's when the first surprise greeted us.

Trina had come up the stairs on Friday morning and then hesitated. It looked as though she was about to go down the stairs again but she changed her mind and came to my door instead. She stood outside my door for a few seconds but didn't knock – just stood there looking undecided. Then, for whatever reason, she turned abruptly on her heel and headed back to the stairs. The next few images were of her disappearing from view as she went down the stairs.

"That was one troubled young woman," Emily commented, "and it seems whatever was bothering her was still a problem when she did come to see you on Monday. Maybe we need to listen again to the recording of her interview. Perhaps we missed something before."

"Good thinking, Emily," I said with just a hint of sarcasm. "I've listened to it twice this morning and still am none the wiser for it."

"Okay, for now, let's just keep the footage rolling until the next person appears on the screen," Ben said.

It was Monday morning before the camera captured anyone else out in the corridor. The first person was me when I arrived at my office. Then, a while later, the next images were familiar to all of us: Trina arriving at my door and Trina leaving my office.

"You can see she remained troubled on that Monday morning, and she looked quite tense when she left this office," Emily observed.

"Keep it rolling," Ben demanded. "The next image should be you, Sonny, leaving here. Whatever is recorded after that will be stuff we haven't seen previously."

He was right. A long recording of nothing appeared after the image of me racing out of my office to go to Trina. It was early Tuesday afternoon when the camera captured the image of a man striding along the corridor. He appeared to hesitate as he passed my door before continuing along the corridor and out of range of my camera.

"Could have been anyone going to one of the other offices on this floor," Emily commented.

"Possibly… but I don't think that is the case," I murmured.

"Why do you say that?" Ben demanded. "Why couldn't it be someone going to one of the offices further along the corridor?"

"The tenant of the next office, along on the other side of the corridor, rarely comes into his office, and the camera hasn't captured him in the corridor in recent times. The other big office that runs right across the end of this floor is vacant and has been for some time."

"What about that small area between this office and that big one at the end of the floor? Who rents that?" Emily asked.

"It's not an office. It's too tiny. The janitor uses it to store his clearing gear and materials… Not that he does much cleaning up here other than the corridor and that big area at the other end of the floor where the company that owns this building and several others in the city heart has their headquarters."

"So you are saying there was no reason for a strange bloke to be wandering along the corridor?" Ben confirmed. I nodded my agreement. "Let's keep the recording rolling to see when he leaves. If what you say is right, we would expect him to turn around and go downstairs again when he finds there is no one around."

Some minutes later, the next image to scroll across the screen made Emily and me gasp.

"That's Justin," I blurted out, "Justin from the bakery downstairs."

"Yeah, that probably is when he came to try to return your watch," Emily added.

"Does he often come up here?" Ben asked.

Emily and I exchanged a look before both shaking our heads. "No, I don't think I've ever known him to come up here," I told Ben.

We watched Justin try knocking on my door a couple of times before disappearing down the stairs again.

"Right… logically, the next image we see should be that unknown bloke leaving," Ben announced.

"If you're right, Ben, he is a long time leaving," I observed. "He's been up on this floor for quite a while, and we still haven't seen him leave. What the hell was he doing up here? And where was he doing it?"

"Might he be a new tenant for that big office, or even a new tenant for that other office if the previous tenant didn't use it much?" Emily suggested.

"He didn't look like he was moving in," Ben murmured. "Arrived empty handed…. What did he do? Sit on the floor while pondering how to furnish the place?"

The unknown man wasn't the next image to fill the screen, but that image did cause a few giggles.

"Ah hah, caught in the act, eh, Emily," I laughed as we watched the image of Emily unlock my office door and go inside.

"That would have been Wednesday morning after Ben asked me to look for your phone and check everything was okay in your office. Was that bloke still up here somewhere while I was here?" she asked, tension apparent in her voice as she asked the question.

"Well, as we haven't seen him leave, I suppose he had to be up here on this floor somewhere at the time," I replied. I gave Ben a meaningful look as I continued. "I don't know where he would have spent the night."

"Keep the footage rolling," Ben ordered.

When the stranger did finally appear on the footage again, it was close to lunchtime on Wednesday – and he was only then on his way downstairs.

"He did spend the night up here somewhere, didn't he?" Emily asked. "How was he able to do that?"

"How often does the janitor clean up here? I mean, how often does he clean that corridor specifically?" Ben asked.

"Hmm… If there's been a bit of traffic, he might clean it

once a week but, most of the time, it's only every two or three weeks," I told Ben.

"Freeze the recording at that point, please, Sonny. I'll be back in a few moments," Ben said as he headed for the door.

"Mystery solved," he announced when he returned. "The door of that big office at the end of the floor has been forced. Our mysterious friend spent the night there by the look of it … or someone inhabited it for some time judging by the mess left behind."

He turned to say something to Emily, but she was speaking to someone on her phone. It was a short call. As soon as it ended, she told Ben, "My team is on its way to go over that office space."

I don't know if Ben heard her or not. By then, he also was busy with his phone. When his call ended, he confirmed his people also were on their way.

"A couple of uniforms and a detective will be here in a few minutes and will seal off that end of the floor. I might go and have a word with the building's management mob about their busted door."

If only I could have been a fly on the wall when the man-mountain that is Ben Richards, resplendent in his superintendent's uniform, waltzed into the management's administration office to acquaint them with what had happened under their noses.

Ben was gone a while before we saw him appear on my screen as he led a couple of suits past my office on their way to examine the busted door of the end office. The sight of Ben triggered another concerning train of thought.

"Emily, did you know Ben would be here this morning?" Emily looked confused and shook her head. "Hmm… I wonder what prompted his visit. It had to be for something more than a free coffee and cake."

My curiosity would have to persist for longer than I liked. It seemed to be taking Ben an inordinately long time to show people a busted door.

Chapter 13

"What are you doing here this morning, Ben," I demanded as soon as he walked back into my office.

I saw concern plaster itself across his face. "I was just out there further along the corridor for a few minutes. I was here with you and Emily before that. Don't you remember my being here earlier?"

"Eh? Of course, I remember you were here before you went to show those people the busted door. My mind hasn't been damaged to that extent, Ben. After you dropped me here this morning and went to your office, what brought you back here so soon after you left?"

"Oh, I see. Didn't I say? No, obviously not… but that's your fault for distracting me with other information. Right, I came to tell you it looks as though we might have a lead on Greta Lomax."

"Excuse my ignorance," Emily began hesitantly, "but who is Greta Lomax, and what does she have to do with what happened to Sonny?"

"She was the nurse who called herself Lisa and told Sonny the story about her best friend, Zali," Ben explained.

"Ah hah, so she does exist. When are we going to speak to her?" I asked.

"It's not that simple, Sonny. It is believed she is somewhere in the district to the north of here. The police there are trying to locate her, but she is either aware they are looking for her or something has her spooked, and she is constantly on the move. They will let me know as soon as I can talk to her. And, before you ask, no, you will not be coming with me to talk to her – not at first, anyway."

"If you will excuse me for a few minutes, I should go and organise my team to go over that office with the busted door," Emily said as she stood up to leave.

"No need, Emily," Ben told her. "Two of your team arrived at about the same time as my detective and a couple of uniforms. I have them all going over that area now. I don't know that we'll score much more than fingerprints from that office, but at least we have Sonny's camera footage."

"My blood just about runs cold every time I think about the bloke hiding in that office when I came here on that Wednesday morning. What if he had mistaken me for Sonny? I might have ended up dumped somewhere too, or left here on the floor somewhere for days before anyone found me," Emily admitted and gave an involuntary shiver.

"Ah, well, that's one scenario, but there could be another situation to think about," Ben murmured as though deep in thought.

"Like what?" I demanded. "Come on, Ben. Both Emily and I need to know what the risks were… and if they still exist, for that matter."

"Okay. Yes, there was a chance – a slight chance – he might have mistaken Emily for you, but two other possibilities are more likely. He might have thought someone else was here at the time and heard whatever Trina told you while she was here. Having that 'somebody else' roaming around would pose just as much risk to them as Sonny. Then, of course, there is the third and most likely scenario: They (whoever they are) might be aware their attack on Sonny didn't finish her off, so they had someone watching and waiting for her to appear again at her office."

"So, I might have been attacked again? And we know they would make sure they did a proper job of it the next time." It was my turn to feel an icy wave run through my veins. "Are they still waiting for me to be here alone? Or, maybe they are watching everywhere I might go and are waiting for an appropriate opportunity to occur."

"What are we supposed to do, Ben?" Emily demanded. "Do we just sit on our hands until they try again, or do we lock Sonny away in some safe place until your guys sort out what's going on?"

"No, we are not going to do either of those things… although I'm still not convinced about what we are going to do. But, for the moment, Sonny will not be here or at home alone at any time."

I groaned. The prospect of being 'under guard' the whole time did not thrill me. My arguments against such a move fell on deaf ears. It meant Ben would continue to spend nights at my house, and a police officer of some sort would be allocated to 'minding' me during the day. Emily found the prospect of such a situation hilarious.

"Oh, I do want to be a fly on the wall while this regime is in place," she giggled. "Ben, your police officer 'minder' will need to be of strong constitution to survive what is dished out to him for doing what he has been assigned to do."

Her comments brought a few terse words from me to point out it would not be his fault his boss had given him such a shitty, pointless assignment. Further discussion of the matter was avoided when Ben's phone chirped. He took the call outside, but the set of his jaw as he walked out told me the call was significant. What it didn't tell me was whether it was significant in relation to me or not. It proved to be a short call. He returned after only a couple of minutes but did not refer to the call. I assumed it might have been about some other matter and had nothing to do with me or what happened to Trina.

"You know," Emily began, "it seems that everyone involved so far in what happened to Sonny has an alias. The nurse, Lisa, turns out to be Greta Lomax and Trina's real name is Zali. I know I am Emily, but I am beginning to wonder about you, Sonny, and Ben. Who are you really?"

"If I might stop you there for a moment," Ben interjected. "You've fallen into the trap of accepting an assumption as a fact. Yes, we seem to have established that Lisa is, in fact, Greta

Lomax. But there is nothing to confirm Trina is Zalika Standish, as Lisa asserted. So far, we have been unable to identify the person run down in the street in front of here, and we have been unable to establish that a Zalika Standish ever existed."

The implication of Ben's words hit me like a thunderbolt. It had been poor investigative practice on my part to accept the information the nurse gave me.

"You're right, Ben. It's back to the drawing board for a fresh start. But what do we do next? Where do I start?" I pleaded, hoping for some inspirational guidance from Ben.

None was forthcoming. Instead, Ben wandered over to stand and gaze out of the same window from which I had witnessed Trina's accident. After some moments, he appeared to remember I had asked a question. He chose to answer me – after a fashion – without taking his eyes off the street below.

"Who was on the street at that time? Who did what? Who saw what?.... We need CCTV footage of that street on the day Trina was killed. That's *all* we need to make headway. It doesn't sound impossible… If only there were such a CCTV camera somewhere in the vicinity that covered that area below. My officers, going door-to-door, haven't managed to locate one yet."

"It's not surprising if you think about it," Emily suggested. "Most businesses would have their cameras set to record what was happening inside their premises, not focused on what was happening on the street."

"Uhmm… there might be one, if it's still there," I volunteered after giving the matter some thought.

"Where?" Ben barked.

"*Gianni's*… the restaurant a couple of doors down from here."

"I just told you, my officers have checked every business along both sides of the street for any with a CCTV camera. They found none. So, Gianni, or whatever his name is, doesn't appear to have one, not now, anyway."

"Did they speak to Gino?"

"Who the hell is Gino, and why should they speak to him?"

"Gino owns the restaurant and lives in the unit above it. When he first installed the camera downstairs, he also installed one on that little balcony at the front of his unit. They had some problems with diners playing up and slipping away without paying. So, the camera he installed upstairs was designed to look down on and record activities in the outside eating area. If that upstairs camera is still there and functioning, it might have captured enough of the street below to be of some use to us."

"How do I get hold of this Gino to ask him about that camera?"

"Seeing as you asked so nicely," I said, heaping on the sarcasm, "I'll give him a call."

As I was about to end the call, Gino answered. With my phone on speaker so Ben could hear Gino, it only took a few moments to gather the information we needed. Yes, his upstairs camera was still in place, and yes, he believed it still worked okay, although he hadn't looked at any of its recordings for some time. I thanked Gino and told him Millhaven's top cop was on his way to talk to him.

"What for? What am I supposed to have done?" he demanded.

"Relax, Gino. He just wants to have a look at that camera's recording from last Monday morning – if it still exists."

"Huh, okay; it should still exist. The camera isn't set to start overwriting until the first of next month. I don't know what you hope to achieve from the recording. It's not great since we installed those umbrellas over the tables in the outdoor dining area. The umbrellas kind of defeated the purpose of the camera. It gives a better view of what's going on in the street than what's happening in the dining area."

"Well, from our point of view, that's good news. We are not interested in what your diners get up to. We're more interested in what was happening in the street at the time."

With Gino's mind set at rest, Ben headed for the door. I called him back and handed him a memory stick.

"In case there is something worthwhile on that recording,

you could take a copy of it while you are there. Gino is a bit of a genius with this sort of stuff, so he should be able to put a copy on the stick for you."

"Right, good thinking. Keep this door locked until I get back, but while I'm away, the detective leading the team going over the office at the end of the floor will be keeping an eye on anything happening in the corridor outside."

"I'm sure we don't need anyone to babysit us," I said a touch tartly. "Who is this detective, anyway? What's his name – in case something does happen and we need to talk to him?"

"It's Detective Galbraith who will be keeping an eye on things while I'm gone."

"Brett? Is Brett working the crime scene on this floor?"

"Ah, yes. I'd forgotten you know Brett from that earlier Thomlinson case. I was surprised when he seemed so keen to keep an eye on you. Now I understand why. Didn't you save his life in the shoot-out at the wrap-up of that case?"

While it would be nice to catch up with Brett again after all these months, I still resented having been allocated a minder. I could see Ben and I having some really serious words if he insisted on my having a full-time bodyguard. As soon as Ben left my office, I turned my attention to Emily, who had sat quietly all through my conversation with Gino.

"Emily, I'm sorry your day off appears to be ruined. Now might be a good time if you want to escape. I doubt Brett will be too interested in anyone leaving this office. His focus will be on anyone trying to come in, not leave."

"Why would I want to leave? I'm just as interested in what Ben might find on Gino's recording as he is, and I suppose you are, for that matter. Anyway, while we are left to our own devices, it's an opportunity for us to go through your recording of your interview with Trina. We haven't achieved much else this morning, so anything we can do without Ben's interruptions might stand a chance of producing something for us."

Although it was sound thinking on Emily's part, and good intentions drove us, we hadn't achieved much more than a fresh coffee before Ben returned – looking pleased with himself.

"Right, Sonny, as soon as you make me one of those," he said, pointing to my coffee, "let's get this footage up on your big screen to see if there is anything of interest on it."

Grunts, sighs, and murmurs were the only sounds to be heard for the next half hour as the three of us studied the recording frame by frame. By the time we reached the end of the footage, my mood had turned dark. I don't know what I had expected, but we had found nothing at all of interest. As I was about to ask what we might try next, Ben pre-empted my question and answered it.

"Rewind it to the approximate time you saw Trina run down out there. Maybe take it back to a bit before it happened. The camera might have captured someone or something out there somewhere on the street just before it happened."

"But we've studied every frame and found nothing. What are we likely to find by going over it again?"

"We won't know until we have a look, so let's do that without an argument, shall we – please?"

Time dragged on and my grumbling stomach had alerted me to the fact lunchtime had been and gone. For the last five minutes, Ben had focused on three frames of the recording and we had been forced to study them in detail at least four times so far. I felt as though my eyes were hanging out. I needed a break.

"Ben, I can no longer concentrate. I'm starving and need lunch. You and Emily continue studying the footage while I duck out to fetch us lunch."

"That's not going to happen," Ben announced. "I'll organise one of the uniforms working the crime scene to go for something. Where should he go, and what do we want for lunch?"

There was no changing Ben's mind, so I said I would order whatever we wanted and pay for it over the phone to simplify things for the unfortunate uniform sent to collect food. The consensus was that fish and salad lunchboxes would be nice. I ordered and paid for three of them from the fish bar across the street, and Ben dispatched a young officer to collect them. It was agreed yet another coffee probably would go well with lunch, and I was happy to go along with that suggestion. Making the coffee gave me a break from staring at the images on the screen. But, as soon as food and coffee were dealt with, Ben dragged Emily and me back to the big screen and Gino's camera footage.

"Now, which frame were we … Oh, yes, that's the one we were looking at. It's the next frame I want to look at again… Yep, that's the one. There is something in this image. I don't know what it is. I can't put my finger on it, but I know there is something in it." Ben almost had his nose up to the screen as he spoke.

Emily and I exchanged a look before sitting back in our chairs to relax while Ben continued to examine the image on the screen.

"Do you have a magnifying glass?" he demanded after a few moments.

Without asking why he needed one, I rummaged in a drawer and handed him the larger of the two magnifying glasses I kept there. Again, Emily and I exchanged a look and raised eyebrows, but said nothing. Several moments later, there was a strangled yelp that almost startled the life out of me.

"Ah hah, there it is," Ben yelped. "I knew there was something about this image. Well, that answers that question, I think."

"Would you care to share your Eureka moment with us?" Emily asked quietly.

"Yeah, yeah; come and have a look at this," Ben said, gesturing at the screen with the magnifying glass he was holding. "Now, if I could just work out who that bloke was, it might lead somewhere."

"Sonny, come and have a look at this," Emily said. "Do you know that bloke at all?"

Although I took my time to peer at him through the magnifying glass, there was no recognition at all. I couldn't recall ever having seen him previously, and there wasn't anything that stood out about him to help trigger a memory.

"No-o, I don't think I recognise him at all. Of course, he could just be another missing bit of my memory. Ben, you obviously think he is important for some reason. Why? And what does he appear to be looking at so intently?"

"At a rough guess, given where he is standing and the way he is looking up, I'd say he was looking at you standing over there at your window. If I'm right, it would explain why you ended up dumped at that abandoned mine site." Ben finished his speech with a knowing nod… while appearing to have developed an idea as he was speaking.

He rushed over and stood at the window and, for several moments, appeared to be studying a point on the opposite side of the street. Emily and I didn't have to be geniuses to work out that was the spot where the mysterious man in the footage had been standing. Suddenly, Ben became excited and started for the door.

"I'll be back in a couple of minutes. Don't move that image that is on the screen while I'm gone."

"Okay, Sonny, what's that all about, and what happens next?" Emily asked. I shrugged in response. "Argh, you know him better than I do. I thought you might know what he was up to."

"You know as much as I do. And, for the record, I have never been able to fathom how Ben's mind works."

Our suspense was short-lived. As he had indicated, Ben returned a couple of minutes later. We heard him finish speaking to someone out in the corridor as he opened the door. Without a word or any other enlightenment, he walked past Emily and me on his way to stand at the window again. Emily looked confused and turned to me in the hope I could shed some light on what was happening. She was disappointed. I didn't have a clue. So we both remained where we were and maintained our silence as we watched Ben drag out his phone and key in a number. Although we eavesdropped on his phone call, the one-sided conversation provided no genuine information but did give rise to speculation.

"Move along a bit… No, to your right… Yeah, that's good. Now, walk out towards the edge of the pavement… Stop. That's about right. Okay, now look up. What can you see?... Can you identify who it is?... Yeah, I suppose the uniform is a bit of a give-away. Hang on a second…."

With that, Ben was motioning me over to stand at the window. I did as he indicated while he stepped away from the window and continued his phone conversation.

"How about now?... Yeah, but give me a description…" I saw Ben look over at me and eye me up and down. "All right, okay… that's good enough… back to work now, thanks."

"Is that it," I demanded as I saw Ben pocket his phone. "May I move away from this window now you've ended your call? And, am I entitled to know what that was all about?" I heard Emily trying to stifle a giggle as I finished speaking.

"What are you in a snit about now? All I was doing was confirming the suspicion I formed after studying that image that's on the screen." Ben grabbed the magnifying glass off my desk and held it up to the big screen. "See that bloke standing on the pavement on the other side of the street? He is looking up at something on this side of the street and not at what is happening – or about to happen – down there on the street. I suspected he was looking up at this window, so I sent a uniform down to test my theory. By positioning the officer exactly where the man was standing at the time of last Monday's incident and having him look up, he confirmed he could see you standing at the window."

"It could have been anyone standing here. If it was this window the bloke was looking at, how did he know who was standing there watching what was happening below? I mean, how did he know it was me, and not some other woman, who was the potential risk?"

"The young officer involved in the re-enactment had no difficulty describing you."

Emily had remained silent for so long that I'd almost forgotten she was there until she asked her question.

"So, Ben, are you suggesting that man saw Sonny observe what happened on the street and decided action was required to eliminate the risk she presented?" Ben nodded, and Emily continued. "I'm struggling with that theory. Sonny rushed straight out of her office when she saw what happened to Trina. There wouldn't have been more than a minute or so in it, yet they, whoever they are, had people in place and were able to deal with that perceived risk almost immediately. Let's go through Sonny's account of what happened… no, let's do a re-enactment of what happened from when Sonny went and stood at that window."

I was taken by surprise when Ben readily agreed to Emily's proposal and I was bustled back to stand at the window as I did on that Monday morning.

"Now give us a running commentary as you replicate *exactly* what you did that Monday morning, and try to keep the timings as near as possible to how you remember things played out on the day," Ben told me.

Within moments, all three of us were clattering down the stairs at breakneck speed as I did on the day. Then, I went through the charade of not being able to open the door to the left of the bottom of the staircase before giving up and racing to the back door instead. In the interest of authenticity, I keyed in my code, listened for the door to unlock, and then ran out into the carpark.

"Is that exactly as you came out of that door that day?" Ben asked.

"Yeah… exactly. The righthand half of the door is the bit that unlocks. So, you pull it in towards you, step around it, and race out. Because I was in a rush, I would have pulled the door open only far enough for me to race through it."

"And that meant you came out into the carpark at the angle you told us about earlier. You would have come out already facing towards the corner of the building and the alleyway beside it." Emily confirmed as Ben checked his watch.

"As you suggested, Emily," he began, "that is very tight timing for anyone to have blocked one door and be out in the carpark waiting for Sonny to emerge through the back door. Ladies, we will discuss this again later. Now, I am taking you both back upstairs to Sonny's office, where I want you to remain until I return later this afternoon. Emily, if you need to leave, do so. But, Sonny, you must not leave your office again until I return… and Brett will ensure you don't."

"Where might you be in the meantime?" I demanded. "If what we have discovered in this little while has given you a possible line of inquiry to investigate, shouldn't we know about it?"

My words fell on deaf ears. Ben remained silent until he was on his way out of my office. Then, he turned and reissued his instructions, "Stay here, and do not try to leave this office until I return."

Tempted though I was to argue, I know Ben well enough to recognise when his tone of voice and body language counsel against doing so.

Chapter 14

With Ben now out of the way, the question was how to make the most of the afternoon available to us without his interference. It was almost a foregone conclusion that listening to my interview with Trina might be the best option. We made ourselves comfortable and played the recording.

At the end of the recording, two glum faces looked across my desk at one another. The exercise had produced nothing new, not even a possible new clue. After a few moments of disappointed silence, Emily sat upright and slapped her hand down on the desk.

"What's wrong with the pair of us? Did we really think some amazing new clue that we hadn't identified before would suddenly emerge today? Let's listen to it once more – slowly and analytically – before abandoning it as a lost cause."

Ever the sceptic, I made an 'as if' comment but, lacking any better suggestion, I returned to the start of the recording and pressed PLAY. Although nothing had changed, and the recording still sounded the same to me, Emily appeared to be more invested in what was being said – or not being said – as she listened to it the second time. At several points, she called for the recording to be stopped and for the last bit to be replayed. Whenever that occurred, it was usually accompanied by questions difficult to answer.

"How did Trina react to that question? I heard what she said, but how did she physically react?" And then there was Emily's other frequent question, "How did she act when she struggled not to tell you what she really wanted to tell you?"

The first time I encountered those questions, my response was a shrug and a shake of my head, but that wasn't good enough for Emily.

"No, Sonny. Think about how it was. Close your eyes. Right, now think about Trina on that Monday morning sitting here where I am now. What was she doing? How was she acting? Was she stony-faced and calm? Was she fidgeting and wringing her hands or whatever? Picture her sitting here, Sonny."

"She certainly wasn't calm. She was twitchy and restless. I half expected her to jump up and dash out of my office almost as soon as she sat down."

"But she didn't, Sonny. And she doesn't seem to have settled down either."

"Argh, no, she didn't. She stayed for about an hour, but she never settled down at all. Her agitation level fluctuated throughout the interview, but it was always there. It's just that on some occasions, it skyrocketed. When that happened, I wouldn't have been surprised if she had run out of here screaming."

Emily's questioning proved intuitive. Instead of just listening to the recording, it was as if she was watching the interview in progress. Whenever she had the recording stopped so she could ask questions about what had just been said, it was always at one of Trina's periods of elevated agitation during the interview.

"Sonny, she sounds scared stiff," Emily observed. I agreed, and Emily continued. "It's obvious she wants help – needs help – but she seems as though she is not game to ask for help or say why she needs it. Sonny, go back and play the last couple of minutes of so of the recording, please."

"Why? It won't have changed. They will still be the same words you've listened to twice already. All right, all right. Don't fuss. I'll play it now."

In the end, I replayed that last bit of the recording three times and was quite determined I wasn't going to play it again. As it turns out, I wasn't asked to.

"There… Did you hear it?" Emily demanded

"Did I hear what? All I heard was what we listened to three times already this afternoon." My frustration was apparent in my response, if not so much in my words.

"I think I can hear a noise in the background. Maybe it's outside somewhere. When it happened, it seemed to have further unsettled Trina and caused her to hurry up and leave. I know you've told me what you think you know about Trina – or the real Zali if you would prefer – but tell me again, please."

For the next few minutes, Emily and I discussed everything the nurse, Lisa (a.k.a. Greta Lomax), had told me about her 'best friend', Zalika Standish, particularly the physical description Lisa had given me. I found myself struggling with the discussion as it progressed.

"Apologies, Emily, I know I'm not doing this very well. It's just that I've been over in my mind so many times everything Lisa told me. It has now lost its immediacy, its impact. I'm now beginning to wonder if I'm remembering it accurately. Maybe my head injury has somehow scrambled my recall, and I'm now remembering what I want to hear, rather than what I was told."

"No-o, I don't think that's the case. Your description of Trina's demeanour during the interview is exactly in keeping with the way she sounds on the recording. If only there was something else she said – or hinted at – that might give us a clue as to why Trina had come to see you in the first place, we might be able to move forward with this thing. At the moment, it feels a bit like only knowing half the story. And before you get all excited, that comment wasn't about your recall. It was about Trina's strange behaviour."

While I accepted Emily's explanation, her comment did sting for a while and a short period of silence followed. Something niggled me about the recording.

"Damn! There is something else about that recording, but I can't seem to put my finger on it. Bear with me, please. Going to go back and play the first bit of the recording again. If anything jumps out at you, yell."

Emily didn't make a sound, and I was no wiser for having listened to it again. But something still suggested whatever I was looking for was to be found in those first few minutes of the interview. I rewound to the start of the interview and started it playing again. Then it hit me….

"That's it! That's what's wrong. Emily, nowhere in that recording does Trina introduce herself or give me her name. How do I know that woman's name was Trina Blewett if at no point she told me?"

It's fair to say we both were equally astounded by that revelation, and neither of us had an immediate answer to the question. How did I know the woman's name? We discussed that for a few moments before a stray thought wriggled through to the front of my thinking.

"This recording doesn't start at the beginning of the interview. For some reason, the very first part of the interview seems to be…."

Finally, that niggling thought came through, and I understood what had happened.

"Oh, hell… Now I remember. Of course the first part of the interview isn't on this recording. Because Trina didn't have an appointment and wasn't an existing client, we sat over here at my desk and not in my interview corner as we might normally have done. It wasn't until after the interview had started and I realised how strange everything seemed, that I started recording it on my phone at my desk. I remember I had to create a pretence of having to pick something up off the floor in order to cover my reaching in under the desk to start my phone recording. So, you see, that's why the early part of the interview isn't recorded. "

"Okay, I understand that bit, but how does it matter that you interviewed her at your desk and not in your interview corner?" Emily asked and continued. "I suppose we should count ourselves lucky that you did sit at your desk, or we might not have had a recording at all."

"Well, no, that's not the case. It had nothing to do with luck – well, not much, anyway."

"Right… I still don't understand. Humour me. How would we have a recording of the interview if you had conducted it in your interview corner?" Emily was sounding exasperated, so I rushed to explain.

"Some time ago, I started the practice of recording interviews I conducted in that corner of my office. I have a digital recorder set up behind one of the lounge chairs over there and I turn it on as I go to let in the client. It records very well even though we just speak normally. In Trina's case, I did turn the recorder on as I went to answer the door but, as she wasn't an existing client, I took her through to my desk rather than interview her in that corner. There was a brief period after she first entered the office when she spoke to me as we stood just inside the door. That was when she would have told me her name and apologised for turning up without an appointment. I think the only other thing that was said while we were standing there was that Trina mentioned a couple of times that she wasn't sure I could help her and that she wasn't sure exactly what I did."

"So, after you showed her through to your desk, was there much conversation before you managed to start recording the interview on your phone?"

"Probably not. Hmm… We might have spoken for about five minutes, I suppose, before I started the recording, but during that time, I think Trina mainly repeated the stuff she said when she first came into the office. Yes, that's when I gave her the copies of my brochures and tried to reassure her there was a fair chance that, whatever her problem was, it would be within the scope of the work I do."

"Why are we still sitting here? Why aren't we checking whether that digital recorder managed to capture anything immediately after Trina arrived?"

"I had started playing what was on the recording for Ben, but we soon realised it was no good and didn't persist with it. We hadn't listened to any more than about a minute of the recorder's efforts. I haven't been back to it since."

"What have we got to lose?" Emily said, throwing her hands in the air. "Get the recorder, and let's see if we can't coax something useful out of it."

No miracles had occurred in the interim. The recording still sounded as bad as it did when I tried to play it for Ben. But persistence sort of paid off. After rewinding it and tinkering with the playback settings a few times, the recording did seem a little clearer. After some solid persuasion by Emily, I started the recording playing again as we both hunched over the machine in the hope of hearing it more clearly. We did pick up a few words, but it was hard work.

"This is hopeless. I'm going to try to produce a transcript of it." Emily looked confused, so I explained what I meant. "This recorder connects to my computer and, using part of the voice recognition program I use, it's possible to produce a transcription of the recording. Please don't get your hopes up too high, though. It doesn't work miracles. If nothing is recorded other than static noise, there won't be anything for it to transcribe."

While it didn't produce any miracles, it did manage to transcribe quite a few disjointed words, including those of Trina introducing herself to me. With each of us armed with a copy of the transcript, we prepared to spend the next few minutes studying it in detail. We had barely started when a knock at the door halted proceedings. My CCTV camera showed Detective Brett Galbraith waiting to be let in.

"Brett, is there a problem?" I asked as I peered around him to check up and down the corridor.

"Everything is fine. I didn't mean to alarm you. I just wanted to check that everything was okay with you and to let you know the crime scene has been closed down. The others have left already, but I will continue keeping an eye on things until Ben returns."

He started to walk away, but I called him back. "There's no point hanging about out there when you can come in here and be comfortable. Go and sit at my desk. You can monitor the corridor by watching the camera feed on the screen on my desk. Would you care for a coffee while you're about it?"

Still reluctant to leave his post outside, Brett suggested he could take a coffee outside to drink it.

"Oh, for God's sake, Brett… Go and sit at my desk while I make you a coffee. Don't worry about Ben. We'll tell him that, although you put up a good struggle, we held you captive."

With Brett installed at my desk with a coffee and a cake leftover from this morning, Emily and I took our copies of the transcripts and retreated to my interview corner. Ben's persistent complaints about my lounge chairs were justified. The ancient lounge chairs that inhabit my interview corner could never be described as comfortable, not at this stage of their life, anyway.

The recorder had picked up Trina introducing herself and apologising for arriving without an appointment.

"Interesting that she doesn't ask if you have time to see her or if she should come back later," Emily commented.

"Hmm… No, I don't recall that being an issue, or that there was even a thought given to the possibility that I might refuse to see her then."

After the initial introduction bit, the transcript consisted of a few separate words, but they were enough to confirm that they were from Trina as she asked about what I did. Then, there was a collection of jumbled words that we couldn't make sense of before I was encouraging Trina to sit at my desk and tell me about her problem.

"This looks like when you persuaded her to go over to your desk. That was before you started recording the interview on your phone. But it appears you were also too far away for the digital recorder to pick up anything being said at the desk. Did she have anything enlightening to say during that gap between the recordings?" Emily asked hopefully.

"No, it was a strange interview. People often are awkward when they first come to see me. They're embarrassed to be talking about whatever the problem is that they want me to investigate, but they soon relax. Trina didn't. I gave her my brochures, but she wasn't interested in them and handed them back. I pushed them back to her and told her to take them home and read them later. To get the ball rolling, I encouraged her to tell me about her problem so I could tell her whether I might be able to help or not. That brought forth just a jumble of words. I couldn't make out what she was telling me, and she really didn't tell me what her problem was.

The interview consisted of Trina supposedly telling me what was wrong. In reality, she started and stopped, paused and started again several times, and ended up not telling me the nature of her problem. She was quite distressed. I was concerned for her, but nothing I did seemed to relax her or coax her story out of her."

"Why did she even bother to see you if she wasn't going to tell you what she wanted you to investigate? I know that's a silly question, but I can't understand her motivation in coming to see you if she wasn't going to tell you why she came."

"Good question… and one I can't answer. Anyway, after this had gone on for a while, I was running out of patience. I again pushed the brochures across the desk to her and asked her to bear with me while I grabbed something else out of the drawer for her. My thinking at the time was that she would either open up, or she would grab everything and leave. If I'm honest, I would have preferred the latter option as I was getting nowhere with her, and I wanted to get away. But, in case she did decide to open up, that's when I reached under the desk and started my phone recording."

Emily was silent for a few moments. She appeared to consider all I had told her before delivering her assessment of Trina's visit.

"Despite the missing words from the recording of when Trina first arrived, it's clear she never actually said what her problem was or why she thought you might be able to help. There was something I did pick up on, though. Trina used the word 'they' a few times, but without providing any clues as to who 'they' might be or why Trina was concerned about them."

Further discussion was prevented when Brett interrupted. "Uh oh, here comes the boss."

Brett had no sooner finished speaking than Ben, looking concerned, rushed into the office when I opened the door for him. As he rushed through the door, he was looking back over his shoulder.

"Have you seen Brett?" he demanded. "He's not outside."

"That's probably because I'm over here," Brett replied and gave Ben a wave from where he was sitting behind my desk.

"He has been keeping an eye on us in here while monitoring the corridor outside via the CCTV camera. That's why you didn't have to knock for me to open the door. We knew you were out there," I explained.

Ben never likes being wrong-footed. Today was no exception, so I rushed on before he could say anything… and probably take Brett to task for not following Ben's instructions to the letter.

"While you were away, we weren't allowed to leave because Brett hadn't been told we could. Now you've returned, may we go home, please? And I suspect Brett might like to leave, too."

"Well, if I'm no longer needed here, I'll leave you to it," Brett said as he made a move towards the door.

"Yes, of course… Sorry for having kept you, Brett, but could I have a quick word before you go?" Ben said, and added a quick jerk of his head to indicate 'outside'.

Brett gave me a knowing wink as he passed me on the way out. Ben followed him out, and I watched the CCTV footage of the two men having a brief conversation in the corridor outside my door before Brett headed for the stairs and Ben came back into the office.

"So, Ben, while Emily and I were held captive in my office all afternoon, where were you and was it in any way relevant to Trina's case?" I demanded a bit sharply.

He attempted to duck the question, but I wasn't having any of it and continued to demand an answer. Finally, Ben heaved a sigh of resignation. I thought my answers would follow. I was wrong. He turned to speak to Emily.

"Do you have to be somewhere else, or are you planning on having dinner at Sonny's this evening?"

"I was going to take Sonny home and probably stop somewhere on the way to pick up something for dinner. Are you going to join us for dinner?" Emily asked. Ben nodded.

"Oh, good… Now we know what everyone is doing tonight, may I just go home, please?" I demanded, my voice reflecting my frustration level.

"There's no need to be like that, Sonny," Ben reprimanded me. "Of course, you can go home. Emily, give me about half an hour and then take her home. I'll bring something for dinner when I come, but I don't want you pair hanging around there for too long before I arrive. So, allow me that half hour before you leave here." There was little opportunity to argue, so we complied with his instructions.

The aroma of the roast dinners he had brought preceded him into the kitchen. The dinners went into the oven to keep warm while we took drinks out onto the back deck. I had hoped that, while we relaxed on the deck, we might find out more about what Ben had been up to this afternoon. Again, I was wrong. He refused to discuss work, and there was no way he could be persuaded to talk 'shop' until we were settled in my lounge room after dinner. But that was as long as I was prepared to indulge him.

"Right, Ben, I will not be put off any longer. Where did you go this afternoon, and was it related to my case?"

"After a quick trip to the precinct, I took a run up to Everton and spent a couple of hours or so there."

"Everton? What's so special about Everton that you would want to spend the afternoon there, instead of here enjoying our company? What have they got that we don't have?" I demanded.

"A police station…."

"Ben…," Emily began tentatively. "Now might be a good time to stop playing silly buggers and tell us about Everton… And preferably before Sonny blows a gasket."

"Argh, okay… I went to Everton because they had located Greta Lomax and brought her in for questioning. Because it wasn't their case, they hadn't tried to question her, and just held her until I arrived."

"Fantastic…," I yelped. "That's the first real breakthrough we've had so far. What did Lomax have to say?"

"Nothing… She was rude and difficult and refused to say anything. I persisted for as long as I could before telling her she was about to be transferred to a cell here in Millhaven, where she would be held for however long it took for her to realise how much trouble she was in. I will keep trying to get her to talk, but as a last resort, if she continues to refuse to answer questions, I will threaten to charge her with conspiracy to murder… And I will do so if I don't get answers."

"Is there anything I can do to help facilitate the process? I mean, would bringing me in to talk to her help loosen her tongue a bit, do you think?"

"That's not going to happen – for any number of reasons – so don't press your luck on that one. However, I also managed to pick up another gem while I was in Everton. When I left your office this afternoon, I called in to see the tech boys at the precinct and asked them to print off a copy of the image of the man who was standing watching your window when Trina was killed. I flashed a copy of the image around the officers at Everton. They identified him as 'well-known' in their area. An all-points bulletin has been issued for his capture."

"How do you rate your chances of his being picked up?" Emily asked.

"*Reasonable* might be my best assessment. Everything that's occurred at Everton so far has happened quickly and without any fuss and bother. The hope is that the bloke will be unaware that Greta Lomax has been picked up and that he has now become a 'person of interest' to us," Ben replied and added a knowing nod.

"While you're in such an expansive mood, Ben, perhaps you might tell me what your plans are for the immediate future," I suggested. "Do you intend to continue spending your nights in my spare room?"

"I do, and that might be the case for some time to come. During the day, while I'm at work, a young uniformed officer will be with you at all times. And I don't expect you to go gallivanting around the countryside. You are to be either at home here or in your office in the city, but not roaming around anywhere else."

"For God's sake, Ben, I don't need a babysitter. I am fine. I can look after myself. Oh, and I intend to start driving myself to wherever I need to go. I would think a uniformed officer would stick out like the proverbial, and I would probably do better not to draw attention to myself by having him around."

"He won't be in uniform. He will be in civvies while he's on this assignment. And, I will say at this juncture, I will not tolerate any nonsense from you in this matter. Is that clear?"

No response was required from me – and definitely no point in arguing any further. But Ben's attention already had swung to Emily.

"Unless you must go home tonight, I suggest you stay here too and maybe for the next few days as well. Feel free to go to work during the day and to collect some personal belongings from home, but I want you here at night."

Emily also knows Ben well enough not to argue when he is in police superintendent mode. We left him on his own in the lounge room while we went to make up Emily's bed in my other (smaller) spare room.

Chapter 15

"I'm not happy about imposing on you like this, Sonny. In fact, I'm not happy about this arrangement at all. After tonight, unless Ben can explain why it is necessary for me to stay here, I'll be spending every night at my place," Emily said as she stuffed a pillow into a case and threw it onto the bed.

"Fair enough… I'm not concerned about your staying here, but I am concerned that Ben hasn't said why he thinks it is important for you not to go home. As far as I'm aware, you shouldn't be in any danger from whatever this case is all about."

"Yeah, that's what is bothering me. If I am in danger, for whatever reason, I think I'm entitled to know about it. Now that we're talking about risks associated with your case, Sonny, I'm wondering if Ben discovered something during his trip to Everton, something he hasn't shared with us," Emily suggested.

Now, that was something worth thinking about. Would Ben hold back information he discovered while at Everton? You bet he would… and he would probably say he withheld it to avoid causing any undue concern until he had verified whatever information he had obtained. I shared my thoughts with Emily.

"So where does that leave us?" she demanded.

"Vulnerable…," I replied. "Because we don't know what we might be up against, we can't be prepared for it if, or when, whatever it is happens. Perhaps we need a few terse words with Ben before we all head off to bed tonight."

"Good thinking, Sonny. It's not too difficult to see why Ben has organised someone to guard you when he is not around. He's concerned they might make another attempt after their first one didn't quite deliver the desired result. But, I have had no part in any of this, and those involved probably haven't even seen me with you to suspect I might pose a risk."

To our dismay, when we ventured back to the lounge room to demand information from Ben, we discovered that, while we had been otherwise engaged, he had showered and gone to bed. Emily and I took a nightcap out onto the back deck and sat chatting for a while before we also called it a night and went to bed. As I waited for sleep to come, I ran my mind back over today's events.

My eyelids started to droop as I did so – until I came to the bit where Ben announced he had a bit of a breakthrough about the man who had been standing watching my window when Trina was killed. All Ben had said about the man was that he 'was known to the Everton police'. If he was known to those officers, they must have known the man's name… and they would have given it to Ben. Why didn't he mention the man's name to me? Was there a chance I might recognise the name? I doubted that would be the case. The image on the camera footage was not of anyone I recognised.

Wide awake again, it was a long time before sleep elected to revisit me, and that gave me plenty of time to mull over Ben's actions. By the time I did fall asleep, I had formulated a string of questions to put to Ben at my first opportunity. And, trying to convince myself Ben might have been withholding information so as not to frighten me just didn't work. We both share the philosophy that we can deal with anything, if we know what it is.

Despite my lack of sleep, both Emily and I were up before Ben left for work this morning. He didn't seem in a hurry to leave, so I took the opportunity to ascertain his plans for the day.

"Ben, if your plans for today involve anything to do with what happened to me or Trina's death, I want to be involved," I told him. "I'm sick of not knowing the whole story of what's going on, and being hampered in my efforts to progress things."

"It might surprise you to learn I have other things to do besides looking into your incident or Trina's death. If anything happens that you should know about, I'll let you know," he growled.

Although, earlier, Ben had appeared in no hurry to leave, he now bustled about preparing to leave. In the midst of it, he spoke over his shoulder to Emily.

"I'm sure you are anxious to return to your lab, Emily. Feel free to leave whenever it suits you."

"That's most considerate of you." Emily's reply dripped acid.

With a confused look plastered across his face, Ben spun around to face Emily. What he was about to say will forever remain a mystery. The sound of a car pulling up outside prevented Ben's possible response. I sprang off my chair and hurried to open the door, but Ben charged off and beat me to it. He flung open the door and ushered in a young man, someone I had never laid eyes on before.

"Right… I need to be off, but this is Nick. For the foreseeable future, he is to be your daytime minder, Sonny. His duties include driving you to your city office, if you should need to go there. He will not drive you anywhere else… and you will not drive yourself anywhere. Is that clear?"

As he finished speaking, Ben gave both Nick and me a hard look. I half expected Nick to click his heels and drop Ben a salute. He didn't. He just gave Ben a nod instead. I was unable to say anything in response. I was so busy biting my tongue to prevent me from saying anything to embarrass Nick in front of his boss. Instead, I tilted my set jaw upwards and fixed Ben with a filthy look. He gave me the courtesy of uncomfortably shuffling from foot to foot for a moment before striding out the door. As Emily picked up her bag in readiness to follow Ben out the door, my thoughts were on Nick and what had not been the most auspicious start to his new assignment.

"Nick, help yourself if you would like a coffee, and there is a fruit loaf on the bench if you would like toast to go with it. Feel free to help yourself while you are here." He smiled and headed for the kitchen – probably relieved to escape from me.

I followed Emily out to see her off. She opened her car door, threw in her bag, and then turned to face me.

"What are we going to do about him?"

"Him who? Nick…?"

"No, you ninny. What are we going to do about Ben? I'm not about to put up with his behaviour any longer."

"Aah, yes, Ben… I intend to devote some thought to that matter today, but you need to tread carefully. You do have to work with him, and any tension between you will make that difficult. As for Nick… well, it's not his fault his boss has given him a shitty assignment."

There was only one thing occupying my mind as I walked back inside. How do I entertain Nick all day today and every day until Ben calls him off? When I came back into the kitchen, I found Nick had mastered the coffee machine and was waiting for his toast to pop up. I decided another coffee might help stimulate my grey cells and result in creative thought. As Nicked munched his toast and I dawdled over my extra mug of coffee, My thoughts were about not only what to do with Nick, but what I was going to do today. There was no point in going into my city office with nothing more to progress my investigation I could do there.

After driving my empty coffee mug around in circles on the table for a few moments, I looked over at Nick, who was watching me intently. Now I had stopped studying my empty coffee mug, he seized his opportunity.

"I'm sorry, Miss Whittington, but I have to admit I don't know much about this assignment. I'm not sure what it is I'm supposed to do. Maybe, if you could explain what it is you do and why you find yourself in need of a bodyguard, I might have a better idea of what it is I have to do." Poor Nick looked so embarrassed as he voiced his predicament.

"Well, Nick, that only makes two of us so far. I'll confess upfront that I don't know what you're supposed to do either. I suppose, in broad terms, your role might be to protect me from any bad guys who might come to do me harm. Don't get too excited about the role because it is unlikely to occur. And, if it does, I'm more than capable of dealing with it myself. If I'm honest, I don't know why Millhaven's top cop suddenly decided I needed a babysitter.

Nick, I'm concerned about what you might be able to do all day. The hours crawl by slowly if you're sitting twiddling your thumbs, while waiting for something that probably ain't going to happen. What were your instructions when you were given this assignment?"

"There weren't any instructions, not really. All I was told was that it was a protection detail, that I was to wear civvies, and it would be in place for an indefinite period. What to do with my time won't be a problem, but I suppose it would help if I knew what you do and what you are planning to do today."

The next few minutes were taken up with what amounted to an executive summary of my life as a private investigator, and an overview of recent events, including Trina's death and my abduction. As to what I was going to do today, I was still waiting for inspiration to arrive. Then, it was my turn to ask if Nick had any ideas about how he would occupy his day.

"Uhmm… Well, unless you have a problem with it, I could work on a couple of assignments that are fast approaching their deadline."

"Rest assured, I have no problem with that at all. Are your assignments associated with a possible promotion in the police service?" It was of no consequence whether they were or not. I wanted to sound interested and establish some sort of rapport between us.

"God, no; they're part of my university studies. I do have a bit of work to do in preparation for my next police exam, but that's still a fair way off.

If you don't mind my asking, why are you not allowed to drive?"

A brief explanation followed about the amnesia I suffered from the injuries involved in my abduction and how I have been struggling over the last couple of weeks to regain fragments of my missing memory.

After appearing to sit in silent thought for a few moments, Nick seemed to become a little excited – and then the questions flowed.

"Did the doctors say it was amnesia? I mean, did they use the actual word *amnesia*, or was there some other term they used?"

"Hmm… Good question… I don't know that it ever was referred to as amnesia as such. They talked about memory loss and the possibility that some or all of my lost memory might never return. But, no, I don't think they ever used the word amnesia when discussing my loss of memory as a result of the blow to my head. Does it matter what they called it? Isn't that what it is, amnesia?"

"Yeah, it is a form of amnesia, but *dissociative amnesia* is the correct term for what you suffered. I know it sounds a bit pedantic, but there is a difference."

Nick then went into something akin to therapist mode and ran through a long list of questions with me. Questions about basic personal information: where did I live, where was my city office, where had I worked in the past, how long have I known Ben Richards, and what was the case I was working on at the time? Having worked our way through that lot, he threw in one last request for me to tell him about my beach place I had mentioned to him. Then, there were a final couple of questions relating to the part of my memory I had lost that fateful day and how much of it, if any, I had recovered since then. All through that question and answer session Nick had remained quite focused and switched on as he quietly asked his questions and noted my answers.

"I don't know how any of that is going to assist you with this babysitting assignment you've been lumbered with," I told him when we appeared to have reached the end of his questions.

"Perhaps it doesn't have anything to do with my current assignment, but it does have plenty to do with what happened to you. As I thought, you suffered dissociative amnesia. That is a form of memory loss often associated with severe trauma. It's a defence mechanism the brain uses to protect you from the memory of the trauma you experienced. It's often seen in victims of severe road accidents and mugging cases involving significant trauma.

In many cases, including yours, the brain hides only the memories from a specific time period. In your case, your brain hid the memories of the day leading up to and during the trauma of your abduction. You remembered everything else, including going into your office in the morning and your plans to go to your beach place as soon as you could get away from the office. And you quite clearly remember regaining consciousness at that abandoned mine site sometime during that night."

"Is this form of amnesia fully reversible? I mean, is it likely I will recover all of my lost memory of that day?"

"If you think about it, you will realise you already have done that. You've recovered your memory of that unexpected visitor, the difficult interview with her, watching her being knocked down and killed out on the street, and desperately trying to go to her. You seem concerned that you don't remember what happened after you stepped out the back door on your way to the alley beside your building. The reason you don't remember it is because you never had any memory of it to regain. There never was any memory of what happened from between the moment you stepped out of that door and when you regained consciousness at the mine site."

Stunned, I sat staring at Nick as I tried to comprehend what he had told me. Although it made sense, I was struggling to take it all on board. But he was right. I hadn't lost any of my memories prior to Trina's arrival, and I've had no memory problems since I woke up in hospital. Given all I've managed to recall over the last few days, there are only those several hours of that Monday afternoon/evening that are a blank in my memory banks.

"How do you know all this, Nick? I'm sure coppers don't get taught this stuff these days. Has it something to do with your university studies?"

"Yeah, it's part of my psychology studies. While there is nothing in the rule book that says I shouldn't do this, I would prefer work didn't know about my extracurricular studies. Anyway, enough about that for now. What are you going to work on today, Miss Whittington?"

"The first thing I'm going to do is persuade you to call me Sonny. After that, I'll try to find out what I can about Greta Lomax."

"Greta Lomax? The woman they had transferred from Everton yesterday?"

"That's the one. Do you know anything about her?"

"Not a lot. I was one of the officers sent to collect her... Not a particularly friendly encounter. I don't think she is being any more cooperative at Millhaven than she was at Everton."

"Ooh, good… that means Ben is unlikely to be a happy chap this evening, and I can look forward to another torrid evening of his bad temper."

Nick chuckled as he surveyed my kitchen and lounge room areas. I guessed he was looking for somewhere to sit and work, so I stepped in to help him out.

"Depending on how much room you need to manage whatever you are going to do today, there is a small spare desk in my office you can use, or you could work out here on the dining room table if that suits you better. Regardless of whatever you decide, I will be at my desk in there," I said, pointing towards my office.

"Would it annoy you if I worked at that spare desk in your office? I'm interested in what you do and how you do it. Would it be a problem if I asked questions occasionally?"

I was about to say no because I would find it too distracting, but I realised I didn't have a real plan and using Nick as a sounding board might prove beneficial… at least until I gain some traction on whatever I am going to do today. So, I agreed, and Nick went about setting himself up at the spare desk in my office. He had barely sat down when he fired his first question.

"You suggested you were going to focus on Greta Lomax today, so what is your plan of attack?"

"A plan – any sort of plan – would be good. Basically, I've hit the proverbial brick wall with my investigation into Trina Blewett and the associated attack on me. I know it's a long shot, but I thought I might try looking into Greta Lomax's background to see if that gives me something more to work with."

"Sounds like a plan to me," Nick commented before asking, "What is Lomax's involvement in all this? How crucial is it to know what's in her background?"

My first reaction was that Nick was wasting my time with his questions, but the little voice in my head pointed out that, as I didn't have anything better planned, I should at least give him an outline of Greta's involvement. At the end of it, I was surprised that outlining everything for Nick had clarified events in my mind and given me a couple of other ideas to explore – after I've looked into Greta Lomax.

As Nick began work on his assignment, I sat pondering where to start my research. Snippets of my conversations with Nick this morning floated through my mind, most of them related to how most of my memory loss already had been reversed. It occurred to me that, as it was no longer a problem, instead of continuing to bleat about my loss of memory, I should be concentrating on *why*... Why did it happen, and by whom? It reinforced in my mind that concentrating on finding out about the people who we knew were involved in some way was the best way forward.

"Right… Greta Lomax…," I murmured. Nick jerked upright on his chair in response. "Sorry, Nick. I was thinking aloud. I'll try to keep my thoughts to myself in future." He gave me a grin and went back to whatever he had been doing.

The one definite piece of information I had on Greta Lomax, and that was confirmed by the hospital staff, was that she was a registered nurse who had worked at Millhaven's hospital some time ago. I thought back to the conversations I had with her. The 'Lisa' I spoke to had no discernible 'imported' accent, so I reasoned there was a fair chance she had been born in this country.

Births indexes compiled by the various states' archives were the logical place to start my search… or so I thought until I realised she wasn't old enough to appear on the indexes yet. Seeing as I was already working on those records, I decided to check the states' marriage indexes… and that proved nothing more than a waste of time. Although there were quite a few Lomax marriages recorded during approximately the right timeframe, without Greta's parents' names, there was nothing to be gained from that exercise.

Electoral rolls were the obvious next resource to search, but I dreaded the thought of having to wade my way through them. Almost as a last resort, before searching for records of registered nurses, I thought of Trove, the National Archives digitised newspaper repository. I have a love/hate relationship with Trove.

Trove is a fascinating place that can chew up lots of time if you let it. Often, the stuff you find yourself engrossed in has nothing to do with the topic you set out to research. Keeping that in mind, I resolutely typed 'Lomax' into the search bar and sent it off to find whatever lurked in its contents. Not a wise move, I discovered as the list of Lomax references numbered in the hundreds. Okay, bad move, I told myself. This time, ask it for exactly what you want it to find. I changed the search criteria to 'Greta Lomax' and defined a fifty-year period for it to search. Few hits were identified this time, but I hit the jackpot.

There it was, included in a brief paragraph in the social jottings column of a Sydney newspaper: *After a number of years as the paediatric specialist at a major hospital on the south island of New Zealand, Doctor Bertrand Lomax, accompanied by his wife, Sylvia, and their baby daughter, has returned this week to take up a position in Sydney.*

So, she wasn't born in this country but, having spent basically all her life here, she had no English accent and sounded as Australian as the majority of the population. Having discovered Greta and her parents had emigrated from England, it's as well I didn't waste time trying to find the family in the births, marriages and deaths indexes. That now left me with two possible avenues of research to pursue if I wanted to know more about Greta: the Federal electoral rolls, and/or the Nursing and Midwifery Board of Australia's national register of nurses. Since searching the electoral rolls can be a tedious and frustrating exercise, I decided to look for Greta's nursing registration first.

In less time than I had expected, I located her details in the register. A search of various other relevant registers told me Lomax had maintained her registration as a nurse but that she appeared not to be currently employed in her profession. That then begged a question about her current source of income. Maybe she was married (but maintained her maiden name) and was supported by her husband, or she was earning an income from some other form of employment. Oh, well, maybe the electoral rolls will shed some light on where she has been living in recent times. Somehow, I doubted the Everton area had been her longtime base.

Nick's phone shattered the silence of my office. He gave me an apologetic smile as he walked past on his way out into the lounge room to take the call. I couldn't read his body language when he returned. He flopped onto his chair and spent the next few heartbeats apparently mulling something over in his mind before he spoke.

"That call was from the boss. He…."

"From Ben? Superintendent Richards, I mean?"

He nodded but continued to appear to struggle to find the words he needed. "He… Uhmm… He said he would be here in a few minutes and wants you to have coffee waiting for him."

"The cheek of the man! Did he say why he was coming here?"

"No, but he sounded… Uhmm, I don't know how to describe exactly how he sounded, but I think something might have happened to prompt the visit."

I groaned. The prospect of Ben in full-on officious mode wrecked any thoughts of further research I might have planned for this morning. "Nick, can you repeat verbatim what he said, please?"

Although Nick did his best, it told me nothing more than I already knew. As I walked into the kitchen to prepare the coffee machine for action, I felt my stomach morphing from a squirming mass into a lead ball. Ben's visit would not be good news.

Chapter 16

As I half expected, Ben arrived all business-like and barking at everyone – and, of course, voiced his disappointment at no cake to have with his coffee. Nick, who had come out into the kitchen to acknowledge Ben's arrival and drop him a salute, retreated to my office while Ben and I remained at the kitchen bench.

Then Ben was bellowing for Nick 'to get out here', and demanded to know why Nick was lurking in the office instead of joining us to hear what Ben had to say. Poor Nick stammered that he thought Ben wanted to talk to me privately and he was keeping out of our way. The next few moments were taken up with me taking Ben to task for his behaviour and settling him down a bit, before demanding to know why he was here.

"We had an incident this morning," Ben said and then paused and appeared to be trying to find the words to tell me about the incident.

I felt my blood run cold. His demeanour told me it was unlikely to be good news he was about to share with us, but I remained silent until he was ready to continue his story.

"When we brought Greta Lomax in for questioning yesterday, she had a couple of blood pressure medications in her handbag. Lomax became agitated when she was told she was being kept in the cells overnight and wanted her handbag, claiming she needed to take her medication twice a day at about the same time every day. She was told to give the sergeant on duty the relevant information, and he would ensure the appropriate medication was delivered to her at the right time.

As it was quite late by the time we ended the interview and we still hadn't extracted any information from her, we decided to keep her in the cells overnight. But, because at that stage, it was only going to be overnight and she hadn't been charged with anything, she continued to wear her own clothes. Despite all the usual precautions and procedures, it appears Lomax had secreted a supply of one of her blood pressure medications in her bra. Early this morning, she deliberately overdosed on that medication. It resulted in her blood pressure dropping to a dangerously low level, and Lomax became unconscious. She is now in hospital in a critical condition but, so far, still alive."

"Christ, if she hadn't even been charged with anything, why would she do that?" Nick murmured.

"Because of what her 'friends' might think she had told the police while she was their overnight guest," I explained.

"Yeah, her actions serve as a reminder. She knew how ruthless the mob might be in dealing with what they perceived to be a risk at large. She chose to take her own life in her own way rather than leave it to the mob to extract it from her in their way. If we had any doubts about those who might be associated with this case, be aware they are ruthless and we must be prepared for whatever they try."

Ben gave Nick and me a hard look in turn as he finished speaking. He needed to be sure we understood the danger we might all be in, thanks to whatever this case was all about. Then, the question Nick asked gave Ben to chance to reinforce his message.

"Sir, what does that mean in terms of my current assignment as Miss Whittington's minder?"

I noticed Nick had become a bit agitated, and I felt for him. When Ben is in one of these moods, he is formidable to deal with, even for those who know him well. This young constable was feeling the pressure of the boss's expectations.

"With utmost urgency, I want Sonny's protection increased – after she is moved to somewhere safe and she is hidden safely away."

"Well, that ain't gunna happen," I chirped and set my jaw defiantly in preparation for the battle I thought would follow, but Ben wrongfooted me by keeping his attention focused on Nick.

"Did you sign out a weapon before you left the precinct this morning?"

"No. No one suggested I needed one and, based on the information I'd been given, I didn't think one would be necessary."

"Sonny, is your Glock in the floor safe in your bedroom?" I gave him a curt nod. "Good; fetch it and give it to Nick so he has time to familiarise himself with it."

A brief war of words ensued, which I lost before flouncing off to retrieve the weapon from my floor safe. I returned and handed the weapon to a very unhappy Nick, who tried desperately to explain to Ben that he had never as much as held a Glock, let alone fired one. I know Ben well enough to read the signs. At that point, he was preparing to tear a strip of Nick about his less-than-cooperative attitude. I stepped in to prevent the debacle.

"He will be fine after I take him through all the finer points of the weapon, but he should have a vest. If you're so concerned about a possible firefight occurring, he needs to be as protected as possible. He won't be much use to me if he becomes incapacitated, or worse. Ben, it might be a good idea if you return to the precinct to collect a weapon and a vest for Nick. By the time you've done that and returned, it will probably be lunchtime. I'll try to rustle up some sandwiches for us." Although somewhat reluctant, Ben agreed to return with the required equipment for Nick – and for lunch.

Before Ben left for the precinct, I took the opportunity to ask a few general questions about Lomax, her prognosis, and whether she was in ICU. My questions stirred up Ben's curiosity.

"What's with all the questions? Why are you so interested in Lomax's present situation?" he asked.

"Look, I know she is a key figure in this investigation but, despite that, while she was being 'Lisa', she was a competent nurse, and she was good to me while I was in hospital."

"Yes, she was being 'Lisa' and paying you special attention because the mob had put her up to it once they discovered you were still alive."

It was time to throw in something from left field and hopefully throw Ben off balance.

"Ben, has there been any progress on that bloke… Err, you know the one, what's his name?... The one who was watching my window from down on the street?"

"Christos…? What about him?"

"Yep, that's the bloke I meant. What's your next move in trying to locate him?" Ben was slow to answer, and I suspected he was going to fob me off, so I fired off my next question before he could. "Do you think Christos played an active role in my abduction? After all, he was down on the street and could easily have raced around to assist a colleague already in position in the carpark."

"Nah, I don't buy that scenario. Timings don't fit. Anyway, I have to go and collect that stuff for Nick. I'll be back for lunch." And then he was gone, leaving Nick looking a little shellshocked.

As soon as he heard Ben drive off, Nick came and handed the Glock to me. "You should keep this in case something happens and you need it. Ben will be back shortly with a service weapon for me."

"Hang on to it until Ben returns, Nick. Ben will not be happy when he returns if he finds you have been without a weapon while he was away, not after he went to so much trouble to put the fear of the bad guys into us," I said as I scrabbled around in my tote bag… and came up brandishing a second Glock. "Besides, I just happen to have a spare one in case of emergency."

"Are they just for show – you know, just to frighten someone off? Do you even know how to use one?"

"Yes, thanks, proficiently. I've taken down a few bad guys in my time with them."

"Sonny, maybe you can help me with something before Ben returns. Who is Christos, and how does he fit into the picture? I hadn't heard any mention of him before you asked Ben about him."

I gave Nick a brief explanation about the man who had watched me from down on the street as I witnessed Trina being run down by a vehicle. "The reason you hadn't heard his name earlier was because I didn't know what it was until Ben told me a few minutes ago."

"How did we get onto him so quickly? Was he already in Millhaven's files?"

Another brief explanation followed about the image taken from the CCTV footage. "The Everton cops recognised the man as someone who is 'known to police' – to put it into police language for you. Ben had told me Everton had identified the man, but Ben did not tell me his name at the time. I didn't know what his name was until I winkled it out of Ben by devious means this morning."

"What's his surname?" Nick demanded.

"Dunno… probably something unpronounceable, and that's why he's just known as Christos. Is it important?"

"It would help locate him on the database."

"If you go digging into those files, won't it leave a trail back to you? Is that wise, given your boss has just mentioned the bloke's name in passing? Won't they start asking questions about why you were digging around in those files?"

"Yeah, probably… and that's not a problem. It would be remiss of me not to check. I would not be carrying out my assignment properly if I did not familiarise myself with all of the possibilities I might have to deal with, including looking into any bad guys likely to land on your doorstep."

"Back deck…."

"What? What about your back deck?"

"That's the route they've always used in the past."

"You're telling me you've had bad guys lob up on your back deck in the past?" I nodded, and Nick continued. "And you live out here in the suburbs alone… still live here? I can see why the boss has based himself here at the moment, and why I was given this assignment. You need protection. You need to be…"

"That's why one of these lives in my bedroom, and one is in my bag," I said as I waved one of my Glocks at him. "Now, if you're done being all excited about my safety, can we see what those police files have to tell us about that Christos fellow?"

As he accessed the relevant database, I walked around to stand behind Nick so I could read over his shoulder. He promptly closed the laptop and then waited for me to take the hint and move away. I didn't.

"I'm sorry, Sonny. These files are confidential. I can't allow you to see them. I will pass on anything I find that I think you need to know."

"No, that's not how it's going to happen, my friend. I make decisions about what is important to me and what isn't, not you. Now, if I am prevented from seeing what's in that file, I will tell your boss you prevented me from accessing information important to my safety. That will probably result in two things. One is, Ben will log in and let me read the file on Christos, and, two, he will then request a full-scale background check on you… Just in case your actions resulted from some association you might have with Christos. They probably won't turn up anything, but it won't look good on your record and probably won't do your chances of promotion much good either."

For the duration of a couple of heartbeats, I regretted having dealt with him in that way – almost regretted. I found the stunned look on his face that resulted bordering on comical. It was cruel of me. Nick is only a lad and not fully aware of how the land lies around here, particularly in regard to my relationship with Ben.

While keeping a suspicious eye on me, Nick slowly eased open his laptop and navigated to the file he wanted. Without looking up, he started speaking. "You were right about his surname…," he said as he looked up in the direction of the last place he had seen me.

The poor bloke almost fell off his chair when I said, "Yep, I wouldn't attempt to pronounce that name." I was standing behind him again and reading over his shoulder, having moved around to stand there without a sound while he was hunting for the relevant file.

"Jesus, this bloke is proper bad news," Nick exclaimed, shaking his head. "His record stretches a long way back."

"Hmm… And, like so many others, he became a bigger fish as time went by," I observed.

"Yeah, it appears he started in a small way with petty stuff and then began expanding his repertoire to become big-time," Nick commented as he moved the cursor down the file. "Looks like he served a bit of time as a teenager."

"And then became Teflon-coated by the time he was involved in the seriously heavy stuff," was my last comment before I stood up straight again.

My back was starting to spasm from being bent over for so long as I read over Nick's shoulder. I had seen enough of Christos' CV anyway to know the extent of the risk he posed. A question slammed in from left field. I didn't feel inclined to return to reading over Nick's shoulder, so I asked him to find the answer for me.

"What about his recent activities, Nick? I saw that Christos seemed to have moved into heavy stuff. What does his police record have to say about his activities, time served, and anything else of interest?"

"Nothing to tell, really. It seems everybody knew Christos was involved in serious crimes that were happening and that he probably was the kingpin in many of the operations over a fair length of time. But, as you said, he was Teflon-coated, and there was never enough evidence to make anything stick."

"I'm interested in his more recent activities, Nick. What has he been up to most recently?"

"Just about everything that is seriously heavy stuff," Nick replied as he continued to slide the cursor further down the screen. "Drugs, people smuggling, money laundering and… oh, shit… It seems he is not averse to the removal of those who get in the way of his operations."

"Removing contingent risks is how you develop Teflon coating," I suggested.

Nick continued perusing the file, but I had heard enough about Christos to give me plenty to think about. I hadn't made more than a couple of brief notes about Christos' career when Ben returned. As soon as Ben walked in, Nick asked if he could have a private word with him. I kept my head down and continued writing so neither of the men would notice the smile on my face. The information in Christos' file was causing Nick serious nervous indigestion, and he was about to share that information with his boss.

Oh, to be a fly on the wall while that conversation occurs! But that wasn't possible, so the best I could hope for was later to receive some insights into their discussions. Having completed my notes on Christos' career, I sat back to ponder everything I had learned this morning. It was obvious I should start with Trina. After all, she was the one definite thing about this investigation I knew anything about.

My mind flew back to my interview with her that Monday morning. Terrified… Yeah, I think that is the best way to describe her demeanour that morning. But terrified of what, or whom? If she somehow knew her life was in danger, why didn't she go to the police? Why did she come to me? How did she think I could help her?

Another stray thought squeezed its way to the front. Who knew she had been to see me? Had I been targeted because of something Trina might have told me, or was it because I had witnessed her being run down? There was something like a two-hour gap between when she left my office and when she was killed. Where had she been, and what had she done during that time? It was obvious she had been to the bakery at some point. She was carrying one of Justin's garish bakery bags when she stepped out onto the road. I probed my memory banks for any other clues that might tell me where she had been.

There was a vague recollection of her carrying another bag. Not just her handbag, but another store's bag – but from which store? Try as I might, a clear image of Trina stepping off the pavement and out onto the road refused to emerge from my memories of that morning. In frustration, I gave up on trying to figure out where Trina had been apart from the bakery.

After allowing my mind to roam free for a moment, it locked onto the image of the car that ran her down. Where had it come from? It couldn't have been sitting out there on the street just waiting for Trina to cross the road. It's a busy street. A high volume of traffic flows along it all day, every day. How did the driver know exactly when to act? I closed my eyes and pictured myself looking down onto the street below from the window of my city office.

"Of course," I yelped, "that's...."

"Would you care to share your lightbulb moment with us?" Ben asked. He and Nick were standing in the doorway to my office and grinning like the proverbial cat.

"No, not really. It was just a random thought that I might consider more fully at some later time," I replied sweetly, as I told myself they didn't need to know.

"Well, do you think you might be capable of at least a random thought about that lunch you promised us?" Ben asked.

"Lunch... Oh, God, is it lunchtime already? See if you can amuse yourselves for a few minutes while I make sandwiches."

"Relax. I picked up salad rolls for all of us before I left town. Now, what about that random thought you had? Do you need some help with it?"

"It's too vague so far to do anything with it. Maybe by tonight, it will have morphed into something more positive. What about you, Ben? What are you doing for the rest of the day after you help us dispatch these salad rolls? Are you hanging around here or going back to your office?"

"Nick is fine on his own here. He doesn't need me looking over his shoulder. Try to be nice, and don't give him a hard time while he is looking after you."

With that, Ben took his leave. Nick walked him to the door and watched him drive away before returning to my office. He heaved a sigh as he sat down at his desk.

"I suppose it's back to those assignments I didn't do this morning for the rest of the afternoon," he said as he dragged over to him the stuff he had been working on before he looked at Christos' file.

"Just as a matter of interest, Nick, did you complain to Ben about my giving you a hard time this morning?"

"Eh? No, why would I? I wasn't aware I'd been given a hard time, as you put it."

We let the matter drop, and both of us worked independently until mid-afternoon. While I assumed Nick was working on his university assignment, I returned to the question of the car that ran down Trina… and the lightbulb moment I had at almost the same time as Ben came to enquire about lunch. I had suddenly realised there is provision for reverse angle parking between the pedestrian crossings along the same side of the street as my city office. *What if* that car had been parked in one of those bays further along the street while waiting for some signal to spring into action?

What sort of signal, from whom, and how far further along the street would the vehicle have needed to be parked? Christ, I just keep finding more questions without as much as the slightest hint of an answer to any of them. Again, I closed my eyes and leaned back in my chair as I tried to remember Trina stepping off the pavement below my window.

"She did have two bags," I snarled when, at last, the image emerged from my memory banks.

Nick had jumped when I shattered the prevailing silence, and then silently studied me for a moment before asking, "Is that supposed to mean something to me, or were you thinking aloud again?"

"Thinking aloud… Get used to it. It happens a lot when I'm trying to find a way around a brick wall."

The longer I held that vision of Trina in my mind, the clearer it became. Yes, she carried another bag as well as the one from the bakery. It was a pink bag that sported bright red words. Which store close by has pink bags with red writing? I took a while to find the answer to that but, at last, it came through. *Bianca's*, the women's fashion store almost at the end of my office block.

"Right, now let's try to put all that together," I murmured. "Logically, Trina would have gone to the fashion store before stopping at the bakery on her way back. So far, so good. But that wouldn't have taken two hours, even if she had tried on several outfits before calling at the bakery." As I opened my eyes and sat up, I noticed Nick studying me.

He blushed and looked embarrassed. "I'm sorry. I'm just intrigued by the way you work… and it sounded as though you might have had a breakthrough of sorts. Is there anything I an help you with?"

"Thanks, but no I don't…. On second thoughts, maybe you can help. How do you feel about being a sounding board?" He shrugged and looked confused. "Okay, let me explain. I'll float ideas past you. You don't have to do or say anything unless something doesn't make sense or something I've said raises a question for you. Of course, if you see a flaw in anything I suggest, feel free to stop me and discuss it with me. Are you up for a few minutes of that sort of stuff?" Of course, he was, thank you very much… and his assignment was shoved to one side.

I gave him a rough timeline of what I think Trina did between when she left my office and when she was run down. "I'm happy with the bits I've nailed down so far, but there is no way I can convince myself those things would have taken up all of the time involved. What else might Trina have done to fill in perhaps another thirty minutes or even as much as an hour?"

"Lunch…!" Nick responded without any hesitation. "During the timespan under review, it would have been lunchtime. Perhaps she dropped in somewhere for lunch. I don't know that area too well, so I can't suggest where she might have eaten."

"There are a few eateries along that part of the street. She could have eaten at any one of them, but you are served quicker at some than at others. I need CCTV footage of her walking along the street to the point where she stepped off the pavement… *And I need to see Justin's camera footage from that day."*

"Who is Justin, and what is so special about his footage?" Nick knew how to play this sounding board role well, I noticed.

"Justin owns the bakery, and I know he has a CCTV camera that records what happens in his shop. He had it installed after he found discrepancies between sales and stocks left at the end of the day. His footage would give us the exact time Trina was in the bakery."

After a phone call, I knew Justin still had the footage from that Monday in question, and he was happy for me to examine it.

"How do you feel about a trip into the city," I asked.

Chapter 17

By the time I was halfway to the door, a stunned-looking Nick scrambled out from behind his desk and loped along behind me to catch up. Flinging open the front door, I stepped outside … And came to a sudden halt, causing Nick to crash into me.

"Where's your vehicle?" I demanded as I surveyed the empty area out front of my house.

"Police compound…."

"Why? What happened to it?"

"Nothing. It's just safe there until I collect it this evening."

"I assume you didn't walk from the precinct to here?"

"Of course not. I was dropped here, and I will be collected later. The powers-that-be thought it best if there wasn't a strange car parked outside your house."

"Best for whom? Best for the bad guys because they would think their target was home alone, and it would be an ideal opportunity for a visit? Or, best for me because, if the bad guys decided to visit, they wouldn't know I wasn't alone, and it could prove a bad mistake on their part?"

Nick looked uncomfortable and offered nothing more than a shrug by way of reply. I continued my rant.

"And, I presume that by the powers-that-be you mean Ben?'

This time, he gave me a nod. I was being unfair, and I knew it. Nick was only a foot soldier obeying orders. It was his idea to leave his car in the compound. I knew that sometime in the near future, I would be exploring Ben's thinking behind his tactic regarding Nick's car.

As I opened the garage, Nick asked cautiously, "Were you hoping we would drive into the city in my vehicle?"

"No." In all honesty, I hadn't given it a thought. "If I thought about it at all, it was that we would take my car. Come on, get in so we can be on our way."

"Uhmm… don't you need me to drive?" Nick asked as he hesitated in the garage doorway.

"Definitely not… Now, get in and fasten your seat belt."

It felt good to be behind the wheel of my own vehicle again and, anyway, I had to resume driving at some point. Today was as good a time as any. Nevertheless, Ben's thinking regarding Nick's car still occupied my mind as I pulled into the carpark behind my city office. Nick leapt out of the car, raced around to open my door, and then stood guard as I clambered out of the vehicle.

"What are you doing?" I asked when I noticed his hand had sought out the weapon in his shoulder holster. "You must be sweating to death in that jacket, but I suppose you have to wear it to hide the holster."

"I'm fine. Now, key in the code, and let's get you up to your office. You're a sitting duck out here in the open… and you don't have a vest. I should have given you mine to wear."

"For God's sake, Nick, you will give yourself a heart attack if you keep this up. Relax. We are not going up to my office… not yet anyway. First, we are going to see Justin."

"Who is Justin, and where do we find him?"

This was becoming tiresome, but I suppose Nick was just doing his job as he understood its requirements. "We are going to the bakery at the front of this building. I will key in my code for the back door, and then we will walk straight through the building to the bakery."

Without waiting for a reply, I strode to the door, keyed in my entry code and marched through the small vestibule area to the next door. Nick rushed past me to push open the door and scan the walkway through to the street before allowing me through the door.

"Nick, you have strained this friendship to almost breaking point. I know you think you are just doing what is required of you as my bodyguard. But, if you keep this up, it won't be the bad guys you have to worry about. I will shoot you. By all means, hang around because that is your job, but keep out of my way." With that, I strode off in search of Justin.

Justin took us through to his tiny office, where he had that Monday's recording set up and ready for me to review. It was a little uncomfortable with all three of us being confined at such close quarters, so I fast-forwarded the recording to midday. Then, at normal speed, I watched the activities in the bakery slide across the screen until shortly before Trina walked out onto the road to her death. I watched Trina come into the bakery and wander around, checking out Justin's work before going to the counter to purchase a small loaf of some sort of bread and a muffin. The young lass serving Trina reached under the counter for one of Justin's garish carry bags and loaded Trina's purchases into it. Moments later, Trina walked out of the bakery.

"Could I have a copy of the part of the recording that has images of that particular customer, please, Justin?" I asked as I rewound the recording to the first appearance of Trina.

"Yeah, of course. Help yourself."

"What? No… I can barely manage my system, let alone try to do anything with yours."

I raised my eyebrows in question at Nick, who sighed and said he probably could do it for me. I handed him a portable hard drive and told him to 'dump it onto there for me'.

After thanking Justin and grabbing some afternoon tea on our way out, we were soon climbing the stairs to my office.

"There is a lift in this building, you know?' Nick commented as I set off up the stairs… while he hesitated at the bottom.

"You can hardly keep an eye on me if you are stuck in that lift for the rest of the day until the company who owns it sends someone to rescue you. Perhaps I should have given you our afternoon tea cakes to carry. That way, you would at least have sustenance while you were imprisoned in the lift." Not surprisingly perhaps, almost immediately, Nick was climbing the stairs beside me.

"Sonny, tell me why that piece of camera footage is so important," Nick asked as I brought it up onto the screen.

"Okay, I suppose it is a bit of a mystery to you. Come around here where you can see the big screen better, and I will show you why it's important." He did as I asked, and I was soon in full explanation mode.

"You might remember I couldn't account for Trina's movements during all the time between when she left my office and when she was killed. If I could create an accurate timeline, I might be able to tie her movements to whatever else was happening in the street at that time.

Right, see… There's Trina entering the bakery and checking out Justin's products. See how she already has a carry bag from *Bianca's*. Now, by checking the time stamp ribbon when she leaves the bakery, I know she didn't have time to do anything else before stepping off the pavement to cross the street."

"So, visiting the bakery was the last thing she did before being killed. How does that help? It doesn't tell you when she was at that fashion place or if she had lunch somewhere."

"No, it doesn't. So, my next move is to have a chat to Bernadette." I saw Nick shake his head and look confused, so I continued. "Bernadette is the proprietor of *Bianca's*. If whatever Trina bought there was paid for by credit card, Bernadette might be able to give me the time of the transaction from the transaction slip."

"Ah hah, so we are off to talk to Bernadette now, are we?"

"In a minute. I just want to check something first, if I can."

I hoped I had saved a copy of the footage Ben had copied from Gino's camera that focused on the street. It probably wouldn't tell me anything new, but it allowed me to match the final period of Trina's life with what was happening in the street then. After only a brief look at the recording, I agreed it was time to talk to Bernadette.

"This does not sit comfortably with me," Nick bleated as we strode along the street to *Bianca's*. "What's this store like, anyway? I've never been in it."

"That's not surprising. I would have been interested to hear about it if you had. In simple terms, it's a women's fashion store. Although Bernadette likes to think she is upmarket, the store is more like mid-range. It sells various clothing lines, underwear, accessories, and lingerie. Not anything I suspect you would buy too often."

The store was quiet, with only one customer being served by the young assistant.

"As I recall, it was a cash purchase, not a credit card sale," Bernadette mused as she led us through racks of clothing and around ironing boards to her office in a back corner of the premises.

A few minutes later, we were on our way back to my office with a scanned copy of the relevant section of the relevant day's cash register's tape – with everything other than the time and date details redacted.

"It's a bit late for afternoon tea, but are you up for a coffee?" I asked once we were back in my office.

Nick claimed to be familiar with my brand of coffee machine and set about making the coffee while I added the transaction time to my timeline. As we nibbled our cupcakes, Nick studied my timeline for that Monday morning and drummed his fingers on the desk as he thought about it.

"She didn't waste too much time shopping, did she?" he commented absentmindedly. "I would have expected her to spend ages trying on outfits and whatever, but she wasn't there all that long at all."

"Good point, Nick. Given what we now know about her other movements, it appears she had a long lunch somewhere and probably at one of the places along this street."

"An hour isn't all that long, not if it is at a busy time and service is a bit slow," Nick suggested.

"If she went straight from my office to an eatery, it would have been right at the start of the lunchtime rush. Service would have been reasonable, and she shouldn't have had to wait too long for her meal. It would be handy to know where she went," I mused.

"Are there any other CCTV cameras along this street?" Nick asked as he went and peered out my window. "Surely there is one somewhere along this street that would have picked her up as she went for lunch."

He was right, of course, and I wished it were that simple. "Maybe this is desperation time," I muttered as I reached for the phone.

Stunned when Ben answered on almost the first ring, I struggled to have my thoughts in order before I opened my mouth.

"Ben, do you know of any CCTV cameras along my street in the city? I'm looking for any that might provide useful footage of that fateful Monday, and I thought your officers might have come across some when they did their door-to-door enquiries."

"Yeah, there are two Council-owned cameras that cover your block and the roundabout at the intersection beyond it. Where are you, by the way?"

"I'm in my office," I said, deliberately not indicating which office, and then quickly continued. "I imagine they would be focused on traffic along that section of the street. I'm looking for footage that might show the pavement."

"You're right about the Council's cameras. What about that Building Society's premises across the road from your office building? Would it have security cameras of some sort?"

"Dunno, but I know it has cameras monitoring internal activity. They might monitor outside the building as well after the hold-up that occurred last year. Any chance you could find out for me, *please*?"

"Okay, I'll try to do something this afternoon. I'll let you know tonight how I got on."

"Uhmm… I was hoping for something before then."

"Of course you were. Where are you anyway? Which office?"

The rest of our conversation probably is best left unrecorded but, suffice to say, I didn't expect I would hear anything more until tonight. About an hour later, both Nick and I were still poring over the two bits of camera footage I had collected when a knock on my door made both of us jump. I stood up to go to answer the door. Nick motioned for me to 'stay' before scrambling off his chair and striding to the door. Ben, I predicted as I did a mental cringe. If Ben had interrupted his busy schedule to come to my office, he was unlikely to be in a good mood.

As Nick cautiously opened the door, I heard him exclaim, "Brett…," before he threw the door open and stepped back to allow Detective Brett Galbraith to enter.

"Brett, what brings you here?" I asked. "Are you still working on that crime scene at the end of this floor?"

"No, I believe you were interested in CCTV camera footage of this street. Ben sent me to the Building Society across the road to copy their footage from that Monday."

"Oh, lucky you… did you have any trouble getting hold of it? I mean, were they reluctant to allow you to copy it?"

"Eh…? Nah, not at all. Ben had spoken to them about it and teed everything up beforehand. All I had to do was front up and copy it. Anyway, I hope what's on this memory stick is useful." Brett didn't hang around after handing over the memory stick. By the time Nick had seen Brett out, I had loaded the contents of the stick and was ready to press PLAY.

It only took me a couple of seconds of the footage to realise it was exactly what I needed. "Keep an eye out for any sign of Trina walking along the pavement on this side of the street," I reminded Nick. "Because it is so far away from the camera, she might not be easy to pick out from amongst the others on the street at the time."

But there she was. "Look there… Trina is stepping out onto the street," I yelped as I froze the recording so Nick could see her. "Ah, see that… Now, that is interesting, don't you think?"

"Yes, I can see Trina. It's not a clear image but, yes, I can tell it's her. What do you find so interesting about that image of her? I don't see anything to get excited about," Nick said.

"Okay, think back to what we already know about her visit to my office. When she left, my CCTV camera followed her as she started down the stairs. That's the last we know about her until this image of her stepping out onto the street. What that tells me is that when she reached the bottom of the stairs, she turned left, went through that door, and then used the same walkway as we've just used to go to Justin's bakery."

"Ri-ight… And that has you excited because…?"

"Because, a couple of hours later, when I raced down those stairs to go to her when she was lying out on the road, I couldn't use that walkway because the door would not open. My only option to reach the street was to go out the back door and around and down the alley between the buildings. So, sometime between when this image was captured and when I tried to go through that door to use the walkway to access the street, the door had been made inoperable. At first glance, it might not seem significant, but it is another point on the timeline I'm developing."

"That doesn't allow much time for someone to tamper with the door," Nick observed. "It almost seems like they knew in advance something was going to happen to Trina and that you might try to rush out onto the street to investigate."

"Yep, that's about how I see it as well. Now, let's see which way she goes now that she is out on the pavement and presumably looking for somewhere to have lunch." As I spoke, I was mentally taking stock of the eateries on this block of the street.

The recording showed that Trina appeared to hesitate for a moment as if she was deciding where to go. "Good girl," I chirped as she turned to her left and headed off. "Now, what's along there that might appeal to her tastebuds?"

"I've no idea," Nick said. "I assumed you would know."

"Aye, I do. There are only two places for lunch between here and the end of the block. One is a sort of health food place, and the other is *Gianni's*. While I don't know much about Trina, somehow, I don't see her as the health food type. I think she is more of a *Gianni's*-restaurant-type diner. And, visiting that restaurant, even during the pre-lunchtime rush, would take longer than a quick bite somewhere else."

"So, what we need to know now is how long it took her to have lunch before she was back out on the street and heading for *Bianca's*," Nick suggested. "Do we just sit here until she appears on the recording again?"

"We could do that, but she has piqued my curiosity. I want to know if she dined alone or with someone else. I might have a chat with Gino."

"Who is Gino, and why do you need to have a chat with him," Nick asked cautiously. "I'm not sure I'm supposed to allow you to go wandering around chatting to people. I'm already nervous about what Ben is going to say about your visiting Justin and Bernadette. And now, you want to go and talk to this Gino bloke."

"Gino owns the restaurant where we think Trina had lunch. He has a CCTV camera covering the dining area in his restaurant. The footage from that camera – if Trina dined there – would show us if she dined alone or with someone else. Hmm… Come to think of it, the footage from the camera he has upstairs on his balcony might be worth another look as well. Right; so, are you coming or not?"

"What? Where are you going?"

"I'm going to talk to Gino… Well, I will after I give him a call first. Do you want to come with me, or are you going to stay here?"

My brief phone call to Gino went much as I hoped it would and I was soon on my way to his restaurant – with Nick in tow. It was that quiet time for the restaurant after the hustle and bustle of the day and before the nighttime crowd of diners arrived. He showed us through to a small office where he had already pulled up the recording I wanted to see.

"The recording has been run through to just after ten o'clock that morning. I know that's a bit earlier than the timeframe you wanted to look at, but I thought it might be useful to see if anything else was happening at the time," Gino explained as I sat down to watch the recording.

"There doesn't appear to be anything of interest to us happening at that time," Nick commented as I scanned the few diners scattered throughout the restaurant.

"Perhaps not, but we shall see if anything changes over the ensuing hour. From the previous recording we looked at, we know Trina would have come into the restaurant about an hour later."

After watching images fly across the screen as I fast-forwarded the recording, I returned it to normal speed when the time stamp suggested it was about the time Trina should appear. About a minute later, we watched her enter the restaurant and then stop and look around.

"Is she looking for someone or just trying to decide which table she wants to sit at?" Nick murmured.

"Patience, Nick... You'll have your answer soon enough, I imagine." Seconds later, the answer was obvious.

A lone diner seated at one of the tables had caught my eye when I scanned those early diners. He had sat stern-faced and seemingly staring at nothing. He wasn't reading a menu, didn't play with his phone, or drink or eat anything while he sat there. Apart from drumming his fingers on the table a couple of times, he just sat there doing nothing. But, somehow, it appeared obvious to me he was waiting for someone. Then, that 'someone' showed up.

I watched Trina make her way over to his table. He didn't stand to greet Trina... never even looked at her or acknowledged her presence in any way. Trina continued to stand beside the empty chair at his table for a while. She appeared to speak to him, but he could have been deaf for all the response she received. Regardless of what was being said, her body language suggested she remained as nervous and agitated as she had been when she sat in my office. Eventually, Trina pulled out a chair and sat down at the table. At first, the man continued to disregard her.

"Not a happy encounter by the looks of it," Nick observed. "What a pig-ignorant bloke… Why doesn't she just walk out again? What's wrong with the woman?"

My withering look made him shuffle on his chair. Although I wasn't about to say so, I did share Nick's opinion. As I watched, a waiter approached the table and offered menus to the couple. Trina took one, but the bloke rudely brushed the one offered him aside before sending the waiter away. Over the next few minutes, I witnessed what I believed was a heated conversation between the two at the table. I watched Trina becoming increasingly agitated as the conversation proceeded.

Then, just as I was beginning to wonder how this situation might end, the bloke, in what can only be described as an angry gesture, pushed back his chair and stood up. Leaning way over the table towards Trina, he appeared to deliver an angry blast that ended with him slamming his hand down hard on the table, before turning and stalking out of the restaurant.

"What a bastard," Nick exclaimed. "I wish I could reach into the screen and thump him one."

"You need to remember that we have no idea what their conversation was about, but there is no way to believe it was anything other than unpleasant. Let's see what Trina does now that he's left her sitting at the table alone."

Almost as soon as I had spoken, we watched a waiter make his way across to the table again. This time, Trina, looking apologetic, ordered something and then sat with her head in her hands while she waited for her order to arrive.

"Well, that's not what I expected to happen," I admitted. "I was sure she would get up and follow him out. I might be misinterpreting something, but she actually looks a little more relaxed since he walked out. Maybe she did sort out to her advantage whatever the problem was," I suggested and raised my eyebrows in question at Nick.

"Hmm… Dunno, but I wouldn't bank on it."

Nothing much worthy of note was recorded after that. Trina's meal arrived (it looked like a small salad of some sort), and she ate it and then left after paying for her meal at the counter on her way out. I paused the recording and checked the time stamp as she left the restaurant. My timeline was now complete. After leaving the restaurant, she had just enough time to walk almost to the other end of the block, choose a couple of items she wanted to purchase, and pay cash for those purchases.

"Are we done looking at CCTV footage now?" Nick asked as I shut down the recording and slumped back in my chair. "If we're finished, what comes next? Are we going back to your office or home?"

"Argh… I'm not sure, but I think there's still something else I need to follow up on," I told Nick before turning to Gino. "I know Ben copied a section of the recording from your upstairs camera, but might we be able to have another look at it?"

Nick threw his hands out, palms up, at me in question and demanded, "Why? What for? I thought your timeline was complete now."

Obviously, watching CCTV footage is not one of Nick's favourite pastimes, but he was just going to have to live with it today. Gino couldn't be more obliging and we were soon climbing the stairs to his apartment above the restaurant. After profuse apologies as he fiddled about with his equipment, he finally had the relevant recording up on the screen.

"Settle back comfortably somewhere, Nick. This might take a while."

Chapter 18

"Take as long as you need to do whatever is necessary," Nick told me as footage from Gino's upstairs camera started sliding across the screen, but his words lacked sincerity.

Poor bloke, I thought. He must be hating this assignment. I've had him feeling nervous all afternoon as I've dragged him up and down this block of the street, and I know he's terrified something will happen that will bring the wrath of his boss down on his head. Can't blame him for being nervous about that, I suppose. Nevertheless, he's just going to have to put up with it for a bit longer. I feel as though I'm closing in on being able to piece together how things played out that day.

I matched up the time I had noted for when the bloke Trina had been talking to left the restaurant with the time stamp on the recording from the upstairs camera. A few moments later, there he was. At least, I felt sure it was the same bloke striding across the street. The question that slammed in from out of the blue shocked me.

Was that man striding across the street – the man Trina had met in the restaurant – the same person who had watched me witness Trina's death? I couldn't be sure. It would take a lot of fiddling with the images before a reasonable comparison could be made. Suddenly, I couldn't wait to go home… although I knew it might take a more tech-savvy nerd than me to achieve that. I asked Nick to copy the relevant piece of the recording onto my memory stick and held my breath as he did so. I wasn't sure I had enough free space left on the memory stick I brought with me, and I cursed myself for not having brought a pocket hard drive instead.

Luck was on my side today I decided when all appeared to go well with copying the segment of the CCTV footage. After thanking Gino for his help, it was time to put Nick out of his misery. "Come on, Nick. It's time we went home."

As we walked out of the back door of my office building, I thought I might redeem myself a little with Nick.

"Do you want to drive this time?" I asked and received a startled look in reply. "As a result of everything we've learned this afternoon, I have a lot going on in my head. I just thought you might prefer to drive."

"If it's all the same to you, I'd rather not. If anything untoward should happen, I need to be free to take whatever action is necessary and not be too busy driving the car to react." Right, that's me put in my place.

My priority when I arrived home was to check the fridge and the freezer. I hadn't heard from Ben, so I was unsure what the dinner arrangements were for this evening. I needed to be able to whip up a meal if, for some reason, Ben was unable to bring something home when he came. While I assessed the state of my larder, Nick went through to my office. When I went to join him, I was surprised to see he had packed up his laptop and cleared the desk he had been using.

"Calling it a day already, are you?" I asked, nodding at his cleared desk.

"Yep… Is there anything you need me to do before Ben arrives?"

"Uhmm… Nick, do you have plans for this evening?"

"What? Er, no, not really. Why do you ask?" Oh, dear, his tone suggested he thought I was prying, and I had ruffled his feathers.

"Oh, I wasn't prying. I just thought you seemed as though you were in a hurry to get away. As you didn't arrive in your own car this morning, I presume someone would need to collect you and take you back to the precinct to collect your car. How is that supposed to work? Is there a set time when your chauffeur will arrive, or do you have to call the precinct when you are ready to leave?"

"Because I didn't know exactly what I would be doing, or anything else much about this assignment, it was agreed I would call the duty officer when I was ready to leave. So, as soon as Ben arrives, I'll make the call."

"Please tell me you don't have any serious plans for tonight. I'm not prying. It's just that Ben doesn't work normal office hours. Most evenings, he doesn't arrive here until at least seven o'clock. As far as I'm concerned, you are free to leave whenever it suits you. I'm not concerned about being here on my own until Ben arrives. But, I do accept that you might find that a bit foolhardy."

"Not foolhardy… Just plain bloody dangerous. I've seen Ben in action when he was unimpressed with something or someone," Nick said and gave me a wry grin. "Well, if I'm likely to be here for a while longer, is there anything you would like me to work on while I'm still here?"

Who knew police officers could be such saints? I gave his question some thought as I strode over and flopped down behind my desk.

"How is your handwriting? I'd like to put this timeline I've developed up on the whiteboard over there so it is easy to refer to whenever I want to check a detail."

Nick studied my scribbled bits of paper before moving to the whiteboard. The next time I looked up, he had filled the whiteboard with the most brilliant-looking diagram showing Trina's movements from when she left my office until her death.

"How's that suit you?" he asked as he stood back to admire his handiwork.

A car pulled up out front. I checked my watch. Too early, but I suppose it could be Ben trying to avoid keeping Nick 'on the job' for too long today. The next voice I heard confirmed it was not Ben.

"Where are you?"

"Come through. We're in the office, Emily," I called out.

"Oh… Hi, Nick," she said as she strode into my office. "I see your boss has you running up some extra hours. Anyway, that does explain my instructions. I was told to pick up three meals and bring them with me when I came here. Ben says he doesn't know what time he will be back this evening, but he will take care of his own dinner arrangements. I'm not sure what that means as far as you are concerned, Nick, but I have brought you an evening meal."

I stole a glance at Nick, who appeared too stunned to speak. "Are you planning on spending the night here again tonight?" I asked Emily.

"Me? No, I'm going home… and preferably before Ben arrives. Just in case he has any fancy ideas like he had last night."

"There you are, Nick. Emily is not staying here tonight, so the second spare bedroom is available."

"Why would I need your spare bed when I have a perfectly good bed at home?"

"Well, Nick, there is no telling how late Ben might be tonight. You can't leave until he returns, and you need to be sharp and alert to keep an eye on me tomorrow. So, if Ben is very late, you will still need to have a good night's sleep. I'll make up the bed again after dinner – just in case."

After we had dispatched the selection of pasta dishes Emily had brought and we had adjourned to the lounge room, it was time to talk 'shop'. Emily initiated the topic.

"Has your investigation progressed much today?" she asked.

"Uhmm… well, a bit, I suppose, but there are a couple of things I need to ask you about." She nodded and motioned for me to continue. "When your team worked the crime scene, apart from Trina's body, what else did they find?"

"Like what specifically?"

"Like a handbag or carry bags from local stores."

"No handbag… it would have been a help if there was one. We would have been able to confirm the victim's true identity. So far, we believe her to be the Trina woman who visited your office not long before she was killed. But, as we haven't been able to identify a 'Trina' in any official records, we doubt that was her real name. So, because we haven't been able to confirm her identity, she continues to be listed as 'Trina'."

"What about clothing? What can you tell me about her clothing?" Emily gave my question some thought before answering.

"Reasonable quality, but not super expensive, if that's the sort of information you want. Better than department store quality, I would think, but not expensive… except for her shoes. They were leather, and that brand doesn't sell for much under three hundred dollars."

Emily then went on to recite the brand names on some of the clothing's labels. She was right. Not quite top-shelf stuff, but definitely not bargain-basement either. I returned to my question about the carry bags from the bakery and *Bianca's*.

"So there was no handbag, but what about carry bags containing her recent shopping?"

"The site was clear, Sonny. While there was nothing to indicate who she was, there also was nothing else lying about to provide any clues as to what she had been doing immediately prior to her death. We thought it odd at the time but, now you've brought it to my attention again, I have to admit it was odd. Some of my team members suspected she worked in an office somewhere along the street and had just slipped out for some reason."

"We might have to revisit those CCTV recordings, Nick. First thing in the morning, eh?" I suggested.

"Why wait until morning? We are not doing anything now, and I wouldn't mind seeing whatever footage you have," Emily said. "You never know, but there might be something on them to help the forensic team's investigation."

No reasonable argument came to mind, so we relocated to my office, and I loaded the footage from Gino's upstairs camera.

"Are we going to see anything useful on that footage?" Nick asked. "We were only interested in the bloke Trina had lunch with and what he did when he left the restaurant. If there was anything captured at the time of the incident, we didn't see it.

And we probably didn't copy it because we didn't watch the recording long enough to realise we needed it."

"True, we were focused on who she lunched with, but I copied a lot more after the bloke left the restaurant," I admitted. "It wasn't intentional. We started discussing what we had witnessed on the recording and I wasn't paying attention to what I was doing. Because of that, I unintentionally highlighted for copying a lot more of the recording than we had watched. The question now is whether the stuff I copied continues far enough to cover the actual incident."

A blur of images flew across the screen in fast-forward mode until I halted the playback and checked the time stamp. With the last image frozen on the screen, I warned the other two.

"Going by the time on the bottom of that image, the next ones that will appear on the screen in a couple of minutes once I press PLAY again will be confronting. Feel free not to watch if you would rather not."

The other two told me in no uncertain terms that they were professionals, and me to get on with it. I sneaked the recording forward frame-by-frame.

"There she is," Nick chirped as an image of Trina stepping out to the edge of the pavement filled the screen.

"Now, let's have a good look at her while she is still alive," I said as I froze the image on the screen. "Right… See, she has her handbag over her left shoulder. It was an expensive leather-looking bag, dark brown in colour, with a well-known brand's logo incorporated in the metal clasp. And, in her right hand, she carries the shopping bags from the bakery and *Bianca's*." My companions murmured their confirmation and offered a few other random comments as I scribbled a few notes.

"Okay… Here comes the horrible bit," I said as I restarted the recording to continue playing frame-by-frame.

We watched Trina pause briefly at the edge of the pavement. The next frame showed her step off onto the road. In the next frame, she was a couple of steps across the road after leaving the pavement. I knew what the next frame had to offer.

"Brace yourselves, guys. The next frame is the critical one," I warned as I moved the recording forward.

I moved the recording through two frames. The first showed the vehicle coming towards Trina. The second image was of the moment of impact.

"A-a-rgh, that's horrible," Emily gasped. "And, it leaves no doubt that what happened to Trina was deliberate."

The recording rolled forward one more frame before I halted it.

"Bear with me," I pleaded, "I'm going to roll it back one frame to when she is hit. This time, try to take in what happens at the time of impact," I urged them. "We know what happened to her. But, this time, keep your eyes on Trina's handbag and her shopping."

"Anything she was carrying would have been sent flying," Nick said. "Those things could have ended up anywhere… Amongst bystanders, run over by other vehicles, even on the other side of the street. It's not surprising your team didn't find them, Emily."

"Here is that image now. Just study it for a moment, please," I asked, and allowed them a few heartbeats before asking, "Okay, what did you notice in relation to those items at the time of impact?"

"It happened as I suggested it would have," Nick said. "Both the handbag and the shopping went flying through the air."

"The weight of her handbag gave it a different trajectory from that of her shopping, Emily said. "I suppose that's only to be expected, and it did have to come off her shoulder rather than just out of her hand as with the shopping."

"Yeah, the handbag was thrown back towards the pavement where she had come from, while the shopping was thrown in the opposite direction, towards the other side of the street," Nick observed.

"Her shopping didn't travel very far," Emily noted. "It appeared to land on the bitumen but up against the edge of that concrete safety island that divides the street. Again, I suppose that has something to do with how heavy, or light, the contents of those shopping bags were."

"Good, good…," I mumbled as I scribbled some notes. "From what we can see in that frame that's on the screen now, the handbag and the shopping were there at the scene at that precise moment of the recording. Emily has confirmed that those items were not found when her team processed the site. Okay, now, I'm going to move the recording forward one more frame. What I want us to watch for is what happens to those items dislodged from the victim by the impact."

A heavy silence filled the room as the next frame filled the screen. I felt everyone around me crane forward a little closer to the screen, just as I had done as the image appeared.

"Take your time to study the image. I know it's hard to focus on anything other than the body lying on the bitumen. Try to examine the area surrounding the body. Try to concentrate on where those missing items landed. Let's see if this image sheds any light on what happened to them."

I shattered the heavy silence when I yelped, "There! Look over here at this edge of the image," I directed them as I pointed to the left-hand extremity of the image on the screen. "See… That bloke seems to reach down to pick up the handbag. I'll come back to this frame if you wish, but I want to move on to the next one to see what he does with the bag."

"Christ, so that's it!" Nick exclaimed. "He hands the bag to someone else. A woman, I think."

"Hang on while I try to remember how to enlarge stuff on the screen," I said as I fiddled with the settings. "Ah, that's better. Now, let's have a look at the woman who received the bag."

The image of the woman still wasn't clear enough to be of any use. I tried enlarging it a little more. That only made the image pixelate. I returned it to the previous setting before scrabbling in my desk drawer for my large magnifying glass.

"Excuse me, guys, while I do my Sherlock Holmes impression and block your view for a moment," I said as, magnifying glass at the ready, I came up close and personal with the image on my big screen. It took me a few moments to focus on the woman well enough to see her relatively clearly.

"Bloody hell, I don't believe it. Here, Nick, you have a look at that woman," I said as I handed him the magnifying glass.

After only a couple of seconds, he handed the magnifier to Emily so she could examine the image more closely. I waited until both had finished examining the image – and were looking a bit nonplussed about it – before I said any more.

"Nick, you're probably the closest thing to an IT guru in this room. Is there some way to print just that part of the image containing the woman?" I asked.

He shrugged and then nodded. "Should be possible. Let me at your computer and I'll see what I can do." A couple of minutes later, he asked, "Do you just want me to print out the image itself, or do you want to save it somewhere as well?"

"Both… And just save it on the desktop for me, thanks."

I heard the printer whirr into life as I finished speaking. After moving Nick from in front of my computer, I located the image he had saved for me and printed off two more copies and then, as an afterthought, I printed yet another copy. I gave each of us a copy and put the extra copy in my file folder.

"That's come up really well, thanks, Nick. I didn't expect we would get something as clear as that. Now, people, please study the image you've been given and tell me if it rings any bells for you."

About a breath later, both my companions were shaking their heads and claiming they had never seen the woman in the image before. Then, I decided to try a long shot.

"In a case like that of Greta Lomax, when somebody is brought in just for questioning, would they be photographed as well as having all their personal details recorded?" I asked Nick.

"Not as a routine procedure. Sometimes, a person is brought in and just asked a couple of questions because it becomes obvious they can't add anything to the investigation that's underway. In other cases, where the officers believe there is a direct link between the person being questioned and a serious crime, the person they're questioning probably would be photographed. Greta Lomax fits in that latter category."

"Is it possible for you to access police files to see if there is a photograph of Lomax, please, Nick?" He shot me a look that suggested he wasn't happy about the request, but after a moment's hesitation, he shrugged and opened his laptop. A few moments later, he demanded to know, "How can I connect my computer to your printer?"

"The printer is Wi-Fi enabled. If you prefer, send me a copy, and I'll print it."

He took the latter option and my printer was soon spitting out three copies of the image he sent me.

"Try comparing the two images you've been given and tell me what you think, please," I asked.

"Shit, that's her," Nick hissed. "That's Lomax. The bloke who picked up the handbag handed it to Lomax, who was standing close to a small group of onlookers."

"Yeah, there's no question about it being the same woman in both images," Emily commented. "She is standing a little off to one side of those couple of people who appear to be rushing towards the body, so she wasn't *with* them. I know it will sound a bit far-fetched, but it looked like she was strategically placed for just that purpose – to receive the handbag."

For the next few minutes, we discussed the logistics involved in setting up such a scenario and its likely chances of success. Were those involved so confident it would work, or were they just plain lucky? While none of us had a firm answer to the question, we all agreed that the whole operation looked so polished, they appeared confident they could pull it off."

"What do we do now?" Nick asked as he sat gazing at the two images before him. "What's our next move?"

"We go to bed," I assured him. "There is nothing more to do here tonight. Our next move will be to catch Ben in the morning before he goes to work to show him what we've discovered."

"Good," Emily exclaimed. "If there is nothing more to do tonight, I'm off home. I do want to be gone before Ben arrives. Let me know in the morning if you catch him before he goes to work."

"Would you like a coffee or a nightcap of some sort first?" I asked.

"No, thanks. I want to call in at the lab on my way home to check on progress on another case we are investigating. It wouldn't do to arrive smelling of a nightcap."

After seeing Emily off, Nick and I ended up back in my office. "I'm just going to put everything to bed, and then I'm going to put myself to bed," I informed Nick. "You would be well advised to go to bed, too. It looks as though Ben is occupied with something major tonight, so God knows what time he will come home."

Although Nick took some convincing, once I gave him the guest's bathrobe out of the cupboard in his room and showed him where everything was in the bathroom, he relented and got on with the business of getting ready for bed. I waited until he was in bed before showering and securing the place for the night. There was no hurry for me to go to bed. I knew there was so much happening in my mind, sleep would be a long time coming tonight.

A strange noise woke me. Although muffled, it was loud enough to have me wide awake in an instant. With my ears straining for any further sounds, as I scrabbled around in the floor safe in my wardrobe, I congratulated myself on remembering to put my spare Glock back in the safe after offering it to Nick.

Armed and barefooted, I padded silently out to my office and turned off all the security systems before turning to the bedroom end of the house. I opened the door to Ben's room a fraction as I went past. His bed remained empty. My next move could prove tricky, so I paused to take a couple of deep breaths before easing open the door to Nick's bedroom. He was sound asleep and wearing nothing more than a pair of jocks.

At the same time as I gently shook his arm, I slid a hand over his mouth. As he started to struggle, I whispered to him.

"Ssshh, we have uninvited guests. Where's your weapon?" Nick nodded toward his bedside table. "Okay, as quietly as possible, put some clothes on and grab your weapon. Our night is about to become a bit lively, I fear."

"Where are they?" he hissed.

"Back deck…," I told him as he climbed into his trousers. "Here's what we are going to do. I've turned off all the security." He looked alarmed. I was sure he was about to argue. "Don't say anything. Just listen. When I let you out of the front door, call my mobile number. Do you have that in your contacts?" He nodded. "Okay, call my number. You won't hear it ring because it's set to silent mode but I will answer it so we are connected.

Your job is to work your way around the right side of the house and be in position to take down anyone who shouldn't be on the back deck. As soon as you are in position for whatever comes next, just whisper 'in position' on your phone. As soon as I hear that, I will re-arm all of the security systems. All hell will break loose. Lights will come on. Alarms will go off. You must be careful not to trigger any alarms until after our guests do. Once I turn on all the systems, even a slight movement out there will trigger the lights and alarms. Are you okay to do this? He nodded. "Good; let's go – and please try not to get injured. Ben would make my life a misery if you did."

"Shouldn't we wake Ben, or is he already in position for what comes next?"

"Ben hasn't come home yet, so it's just you and me tonight, Cowboy."

Poor Nick. No doubt he now was struggling to work out how to deal with a lunatic intent on mounting a full-on offensive against the bad guys.

Chapter 19

As soon as Nick told me he was in position, I slipped out the front door, arming the various security systems with their remotes as I went. Nick had made his way along the right-hand side of the house to take up a position at the rear of the building – while keeping out of sight of anyone lurking on the back deck. Then, I raced across the front of the house and along the left-hand side of the building towards the back deck, all the while keeping well in the shadows.

I had barely started down the side of the house when the place lit up like a fairground, and the alarm probably succeeded in waking the neighbourhood. Whoever was lurking on the deck probably reasoned their safest option was to be somewhere else by the time anyone came to investigate the commotion. After running along past my office wing and the kitchen, I paused to take stock of the situation. I could hear a commotion coming from behind the house as I slowly picked my way to where the back deck railing began at the end of the kitchen.

From a point about halfway along the back deck, a figure vaulted over the railing and landed about three metres in front of me. Hidden in the deep shadow of the house, I was invisible to the escapee as he raced towards me. I stepped out of the shadows with my Glock pointed at him to successfully block his getaway.

"Going somewhere?" I demanded as I took a couple of paces towards him and became fully illuminated by the lights on the deck.

In a moment of rash bravado, he decided to charge at me. I fired into the ground at his feet. He stumbled as he tried to come to a sudden stop. A shot rang out from behind the house. Two more shots and a scream followed in quick succession.

"Oh, Christ, Nick…," I murmured and then screamed, "Nick. Nick, are you okay?"

My blood ran cold. My pulse stepped up a couple of notches. He didn't reply. I tried again. "Nick….?"

"Yeah, all under control," was his laboured reply. "What about you?"

"All good here – more's the pity. I would have loved a spot of target practice. It's a while since I shot anything – or anyone." I realised it sounded like dialogue out of some spaghetti western, but I wanted to bloke on the ground in front of me to understand I had no qualms about shooting him if he did anything silly.

"Take him out to the front of the house," I told Nick as I motioned my quarry onto his feet with my weapon.

I arrived there first and had my bloke face-down on the forecourt at the front of the house before the others arrived. I was waiting for Ben to answer his phone by the time Nick and his hobbling prisoner finally joined me. Nick pushed his bloke down onto the gravel as Ben answered his phone.

"Cover them both," I told Nick as I moved away to talk to Ben, who had just uttered his opening remark again.

"What? Sonny, are you going to talk to me or not… And why are you calling me at this hour?"

"Good to hear your voice, too," I spat back. "Perhaps, if you could spare a moment, you might send someone to collect a couple of prisoners currently being held at gunpoint… Oh, and one of them will need an ambulance or some sort of medical attention."

"Jesus, can't you stay out of trouble for just one night when I'm already busy?" And then, after a couple of heartbeats, he bellowed, "Are you there on your own? Where is Nick?"

"Nick? Oh, he's busy keeping an eye on the bad guys cluttering up my forecourt." That brought the call to an end. Less than ten minutes later, sirens and flashing lights came along my street.

Our prisoners were dispatched to the watchhouse. About half an hour after their departure, Ben arrived… to find Nick and me sitting in the lounge room with large single malt scotches in hand.

"By the look of this, any injuries tonight were sustained by the other team," he said by way of welcome as he marched through to pour himself a scotch before joining us in the lounge room. "Now, perhaps you might like to tell me about the fun and games I missed out on here tonight."

Out of deference to Nick, I waited for him to give Ben an overview of what happened, but Nick appeared to have become incoherent and couldn't find the words to get started. Not for the first time tonight, I thought, 'poor Nick', and jumped in to rescue the situation. My report didn't take long to deliver. Well, it was a case of too much happening over a short period of time, and we ended up with two prisoners now occupying police cells.

"I presume you shot the bloke in the leg?" Ben asked Nick.

"Yes, Sir."

"It wasn't hard to work out which one of you was responsible. The bloke was still alive. That would be an unlikely situation if she shot him," Ben said, jerking his head in my direction. "You know the protocol. Sometime in the next few days, I will need your report on tonight's activities. Tonight's events probably shook you up a bit. Do you feel you need some time off, or are you okay to continue your assignment?"

"No time off required, Sir. I'm fine… And, Sir, I had an excellent partner tonight." I heard Ben chuckling as Nick finished speaking.

"There's not much of the night left before the sun comes up again," I announced. "So, I don't know about the pair of you, but I'm going back to bed." There was the usual flurry of 'goodnights' as I strode off to bed, leaving the two men still sipping their drinks in the lounge.

The house was deathly silent when I wandered out to the kitchen this morning. I had no idea what time the men went to bed, but they were still catching up on their beauty sleep. It was a few minutes before seven o'clock when Emily arrived as I was finishing breakfast.

"Couldn't sleep, eh?" I quipped as she came into the kitchen.

"Haven't been to bed yet… Might our friendship stretch to a long, strong coffee?"

"How about breakfast as well?"

Emily made herself toast while I made her a coffee – and a second one for me. Neither of us felt talkative until we had drained our mugs. Then, it was question time.

"If you haven't slept since you left here last night, what brings you here at this hour of the morning, Emily? Did you decide to sleep here after all?"

"What? No. Did you bring home those CCTV footage recordings we looked at previously?" I nodded, and she continued. "Something has niggled me since we looked at them. I had intended to ask you to play some of it again yesterday, but then we got swept up in what happened with the handbag. There was something else on that same bit of footage that I want to look at again. I don't know whether it'll be important or not but, somehow, I think it might be relevant."

As I loaded the footage, Emily directed me to the bit that she wanted to review. "Go to the frame that shows where the handbag and the shopping landed on the road." I ran the recording through slowly until she shouted, "Stop. Freeze it there… Yeah, that's good. That's the start of the bit I want to see. Take it forward frame-by-frame, please."

The next frame was the one that showed a man picking up Trina's handbag off the road. Emily signalled me to stop and told me not to move on to the next frame.

"Yeah, this is the frame I wanted. Don't worry about the handbag. We know what happened to that. I want to concentrate on those bags containing Trina's shopping. Where they landed on the road would have resulted in them being run over once traffic started flowing again. Now, watch that elderly woman wearing some sort of uniform. In this frame, we see her striding across the traffic island towards the body."

"She is wearing a hairdressing salon uniform from where she works. I can't remember her name, but she works a few hours on some days in the hairdressing salon across the street from my office. I think someone told me she had been a nurse – or an ambulance officer, or something medical anyway – before she started working part-time at the salon. Carla, the hairdresser who owns the salon, or is the boss anyway, is that woman's daughter. Gossip has it that the mother forked out the money to set up the salon and now comes to work to keep an eye on things. Carla is a good hairdresser but doesn't have much business sense. Her mother does the 'meet and greet', all the reception stuff, makes cups of tea and coffee, washes the towels, and generally keeps the place tidy. Why are you so interested in her?"

"I'm not sure yet. Move onto the next frame, and let's see if we should be interested in her."

When the next frame didn't tell us much, I moved it onto the frame after that.

"There!… See what she does?" Emily asked, apparently particularly excited about something that I saw as barely interesting.

"Okay; as she stepped off the traffic island, she swooped down, picked up Trina's shopping, and placed it up on the traffic island out of harm's way. I don't see anything too exciting about that. She spends a lot of her day picking up stuff and tidying up. Maybe she is compulsive that way."

"Sonny, run the recording on slowly, frame-by-frame, until we know what happened to that shopping. I know you don't think Trina's shopping is important, but there is something about it that won't leave me alone."

Emily proceeded to provide a running description of what she saw as significant about each frame as it came up on the screen.

"We need to watch what that bloke does. The one who elbowed his way through the crowd to stand just behind the bags the woman rescued and put up on the traffic island. Now, on the next frame (she motioned for me to roll it forward again)… See how he now has a problem with his shoelace and goes down on his haunches to deal with it?"

"Not particularly convincing, is he? He's not even looking at his shoe. He seems more interested in checking out the crowd around him," I observed.

"Yeah, now watch what he does on this next frame," Emily said as she motioned for me to move the recording on again. "See, having supposedly dealt with his shoelace, when he stands up, he's holding those bags containing Trina's shopping."

After studying the new image for a few moments, I moved it on twice. The first of those frames showed the man spin on his heel and was about to stride off. Then, the next frame showed him striding across the road to the other side, with his phone pressed to his left ear and swinging Trina's shopping from his right hand. Trina's shopping had now taken on a whole new dimension for me as far as my investigation was concerned.

"Why would a bloke want to steal something that was obviously a woman's shopping?" I thought aloud.

"I doubt anything Trina bought from *Bianca's* was likely to fit him," Emily quipped.

"So, why did he take it? What did he think it might contain?" I asked as I moved the recording on to the next frame.

His call apparently ended, and although the bloke was now standing on the pavement on the other side of the road, we clearly saw him rifle through the contents of the bag from *Bianca's*. The little voice in my head was telling me to go back and look more closely at the man's actions. I dutifully rewound the recording to the frame that showed him standing up after having dealt with his shoelace. And, this time, that little voice in my head was telling me to look harder at the image on the screen. I reached around and grabbed the magnifying glass from where it had been abandoned on my desk. I moved forward to have my nose only centimetres away from the image on the big screen.

"Aah, Yes!" I yelped, startling Emily.

"What? What have you found so interesting?" She demanded.

Holding my hand up in a 'stop' gesture, I set about doing something I wasn't sure I knew how to do. But, a minute or so later, I felt pretty chuffed with my efforts as my printer whirred into life. I retrieved the printouts and was studying them when a noise in the kitchen alerted me that at least one of my guests was now up and about. I found Ben standing at the coffee machine.

"Good of you to join us," I said cheerily as I came into the kitchen, "and I suppose you would like breakfast now?"

"Breakfast would be good. What do you have on offer?" Ben asked just as Nick also appeared in the kitchen.

"I'll have whatever he is having – as long as it includes plenty of coffee," Nick told me.

"I'll do the toast while you make the coffee," Emily suggested on her way to get the bread from the cupboard. "Raisin or plain…?" she asked Nick. Nick reiterated he would have whatever Ben was having.

"He always has plain," Emily told Nick. "Is that what you want?"

"Err, well, no. In that case, I'll have raisin toast, thanks."

Over breakfast, Nick asked Ben if he was going to remain at the house for a while. Nick wanted to go home for a shower and clean clothes, but he knew that once Ben left for work, Nick would have to stay with me. I helped ease the way for Nick to leave.

"Ben, if you could spare me some time after breakfast, there are a couple of things I want to show you."

"Are they important, or could they wait until tonight? I need to see how things are going after last night's crime spree, so I don't want to hang around here for too long this morning."

It didn't take too much effort to persuade him we would be finished with what I wanted to show him by the time Nick returned and Ben could leave for his office. I hadn't noticed, but Nick must've called the precinct because, a few minutes later, a police car collected him and took him back to the precinct to get his own car. With breakfast over and Nick gone, Ben, Emily and I adjourned to my office.

As I started to tell Ben about the timeline I'd constructed for Trina's movements prior to her death, Emily was adding a few extra bits we had gathered this morning to the timeline on the whiteboard. I directed Ben's attention to the whiteboard and talked him through the various points listed on it. The first couple of points were not news to any of us. It wasn't until after Trina left my office and went to *Gianni's* for lunch that the exercise became interesting.

I explained her meeting a man who was already waiting in the restaurant. And how it didn't appear a pleasant event before the bloke stormed out and Trina stayed on to eat on her own. Then, after discussing the shopping Trina did, I told Ben how I had played a section of the recording of the incident that killed her. I explained about Trina's handbag and shopping being sent flying when she was struck by the vehicle. As I flipped through my file in search of the printout I needed, I recounted what happened to Trina's handbag.

"… So, after the bloke picked up the handbag, he turned around and gave it to a woman standing behind him. The woman took the bag and promptly headed off towards the intersection at the end of the block.

The bloke who picked up the handbag remained at the scene for a few moments after the woman left. He took a phone call while he was standing there. Then, when he left, he headed in the opposite direction to the woman. He hurried along the street towards my office building."

"Okay, you've grabbed my attention, and at least answered the question about why we found no handbag at the scene. But, the question now is, what happened to the handbag after it was given to the woman?"

"Perhaps it won't be too difficult to find the answer to that question. In fact, you should be able to follow up on it once you go back to the precinct."

He gave me one of his famous sceptical looks, and I continued. I slapped a printout down on the desk in front of him and tapped it with my forefinger. "All you need to do is ask this woman what she did with the bag," I said with a smirk as he stared at the printout. He looked as though he had been punched in the face… and I did understand his shock.

"Lisa – or Greta Lomax, if you prefer. Whatever you want to call her, the woman last known to have had Trina's handbag is recovering from overdosing in your cells. I'm sure you don't need me to make suggestions about how you might pursue the matter of the handbag with her."

For the next few minutes, we discussed the chain of events up to that point in time and how the whole exercise seemed so finely orchestrated. At last, we had exhausted all there was to say and speculated about regarding the handbag.

"That was no coincidence," Ben announced. "Those two people were strategically placed for the specific purpose of grabbing that handbag. You're right, Sonny. I've got plenty to talk to Lomax about, and it will all make good leverage if she still wants to be uncooperative. So, is that the end of the surprises you wanted to tell me about?"

"Not quite… That's only half the story. The other half of the story deals with the shopping that Trina did after lunch and before she was killed."

After explaining about the shopping and how it, too, had been flung into the air and landed on the roadway when Trina was run down, I outlined the subsequent sequence of events that occurred concerning that shopping and mentioned the people involved.

"Ri-ight… That's interesting, but I doubt it's of any real relevance to my case," Ben told me. "We were anxious to get hold of the handbag to help identify Trina, but I doubt her shopping will tell us anything exciting."

"Perhaps women's underwear, or whatever it was she bought, won't be of any interest to you, but it seems like it was to the bloke who made off with the shopping." I told him about the bloke with the troublesome shoelace who, again, happened to be in just the right place at the right time to make off with the carrier bags, and of the bloke's particular interest in the contents of the bag from *Bianca's*.

"Oh, good… So now we've got another player to worry about. Okay…," He said, adding a theatrical sigh, "I suppose we'll have to try to get a look at this bloke who appears to have a fetish for women's clothing."

"Or you could just have a look at this," I said, slapping a printout of the image of the man from the recording in front of Ben. "And, if I'm not mistaken, you've already come across him before in the course of this investigation." There was that stunned mullet look across his face again.

"Christ, it's the window watcher… You know, the bloke who was watching you at your window when Trina was run down. Again, I'll bet his presence and subsequent actions were not a coincidence either."

Discussion of this part of yesterday's results of my investigation was brief. After all, there wasn't much more to tell him. He already knew the identity of the bloke in question, thanks to the officers at the Everton police station. Whatever the operation was that led to Trina's death, Christos appeared to have a starring role in it.

At that point, Nick returned, and Ben started making noises about heading to his office to prepare for a chat with Lomax. Emily also announced she was almost asleep on her feet, and she was going home to bed before she fell over. I gave Nick an apologetic look as the other two gathered up their belongings in readiness to leave.

"I suppose you've drawn the short straw and are stuck with me again today," I murmured to Nick.

"Suits me fine," he replied, grinning from ear to ear. "I am having a ball. The way you operate is fascinating – and the results are amazing. Even last night was a learning experience. I could have been a police officer a long time before being involved in such a takedown. And I'm still blown away by the way you organised and executed the whole operation. Have you ever considered becoming a police officer?"

Poor bloke; I just roared laughing. He wasn't to know he wasn't the first person to ask that question. I didn't honour it with an answer.

As soon as Emily and Ben left and Nick and I were alone again, the inevitable question arose.

"What are we going to do today?" Nick asked as he collapsed on the chair behind what had been designated 'his desk'.

"It would be good if I had a few bright ideas about that, but I don't. If I'm honest, the thing about this case that's gnawing at me now is something I can't do much about. I want to know who Trina is – not just her real name but everything about her." I gave Nick another apologetic look. He nodded knowingly.

Nick appeared to give my comments some thought before firing off his next question.

"Forget about the Standish surname and the Blewett surname, too. Think of someone called Jane Doe and tell me how you would go about finding out all there is to know about her. Where would you start?"

"Well, let's assume your Jane Doe is approximately the same age as Trina. Now… we are unlikely to find any mention of 'Jane' in the official births, deaths and marriages indexes for the various states. All the events likely to be associated with her and her parents are too recent and, under privacy regulations, will not appear in the indexes. Then, there are the various electoral rolls and newspaper archives once you decide on likely time periods to research.

Of course, it's much easier for coppers to undertake such research. They – you have other resources you can access."

"Okay, I'll give it a go. Tell me what they are?"

"No, no… I'll not have you accessing those sorts of records on my behalf. Apart from being chucked off the force, you're likely to end up charged with something as well."

"I wouldn't be searching those records for you. I'd be a copper assisting with an important ongoing investigation and looking for information to pass on to my boss. Don't look like that, Sonny. Ben and I discussed the work you do as a private investigator and how it's your research that often helps solve cases. I told him I was fascinated by how your mind works and how yesterday has helped me decide I want to be a detective. Ben told me to observe, take notes, and help out wherever I can. He said it was an invaluable learning opportunity for me."

"What about your psychology studies? Are you going to chuck all that away to become a detective?"

"God, no, nothing could be further from my mind. I'm studying to be a forensic psychologist. That study and training will be invaluable to me as a detective and, if that is the path I want to follow, I don't have to waste time finishing my doctorate and qualifying, just so that I could hang up my shingle in private practice. On top of that, my psychology studies will help fast-track my rise through the ranks."

"Why are we sitting here talking about it? Let's get you working and learning. Your first job is to make us coffee while I think about what I might give you to do."

Chapter 20

"Right, I'm ready to go," Nick announced as he returned with our coffee. "What have you decided to give me to do… and how complicated will it be? You have to remember I'm new to all of this stuff you do."

I ran through a list of clues we might follow-up on and the resources that might prove useful. My plan was for Nick to decide what he would like to do. Nick was silent for a few moments when I finished my list of potential tasks.

"Well, the usual approach is to start with something you know and to work from there to find out everything you don't know about that fact. So, what do we actually know that we can follow up on today?"

"High on my list of priorities is to find out who the hell Trina Blewett is, where she was living, and what she was doing before she ended up spread-eagled on the road. And, although I know Ben's team will be working on this, I want to know all there is to know about Greta Lomax and whether she knew Trina previously."

"Ye-es, those things are worth investigating, but none of them you mentioned is a 'fact'. If you want to look into identities, the only one we know anything about with any confidence is that the infant daughter of Doctor Bertrand Lomax arrived in Sydney with her parents in the 1980s. But, knowing that, and linking it to Trina's Blewett's death, is a long bow to draw at this stage," Nick told me.

"Good thinking, Nick. We need definite information about the woman we are calling Trina. My preliminary investigation failed to find any mention of a Trina Blewett anywhere. If we accept the assumption that Trina might be Zalika Standish, it might be worthwhile establishing whatever we can about Zali."

"Okay… I can see the merit in that," Nick agreed. "So, how might we do that, and where do we start?"

"Another good question… I think a good starting point might be Trove. Again, the best we might hope for is something in the social columns of the newspapers of the day. The search will be much the same as the one that gave us the information on Lomax's background."

The next couple of minutes were spent explaining Trove and how to use it – and giving Nick some sound advice – before sending him off in search of anything relating to the surname 'Standish'.

"If you don't give it specific parameters to search, you will end up with a lot of interesting stuff to read, possibly none of which will be relevant to our case," I warned him.

While Nick muttered at his laptop screen, I examined everything in my case file in the hope some previously overlooked clue might jump out at me. About ten minutes later, I did jump... But it was in response to Nick's shout and not because I had found anything.

"Gotcha…," Nick shouted. "Yeah, Sonny, I think I might have found Zali. Have a look at this."

Scrambling out from behind my desk, I rushed to stand behind him to read over his shoulder. The information filling his laptop screen appeared as a 'Social Jottings' article in a Sydney newspaper. *Dr George Standish, accompanied by his wife, Mrs Maria Standish, and his infant daughter, has arrived in Sydney to take up his position at Sydney's Royal Prince Alfred Hospital.*

"That is what we were looking for, isn't it?" Nick asked, suddenly doubting the reason for his earlier exuberance.

"Yep, that's a start, but we have a few more hurdles to negotiate yet before we get too carried away."

"I don't suppose it constitutes a real 'fact'. This entry isn't as helpful as the one that clearly identified Greta Lomax's parentage. It is more a tantalising suggestion than a clue."

So soon after his excitement, Nick now sounded disappointed, deflated, and in desperate need of encouragement. I attempted to bolster his ego and encourage him to keep digging for more information.

"You are right. It is both tantalising and frustrating at the same time. That's why I think we need to find out more about that infant daughter. I know it's not a fact, but let's see if we can link that child to the name Zalika Standish. It will help us to know whether we need to keep the name in our investigation or discard it as a red herring. You could start by continuing to explore the newspaper archives on Trove for any further mention of George Standish or his family. In the search bar, you will need to type in his name and a date range from the late 1970s to today."

Nick attacked his challenge with vigour while I sat back to ponder what I might do to contribute something worthwhile. The thought that kept bouncing around in the back of my mind was that the nurse, Lisa, had claimed Zali Standish was her best friend. While that lacks credibility, given the matter of the handbag, was there a genuine connection at some point between the two women? As I took a sip of my coffee, now barely lukewarm, a new thought slammed to the front of my thinking: what if Zali Standish also had been a nurse? And, might there have been a nurse called Trina Blewett?

Moments later, I was logged on to the Nurses and Midwives Registration Board's website. Although I had previously checked on Greta Lomax, I checked her registration again before commencing my search for the other names. It didn't take long to find Zalika Standish's name on the register. My pulse stepped up a notch, but I wanted to check for Trina Blewett before I became too excited.

'Trina' was likely the diminutive of a longer name – Petrina, perhaps – so I concentrated on her Blewett surname. I don't know why, but I was surprised to find the surname didn't appear at all in the register.

"Argh… what does that really mean," I asked the universe, startling Nick, who looked up from the note he was writing and asked what I meant.

"I was playing a hunch," I told Nick. "I reasoned that, if the child's father was a doctor, the daughter could have become a nurse to follow in the family's medical tradition. If that were the case, it might have been through nursing that Lisa and Trina became acquainted. It doesn't tell me whether they were good friends or not."

"No, it doesn't... But it does give some credence to the possibility that Lomax did know something about what was going on in Trina's life just prior to her death."

Nick is making a very good sounding board and is having something of a stabilising effect on my thinking, I told myself as I briefly considered his comments.

"You were writing something when I disturbed you. Have you found something interesting about the Standish family?" I asked, hoping he had something exciting to share.

"A couple of things... But I don't think they are of much use to us. For instance, Doctor George and his wife had a son soon after arriving in Australia. Then, it was not long after that when newspapers seemed to decide that readers had lost interest in social jottings, and scaled back the column inches they allocated to such articles. They quickly start to focus on only major events, or news that will impact only a large segment of the community. Smaller regional newspapers, however, were a bit slower to relinquish the old ways."

"Anything else of interest apart from the new Standish son?"

"Uhmm... George merits a few mentions in the stuff I've looked at so far. He was appointed chief medical officer at the Royal Prince Alfred Hospital, and later was granted a sabbatical to study some new research being carried out in the USA. That's all I have so far, but I still have a bit to go through."

"Yep, a bit like the stuff I've found – interesting but not particularly useful." Then, a new thought slammed in as I was about to move my thinking away from Standish family matters. "Nick, what does that entry about the Standish son have to say?"

"Hang on a minute while I bring it up. Right, here it is... Ah hah... It's just what we needed... *Dr George and Mrs Maria*

Standish announce the birth of Xavier, their first son and little brother for Zalika. That's the link we were looking for, isn't it?"

"Aye, it is. Our only problem now is establishing the link between the information you've retrieved from Trove and our Jane Doe." I saw Nick's confused look and rushed on to explain. "The question is whether Jane Doe, Trina Blewett, and Zalika Standish are one and the same person."

Silence filled the room for a while as Nick and I dealt with our frustration and disappointment. It allowed for reflection on all I thought I knew about the Trina Blewett, who came to see me that Monday morning… and made a mockery of Lisa's information about her 'best friend', Zali. Everything the nurse, Lisa, had said about Zali's father having been ill and Zali giving up her career to go home and run the family business now appeared a long way removed from the reality of Zali's life. I couldn't help but wonder if Greta Lomax, who had posed as Lisa, had ever known Zali at all. Nick brought an end to my thoughts about Lisa's possible motives for the story she had spun me.

"Sonny, what happened to Trina's handbag intrigues me. It must have taken an enormous amount of planning and required precision timing to have everyone in the right position at the right time. And, now I think on it, maybe it also required some degree of 'insider' knowledge. How did they know where Trina would be and that she would attempt to cross the road at that precise time? Why were they interested in her bag in the first place? Nobody would employ such elaborate planning for a simple bag-snatch."

"Christ, you do ask the most interesting questions… And, of course, I don't have answers to any of them. But let's analyse that for a moment, shall we? I suppose the big question is what they thought they would gain from the handbag," I suggested.

"Cash, credit cards, drivers licence, car keys, house keys, and maybe Medicare and health insurance cards… Anything else you can think of as you probably have more idea of what women carry around in their handbags?"

"I'm the last woman you should ask. My bag contains a handgun, digital recorder, camera, small pair of binoculars, several notebooks, and pens and pencils – not exactly what your average woman would carry around. While my bag might be atypical, let's assume Trina's bag was typical. So, what was in her bag that warranted killing her to have it? There would be opportunity for financial gain from any cash and credit cards and, I suppose, they could sell Trina's car and house if she owned those things."

"The killing still doesn't make any sense. They could have whacked her over the head on a dark street and stolen her bag, or followed her home and ransacked her house, as well as hitting her over the head and taking her bag. There has to be something more important – much more important – that they hoped to gain, or gain access to, for them to be prepared to go to the lengths they did." Nick shook his head in disbelief as he spoke.

"We can't overlook Christos' connection to all this. How would Trina's bag and her shopping benefit his sphere of operations? We know he is involved in a wide range of enterprises, but which one would be worth so much effort and planning?" I gave Nick an apologetic look before continuing. "I'm sorry. I know none of that is helpful, but I don't have anything better to suggest."

"What do you think might have happened to her brother?" Nick asked after staring into the distance for a moment. "I mean, did he follow his father into some aspect of the medical profession, or… or, did he fall in with the wrong lot somewhere along the line?"

"Are you suggesting that his life might now be in a precarious position after having done the wrong thing somehow by Christos and his mob?… And they were trying to use Trina in some way to get to him?... Hmm, interesting scenario you've created there…."

"But, one based on nothing more than speculation and creativity… Huh, we still can't be certain Trina even had any connection to the Standish family – or had a brother." Nick paused for a moment before continuing. "Maybe we should wait to see what the police questioning of Lomax produces after they confront her with evidence of her role in Trina's murder."

He made sense – lots of it – but I couldn't just sit around hoping that Ben might tell us something to shed light on what Trina's death was all about. I was immersed in my own thoughts and struggling for inspiration about what else we might try, when I heard Nick calling my name through the fog swirling around in my head.

"Did Trina give you an address or anything – maybe a phone number – when she came to see you?" he asked.

"No. Unless she became a client, I wouldn't…." I sat staring at Nick while I tried to sort out whatever the little voice in my head was trying to tell me. Then, the fog started to clear, and intuition began oozing through.

"Jesus, I'm being a bit slow today, Nick. If we want to find out more about Trina, maybe we should be searching other ancillary records for any mention of her."

"Like which records…?"

"Drivers licence, vehicle registration… Anything that might give us a photo and maybe an address." I gave him a wicked grin and said, "Those are records only police officers can access. Do you feel up to the challenge, or does accessing them pose a risk to your career?"

Nick just shot me a look and dragged his laptop over. "Which surname should I look for?"

"Try Standish first. I doubt you'll find anything for Trina Blewett."

A few moments later, I saw him sit upright and peer at his screen briefly before attacking his keyboard again.

"Don't keep it a secret, Nick. What have you found?"

"Everything, I think. I've found Zali's drivers licence information, so we now have her address – or her address at the time she renewed her licence."

"When was that?"

"Three months ago."

"Right, so there's a fair chance it might still be current. Could you have a quick look for any vehicles registered to her, please?" About a minute later, he read out the make and model of a vehicle registered to Zalika Standish.

"Did you find a drivers licence for Trina Blewett?"

"Err… No. I didn't look. Once I found one for Zali, I didn't look any further, and I just did the same with the search of vehicle registrations." The poor bloke looked so embarrassed. I didn't know what to say, but he saved me the bother. "Sorry… That was a sloppy performance on my part. I'll check for the Blewett name now."

His search seemed to take longer than I expected. Then, he was shaking his head as he told me, "There was only one entry for a similar surname, but it had a slightly different spelling, and it wasn't for a Trina or any other name that might logically be shortened to Trina."

"It still might have been her, but just tinkering with her identity again," I suggested.

"She would have had to tinker with more than her identity. The entry I found was for a fifty-nine year old bloke."

"So, probably not Trina, eh, Nick? Is there a photo with that licence renewal for Zalika Standish?"

"Yeah, I'm opening it now. Do you want me to send you a copy so you can print it out?" The answer was so obvious I just gave Nick a wide-eyed smile in reply.

Both of us sat for some moments just staring at the drivers licence photo before I spoke.

"We can chalk up one more victory, my friend. I can confirm it was Zali Standish, calling herself Trina Blewett, who came to see me that Monday morning," I told Nick and offered him a high-five to celebrate.

"Chalk up *three* victories, don't you think," he asked. "Not only have we established the identity of the woman rundown on your street, we've also discovered her address and details of her vehicle. Not a bad morning's work, I reckon. Are you going to let Ben know what we discovered?"

"Aah, good question… But no, I think I'll tell Emily first so she can start matching forensic information with the identity. Then there is something else I want to do before I talk to Ben."

"Okay, but do we do whatever it is before or after lunch?" Nick asked.

We appeared to have successfully utilised all of the morning. So, as soon as we had a quick sandwich lunch, I suggested we take a drive past Zali's address.

"Your vehicle or mine?" Nick asked as I checked the contents of my oversized tote bag.

"Eh? I didn't think there was a choice."

"Yes, I came back in my car this morning. It's parked outside. So, which one do we take."

So much for my powers of observation, I thought as I confirmed we would take his today. Soon after we took off, he admitted he still wasn't familiar with the layout of Millhaven. "I've only been here less than twelve months and most of that time has been spent working cases, not driving around the place."

For a moment, I mentally kicked myself for not insisting we take my car. I resigned myself to giving him directions as we drove through the suburbs.

"This is a fairly well-heeled part of the city," he said as we turned onto Zali's street.

"Pull into the kerb here for a moment," I demanded.

"Why?... What's the problem? Have you seen something?"

"Do shut up," I growled. "Before we come to Zali's address, I want to search my bag for something that looks like a map. Do you have a map of some sort in this car?"

He indicated the glovebox. Having selected the one that suited my purpose best from the three maps I found, I told him to crawl along the street while I flapped the map about a bit in what I hoped would be an Oscar-winning performance of someone looking for a particular address on this street. Nick shook his head and shrugged, but did as I asked. I flapped the map about where onlookers could see it, and randomly pointed at places as we crawled along the street.

"Zali's place is just up ahead, Nick. See the place that needs a lawnmower… It's the beige-coloured one with the red tiled roof. Just before we come to it, ease to a stop in the middle of the road. Don't be alarmed. I'll just be putting on another theatrical display for a few moments before I tell you to move off again… Here!… This is good. Stop here."

There followed the main act of my performance. After more vigorous flapping about of the map, I leaned forward close to the windscreen and looked around in all directions ahead of us. Then, after exercising the map again for a moment or two, I gesticulated for Nick to drive further along the street – but at not much above a crawl. Just before the intersection at the end of the street, I again asked him to pull into the kerb. I told him we should look as though we were engaged in a brief conversation that perhaps was a bit heated, during which I would frequently throw my hands in the air.

Act 3 of the charade played out, I called curtain time, and we drove out of the street and headed back to my place.

"You are going to have to explain that whole episode when we are home again. I have no idea what it was all about or what it achieved – if anything." He complained. Yet again, I thought, 'poor Nick'.

As soon as we were home again and seated in my office with coffees, Nick renewed his demand for information about this afternoon's expedition. While I wanted to be as succinct as possible when I explained it to him, it wasn't so simple.

"The whole idea behind our drive this afternoon was to have a look at the address her drivers licence gave us for Zali."

"Yes, but what did that give us? I'm not being deliberately thick, but I don't see what it achieved."

"Okay, I wanted an idea of the area in which Zali lived, where it sat on Millhaven's socio-economic scale, and to check if there was anything obvious happening there."

"Like what?"

"I was looking for any sign someone was in the house, or had been there, since Trina's death."

"You're not going to be able to see that by just driving past. If the place had been broken into, the point of entry most likely would have been the rear of the house, away from the street and the prying eyes of neighbours."

"They wouldn't have needed to break in. Zali's keys would have been in her handbag – presumably. So, the bad guys could just let themselves in. And, as for the prying eyes of neighbours, that was another thing I was checking for. Did you see anyone outside, or as much as a curtain twitch as we drove past? No? Right… Then, it is fairly safe to assume there are few, if any, retirees or stay at home mums living near Zali's house. I also was checking for any vehicles that might have been parked at the house."

"There was a vehicle parked up beside the house. Should we call it in and have a patrol car check it out?"

"Nah… It was Zali's car that was parked at the house. Remember, the details you found when you looked for her registration information… and this is the number on the plate of that vehicle at the house. I think you'll find it confirms it was Zali's vehicle." I flipped open my notebook and showed him the registration number I had scribbled down as we drove out of Zali's street.

"It appears I have a lot to learn about being an investigator. Apart from all the details you've already drawn to my attention, was there anything particularly interesting about that address?"

"Yeah, the address itself. It was in a well-heeled area of the city. That is not where a single, young woman is likely to own a house. So, that then gives rise to a few new questions. Does she own the place or rent it? If she owns it, did she buy it herself, or was it bought for her? Does she live there alone? And, if she bought it, what does she do for a living to be able to afford to live there? We know she was a nurse for some time, but would that allow her to buy a house in that part of Millhaven."

"How do you manage to do this all the time?"

"What… be a private investigator?"

"Yes.. no… Argh, as soon as we find one minuscule piece of information that takes us one step forward with the investigation, you come up with a load of new questions that result in us going two steps backwards. I just do not know how you ever manage to solve a case … let alone do it all the time for a living."

Poor Nick, he does keep thinking like a copper and following a copper's set structured approach to everything. I would have made a lousy cop had I gone down that track so long ago now when I was first pressured to become one. But, there was something I – we – must do before our next encounter with Ben.

"Don't worry about it, Nick, just accept we have made progress today. Our next task is to organise all we've uncovered today into a concise report to give to Ben tonight. It's possible Ben might already be aware of some of the stuff we've discovered, but we need to record it for him anyway. Do you feel up to that task?"

Of course, he was up for it. He dragged his laptop over, ready for action, before appearing to stall.

Chapter 21

"Perhaps, before I start work, it might be best if we compared notes about what we've discovered. That way, I won't overlook something or misinterpret anything."

Armed with a list of key points, Nick was soon working his keyboard with renewed enthusiasm. Producing a report was something he knew how to do and felt comfortable doing it. While he was focused on his report, I turned to a new page in my notebook and started a list of all the additional questions today's research had produced. When I sat back to review my compiled list, I was surprised by the length of it. Maybe Nick's comments were justified. I was still studying my list – and waiting for inspiration to strike – when Nick interrupted my thoughts.

"Sonny, is it likely I will have to sleep here again tonight?"

"You are asking the wrong person. That's a question for Ben. But, unless he is involved with a case and likely to be at a crime scene for some part of the night, I would think you should be able to sleep in your own bed tonight. Is there a problem if you can't?"

"No-o, I don't suppose so. Oh, please don't think I don't appreciate your hospitality. I don't know how you put up with having your home disrupted the way it is, but I would like to go home tonight, if at all possible… even if it isn't until after dinner."

I felt for the lad, and I suspected there might be a 'someone' who also would like Nick to be free tonight. Still, it wasn't something I had much say about and I knew Ben wouldn't think to let Nick know in advance what was happening tonight. I had deliberately not stripped the spare bed this morning on the off chance Nick might be spending another night in it.

While I was pondering tonight's arrangements, Nick's voice cut across my thoughts. "I hope Ben comes home early this evening. I'm dying to know how their interrogation of Greta Lomax went today and what they managed to get out of her."

Thank you, Nick, I thought, but I didn't say anything. All day, I had struggled to keep that same curiosity at bay and now Nick's comment had it back squarely centre-front again.

Ben was a welcome sight when he parked out front of my place just before seven o'clock. The aroma of roast dinners preceded his arrival in my kitchen. Nick glanced at me out of the corner of his eye and murmured, "I hope one of those is for me."

There was one for Nick, and there was a spare meal as well. Ben had thought Emily would be joining us and asked if I had heard from her. He seemed concerned when I said I hadn't heard from her all day.

"If you would like to put those in the oven to keep warm, I'll make a quick call, and then we can relax with a quick drink before dinner," he said as he strode out onto my back deck.

Nick raised his eyebrows at me in question but didn't say anything. I just shrugged and did as I was told. I thought there was a fair chance Ben had gone to call Emily, and that had my stomach churning. If Ben thought Emily would be here this evening and felt the need to call her, it told me some unpleasant happening might be a possibility. Ben's call seemed to be taking longer than I expected. After a quick check confirmed Ben was still engaged with his phone, I sidled up to Nick who was still standing next to the kitchen bench.

"I don't like the way this looks. I hope you didn't have anything too important planned for tonight," I whispered. Nick gave me an unfathomable look in return. "All hell is about to break loose, I think… but, of course, I could be wrong,"

My gut instinct wasn't wrong. It was as sharp as ever I discovered, when Ben rejoined us in the kitchen. The look on his face and his set jaw confirmed my building fears. My squirming stomach immediately tightened into a lead ball.

"We might have a problem," he said, confirming the obvious. "Emily was joining us for dinner and said she would be here by about six o'clock. She's not here, and she's not answering any of her numbers."

Dragging my phone out of my pocket, I tried to remember the name of Emily's team leader. I saw his name come up as I flicked through my contacts and promptly keyed him. The news was not good. No, Emily wasn't at work and he hadn't seen her since around mid-afternoon. I called her neighbour. Emily often works cases with me, and things can become hairy from time to time. We both have various numbers on our phones to use to check on each other's whereabouts and safety, if one of those 'hairy situations' occurs. Emily's neighbour confirmed Emily was not at home and she hadn't seen her come home this afternoon. I relayed the information to Ben.

"Dinner is on hold," he announced. "I don't know when I'll be back… or if I'll be back tonight."

"I'm coming with you," I shouted after him as he marched towards the front door. That brought him hurrying back to me.

"You're not going anywhere. You and Nick are staying here. Check your weapons and stay on alert." And then he was racing out the door as I marched into my office.

"Grab your weapon and your phone, Nick, and come with me," I told him as I emerged from my office with my tote bag over my shoulder.

"Where are we going? Ben said to stay here."

"Feel free to stay here if you wish, but I have better things to do. Now, are you coming with me or not."

As I raced to the front door, I thought I heard him murmur, 'I wouldn't dare not go with you'. Nick followed me out and headed for his vehicle parked out front.

"No, we are taking my vehicle," I told him as I rushed past him and opened the garage. "No, not that one, Nick. We're taking the big tank tonight. Come on, get in. Don't muck about wasting time."

I roared out of the garage, closed and locked it, and armed all the security systems using the remotes as I headed for the driveway. Ignoring the speed limits, I roared to the intersection at the end of my street without any real idea of where I was going.

"Where are we going?" Nick demanded.

"Still trying to figure that out, Nick, and that will happen a lot quicker if you just sit there and say nothing to interrupt my thought processes." He went to argue, but I took a corner a bit too sharply, and he opted to grab for the dashboard instead.

It wasn't really the truth. From the moment I left the house, my subconscious had me heading in one direction and one direction only. Continuing to disregard most of the speed limits, I headed across town before easing back to the mandatory speed.

"Isn't this… Uhmm… Haven't we been here before?" Nick hissed at me through the darkness.

"Yep, and we are going there again. Get your weapon out and have it lying in your lap… Just in case we might need it. I'm going to drive down the street at legal speed, so keep your eyes peeled as we go past that house. I won't be slowing down or doing anything else to indicate I have any interest in the place as we go past... And don't talk while we are about it."

We continued past the house and onto the T-intersection at the end of the street, where I turned right to head out of the area and back onto a main road. As soon as I was out of the street, I hit the phone button on the steering wheel and shouted, "Call Ben". After the usual faffing about confirming the number I wanted to call, I heard Ben's phone dialling.

"What…?" he barked

Ignoring him, and with no time to waste, I gave him the address of the house and added a few details to help him locate the right place. "Beige coloured house, red roof, on the western side of the street and about halfway down the northern half of the block. Emily's car is there, and there are lights in the rear section of the house."

"She's probably gone to visit a friend or someone... Strange that she is not answering her phone, though. Why do you think the house is important?"

"Zalika Standish lives there… or used to live there."

"Get out of there," he bellowed at me before cutting me off.

"So, now, what do we do?" Nick asked cautiously. "Do we just go home again?"

"Don't be bloody ridiculous, Nick. Of course, we are not going home. We are going to go around the block. There is a small area – I think it might be a bus stop – a short distance before the entrance to Zali's street. We are going to sit there for a while. Keep your weapon handy. If Ben and his merry men don't turn up soon, we might have some work to do."

"You are joking, aren't you? You wouldn't go racing in there with all guns blazing, would you? It would be ridiculous, not to mention foolhardy… People are likely to be shot, and that might include us."

"Yeah, and that's why, if I do decide to go in, you will remain here in the vehicle. The paperwork I'd have to face if anything happened to you gives me the horrors just thinking about it. And, in case you have any ideas to the contrary, your involvement will not do your career any good."

Every minute we sat parked there felt more like an hour. Suddenly, my phone vibrated. I checked the caller ID before answering it. Ben.

"Where are you and what are you doing?" Ben barked at me. "And where is Nick?"

I gave him quick details of where I was parked and confirmed Nick was sitting beside me. Of course, Ben then wanted to give me the third degree about why we were there and why Nick was with me? He demanded to know why Nick hadn't stopped me from leaving home. I couldn't help but laugh.

"If you couldn't make me stay home tonight, how the hell do you think Nick was going to achieve it?" The call ended at that point.

"Not exactly a happy chap, I assume?" Nick said in reference to Ben's call. "I guess he was letting you know the cavalry is on its way. Did he indicate what they planned to do?"

"Don't be silly. That's not how Ben works. The first we'll know about it is when it happens."

"So, what's the point in just sitting here? It doesn't seem like we will be involved... and I suspect Ben would not be impressed if we did become involved. Why don't we just go home? On second thoughts, why don't you go home and leave me here to help Ben's team when they arrive?"

Poor Nick, he really is still wet behind the ears. He would be unemployed so fast he wouldn't know what hit him. I took a deep breath before explaining another fact of life to him.

"You need to stick with your university studies because you obviously aren't interested in remaining a copper. I am also worried that you might also be harbouring a death wish." He didn't understand and sought clarification, so I explained. "If I left you here, your life would be over as you know it. You will have contravened the rules of the assignment Ben gave you by not being with me at all times, and the reason you did that was so you could gatecrash Ben's offensive on that house. You would not come out of any of that very well.

If you just sit here with me, you are doing exactly what you are supposed to do. You tried to make me go home but, when I wouldn't, you stayed to guard me."

Nick swivelled around in his seat. I knew he was about to argue, and I also knew I was about to snarl at him. But neither of those things happened when loud knocking on the car's window made both of us jump. I lowered my window – and immediately wished I hadn't.

"Why are you still here?" Ben growled at me.

"Just keeping watch in case anything happened, like a vehicle leaving the property or anything," I lied without even a twinge of guilt.

"Well, the police are here now, so you should leave – before I have you arrested. And what's your excuse, Nick."

"Arrest probably is the only way you might get me to leave. As for Nick... Well, he's tried hard to get me to go home but you know how impossible that is when my mind is made up.

He doesn't have any choice but to stay here and continue to guard me. By the way, how many officers have you brought, and where are they?"

"Where they are is not your concern."

"It will be if a number of your people surround this vehicle in the mistaken belief it is a part of your operation. Might prove embarrassing later."

"My men will not surround you. I only have one other officer with me."

"Ben, how come there are only two of you? I don't know how many people are in that house, but you can't go in there with only one other. Emily could be killed, and so could you and your officer. You'll have to leave it until more officers arrive."

"I'm not stupid. I'm about to try to establish what the situation is in that house, but, if needs be, I'll abort the operation rather than put anyone's life at risk. If you two plan to continue sitting here in the dark, don't come any closer to that house, and don't even think about entering that street," were Ben's parting words as he started to stride away from my car.

"Hang about. Come back," I hissed at him.

"What now? I've got things to do, so make it quick."

"Don't abort the operation. You have two more support personnel right here. If we don't do this tonight, who knows what Emily's situation might be tomorrow? Come on, Nick. Bring your firearm. We're about to join the party."

"Jesus, Sonny, you are impossible… Okay, I'm desperate. So, yes, you're in… But you two follow my instructions to the letter."

"Good… Now, how do you want to play this?" I asked while I was trying to think what our role might be.

"As they appear to be occupying the rear section of the house, I'll try going in through the front of the house and maybe take them by surprise. It depends on what we find when we get there. We might have to mount our rescue from the rear of the place. What are your thoughts on this one, Sonny?"

"Give us about twenty minutes to be in place. I'll let you know when we are right to go."

"Not exactly a well developed strategy," Nick commented as we watched Ben disappear into the darkness.

"No time for strategies… I'm going to leave the car behind that parkland that backs onto the house, and we will go in on foot through the park." I had started the car and eased it out of the bus stop area by the time I finished speaking.

Nick continued to babble on about why Ben hadn't organised more officers and how foolhardy this whole exercise was with so few involved. I wasn't paying any attention to him. My mind was fully occupied with trying to work out what our best move would be once we were in the park. But I had something to do … and I was tired of Nick's ranting.

"Be quiet. I have to call someone." The number dialled for what seemed like a lifetime before anyone answered.

"Mitch, thank God you're there. I wasn't sure I'd be lucky enough for you to be in the lab. Do you have any members of your team available tonight?"

"Some of the day shift blokes are at home, but I'm the only one working in the lab. Why? What's the problem?"

"Your boss has been abducted, and I believe she is being held at an address on the north side of the city. It might be advisable to bring your team in and have them on standby. I'm sure you will have plenty to do before too long."

Everything seemed to happen at warp speed after we set off on foot through the park towards the house. I called Ben's phone and whispered, "In position." Within moments, an almighty ruckus broke out. Several shots were fired. Someone screamed. Then, light shone out through the back door and a group of people dived out through it and into the parkland. As I watched from my hidden vantage point, I realised there were three people in the group, and they struggled to make progress.

I caught my breath. One of them was Emily. She appeared to be bound by ropes at her wrists and ankles, and a rag was tied around her face… Probably a gag of some sort, I told myself as I focused on that rag. Two blokes, gripping her arms, half carried and half dragged her into the park. Although she was making it as difficult as possible for her captors, she wasn't having much success – except for slowing them down a little.

One of the men had run out of patience with her. He added a few choice words as he struck her across the face. Emily faltered and stumbled forward. The man who had struck her lost his grip on her and, in his hurry to grab hold of her again, he also stumbled but fell backwards away from Emily and her other captor.

"Show time," I hissed at Nick. "Standby for action."

Having regained his feet, the bloke who had stumbled rushed forward to grab hold of Emily again. I fired. He yelped and went down.

"Take the other one," I growled at Nick.

A second shot rang out. The second bloke fell to the ground.

"I'll take Emily…," I yelled to Nick. "You deal with the one you shot. Then go and help Ben."

After rummaging in my pocket for my Swiss army knife, I discovered the rope around her wrists didn't need to be cut. Similar to clothesline cord, it was not tied too intricately. With a bit of tugging and pulling, the knot came undone. After flexing her wrists a couple of times, Emily reached up and undid the gag while I untied the rope around her ankles. Her ankles were tied individually and then tied together loosely so she could still shuffle along.

Freed of all constraints at last, Emily leaned against a tree for a moment to recover. I wanted her away from there and safe. She was adamant she was staying to help. In the midst of the argument that ensued, the second bloke who had been holding her started to regain consciousness. When I shot him – not fatally – he had stumbled, fell and hit his head, knocking himself out cold. Now, he was coming to again, and it was obvious he was most unhappy about the way things had panned out.

Between us, Emily and I dragged him to his feet and over to a nearby large tree trunk. While Emily held him hard up against the trunk, I used Emily's ropes to lash him to it. Then, as a final touch, Emily tied her gag on him.

"Right, get out of here," I told her. "My car is on the other side of this little park. Here's the key. Take it and go home." I tried to give her the key, but she wouldn't take it.

"No. I have unfinished business here. You don't happen to have a spare weapon on you, do you? I have a few scores to settle." I shook my head – which was pretty pointless in the dark.

"I don't have a second weapon, and you don't like Glocks anyway. But… there is that one over there on the ground. One of your 'friends' must have dropped it."

"Ah, yes. I know how to use one of those," she said as she rushed to pick it up. Then, after checking the weapon, she demanded, "Right, Sonny, what do we do now?"

"Due to a lack of information about what's happening at the house, my thinking is for us to work our way around to the front of the place. Someone in there might suffer a rush of blood and try legging it out the front door."

The neighbouring house was in darkness. There had to be no one at home or, with all the noise coming from Zali's place, every light should have been switched on in that house by now. We worked our way across to and down the neighbour's yard, pausing to check out the situation next door before moving out of the neighbour's yard and into Zali's front yard.

"Look, Sonny," Emily yelped. "One of them is escaping."

A man heading for the street was illuminated in the dim glow of the street lights. Almost as a subconscious but automatic reaction, I raised the Glock and fired. We watched the figure go down before we scurried across to stand one on either side of Zali's front door. We were barely in position before I noticed a crouched figure coming across the front yard towards us. I swung around and pointed my weapon at the figure.

"Police… Don't shoot… Lower your weapon." The man's voice was familiar. "Brett…? Brett Galbraith, what's happening?" I demanded as the figure emerged from the darkness and started across the lawn.

Chapter 22

"Sonny… Thank Christ you didn't shoot, or I would be measuring my length on the grass. I knew Ben would go in anyway, even though he had no support. Give me a quick situation report."

By the time Brett finished speaking, a second officer had joined us. I gave Brett a quick overview of the situation as I knew it. Emily confirmed at least six people had been in the house, but there could have been more.

"We have neutralised three of them, so there are at least three or more still inside," I clarified for Brett.

"So, who is minding the rear of the property?"

"Just Ben and Nick."

"We need to mount a surprise from the rear, but we need Ben to keep them focused on him so we can surprise them from this side," Brett said as he eyed off the front door. "Not locked, I assume, if the body out there on the grass just came out through it."

"Probably not locked," I agreed. "When will you be ready to go in?"

"Now… The sooner, the better, I think," Brett growled.

I dragged my phone out of one of the pockets of my cargo pants and moved a few paces away from the door. I keyed Ben's number. Thank God mobile phones' screens light up even when the devices are set to vibrate only. A moment later, Ben answered in what was becoming his customary manner.

"What? We're a bit busy."

"Get a bit busier and keep them fully occupied for the next few moments," I growled at him.

"Sonny, don't…." I ended the call before he could finish whatever he was going to say.

Within a moment of ending my call, all hell broke loose at the rear of the house. Brett was already standing with his hand on the doorknob when it happened.

"Let's go," Brett hissed at the officer with him.

He shoved the door half open without a sound, and Brett and the officer rushed inside. Screams and shots came from inside the house. My phone vibrated: Ben.

"Are you inside?"

"No... out front."

"Then, who the hell is inside?"

"Brett Galbraith and a uniform."

"Jesus...." That was the last thing I heard before he ended the call, and the intensity of the firefight stepped up a notch.

About then, two vehicles eased up onto the driveway. I heaved a sigh of relief. They were police wagons. Two officers scrambled out of each vehicle and came towards us. Again, I was asked for a situation report. I reported two officers at the rear of the house and two inside, but I couldn't tell them more than that about the situation inside the house… except that, as I finished speaking, I noticed things seemed to have gone quiet. There was a lull in the shooting.

The uniform who appeared to be the most senior of the four officers who had arrived in the police wagons, dispatched two of the men to assist Ben at the rear of the house. The two remaining officers conversed for a couple of moments before rushing through the front door.

"What happens now?" Emily whispered.

"Call Mitch and tell him to mobilise his team. There's going to be a mountain of forensic work to do here." I gave Emily my phone. She walked away to make the call.

Then, the place came to life again. People in handcuffs were being shuffled out and into the waiting police wagons. Some were sporting bandages. Ben and Nick followed two uniforms who were escorting one prisoner to the wagons. I counted four prisoners removed from the house. Then, as the last of them was escorted out by the uniform who had arrived with Brett, I felt my pulse speed up. Where was Brett?

I was about to race through the front door to look for him when, brushing himself down, he emerged and gave me a grin.

"All clear," he called to Ben.

"We can all go home now," he said over his shoulder to me as he walked over to check on the loading of prisoners into the vans.

Ben walked over to Emily. After asking if she was okay, he suggested, "You might want to call your team and have them start going over this place." Emily just grinned and nodded by way of a reply.

"I'll be off now," I told Ben. "I'll be at home if you want me for anything."

"Where's your vehicle? Is it still parked at that bus stop?" Ben asked.

"No, it's on the other side of that park behind the house. Nick and I walked in through the park." *The park...* Oh, God... I had forgotten all about them. "Ben, we left a couple of members of that mob in the park," I said, jerking my head towards the police wagons.

"Argh... They've probably legged it by now."

"Uhmm... No, I don't think that's likely – or possible."

"A bit damaged, are they?" Ben said, adding a disgusted shake of his head for good measure, before calling for a couple of ambulances. "They will have to be transported under guard. Who do I have left here? I need two officers."

"Well, you have the officer who came with you... And there's Nick."

"Right... and while Nick is riding shotgun in one of the ambulances, who will be looking after you?"

"I don't need looking after, thanks, Ben."

"I'll vouch for that," Nick chimed in. "She's amazing and certainly doesn't need me minding her."

"Look, if you don't mind," Emily began, "while you sort your issues out, I think I might check with Mitch and the team and then head home."

"How are you getting home?" I asked. Emily nodded towards her car. "I don't think your car is available. It's now part of the evidence. I'll take you home. While you talk to your forensic team, I'll bring my car around to collect you."

"Sonny is right, Emily. It might be a day or so before you get your car back. Go and talk to your team, and then I will drive both of you around to where Sonny has parked her vehicle," Ben said. Then, turning to Nick, he continued, "When the ambulances arrive, you lead them through the park to those two blokes they need to collect. I'll arrange for someone to take you back to Sonny's place later."

"By the time I drop Emily off at her place, it might be a while before I am back at my place."

"No, Sonny, that's not how it's going to happen. You will take Emily home to your place with you. I need to interview you both, and I will be perfectly happy to do it at your place."

Emily went off to talk to Mitch and the rest of her team, and Brett sauntered up to talk to Ben. I was left alone and feeling a bit superfluous to needs. Damn it, I thought. Instead of standing around here, I could jog back through the park to collect my car and be back here by the time Emily is ready to leave. I started down the side of the house.

"Where the hell do you think you are going?" Ben bellowed after me. "Come back here. Just wait a few minutes until I sort things out here, and then I will drive you both around to your car."

"I could drive Sonny around to where her car is parked," Brett volunteered.

"That's not a bad idea. Thanks, Brett. Sonny, bring your car back here to collect Emily. Then the pair of you should go home to your place and stay there until I arrive… and stay alert. We don't know whether we have rounded up all of that mob tonight. If we haven't, it's possible you might have visitors later."

Nick sidled up to me and whispered, "Sorry, Sonny. I totally forgot about those two in the park." Despite Nick's attempt to keep his comment between us, Ben overheard him.

"Perhaps the pair of you might like to show Brett and me where you rescued Emily," Ben suggested.

The site was much as we left it. The first bloke was still out to it on the ground, while the bloke we tied to the tree didn't look to be in great condition either. Ben untied the gag and removed it… and did a double take. The bloke opened his eyes and glared up at Ben.

"Well, well… Christos, you don't appear to have had a great evening. Never mind, we'll take very good care of you from now on," Ben told the bloke still hugging the tree trunk.

"Christos…." I echoed as Nick and I exchanged a look.

"Yes, this is Christos… And we are going to be looking after him for a long time to come after tonight," Ben confirmed for both me and Christos.

It was the best part of an hour later before Ben joined Emily and me at my place. Nick was still guarding one of the patients in hospital while he waited for a uniform to arrive and take over. Of course, the first order of business was coffee and port, accompanied by thick slices of toasted olive bread slathered in butter. Then, with sustenance organised to sustain us through the next ordeal, it was down to the business of what happened to whom and when and where.

As expected, the key player in this episode was Emily. She delivered a blow-by-blow account of her side of the story.

"…Then, on my way back to the lab, I was run off the road and ended up half in a ditch off the side of the road. My car wasn't damaged. The other car didn't hit me, but in trying to avoid being hit, I ended up half in and half out of a drain running beside the road. I couldn't get myself back onto the road, so I called a towing company to pull me back onto the road."

"Did you have to wait long for them to arrive?" Ben asked.

"No, only a few minutes. They had a truck on its way back to the depot from another job, and it swung by to sort me out. We agreed my car seemed okay, and they left to head back to their depot. While everyone had agreed my car was okay, I needed to reassure myself, so I walked all around it to make sure before I drove off. It was while I was checking it out that a car pulled up. It was angled across in front of my car. Alarm bells started ringing, but there was nothing I could do. Four blokes got out of that other vehicle and strolled around to where I was. I tried telling them I was just checking something and that I was about to leave. They grabbed me, threw me onto the ground, tied me up, and shoved a hood over my head. Then they threw me into the boot of their car and drove off. I didn't know what was happening, but later on, I discovered someone had also driven my car to that house."

"What about after they took you to the house? What happened then?" Ben asked.

"I was kept bound and gagged in a small room with no windows. I suppose it was a storeroom or a boxroom, but there was nothing in it except a couple of bare shelves along one wall. I don't know how long I was there. They took my phone, and somewhere along the line, I lost my watch. During the time I was in that room, three blokes came at different times to check on me. Each of them opened the door slightly, peered inside, and then closed it again.

Later, I thought I heard a bit of fuss and bother happening outside. The next thing I knew was that I was being dragged out the back door and across the backyard. I was still gagged and bound, but the hood wasn't put back over my head. Because I could only shuffle along, I was slow. The two blokes trying to drag me through the park became angry about the slow pace. One of them suggested the other one should throw me over his shoulder. A bit of a debate broke out between them about it. That's when Sonny and Nick arrived. You probably know the rest."

"Emily, did they say anything to give you a clue about who they were or why they had targeted you?" I asked.

"The only thing was something I heard as I was being taken to be locked in that room. I heard someone shouting, 'Well, it must be somewhere'. Then, someone close to me snarled back, 'If you think of any more places to look, let me know'. They're the only snippets of conversation I could make out until they were trying to drag me through the park."

"Any ideas about the 'something' they were looking for, Ben?" I asked.

Ben shrugged and suggested, "Might the same 'something' they were looking for in Trina's handbag."

The place lapsed into silence for a while after that until Nick's arrival stirred things up again. After a couple of minutes of faffing about making Nick coffee and everyone settling down again in the lounge room, Emily started to say something and then stopped.

"Spit it out, Emily," Ben encouraged her. "Even if you think it's ridiculous, tell us about it."

"It's not that I think it might be ridiculous. It's just that I don't know all the finer details." Ben waved his hand to indicate Emily had the floor. "Okay, here goes. When I went to talk to Mitch before I left that house, he told me about something that happened at the forensics building this afternoon. We didn't have time to discuss it, but it seems there was an attempt to break into the forensics facility, and it was at around the same time as my drama on the roadside was happening. Two blokes tried to force their way in, but all the security gear did its job. Alarms went off everywhere, and the electronic locks flew shut. A scuffle broke out between the two security guards on duty and the two intruders. One security guard was injured and later went to hospital. The other guard discharged his weapon. It's believed he winged one of the intruders."

"Why would someone want to steal bits of dead people?" Nick asked. "There's nothing in the forensics building worth flogging off, so why would anyone want to break in?"

"Break-ins aren't always about stealing stuff to flog off later," Ben told him. "What there is in that building by the truckload is evidence… and not just 'bits of dead people' type evidence."

"You think whatever they were after had something to do with Trina's death?" Emily asked. "By the way, just so I get it right, are we now calling her Trina or Zali? Sonny, you seem to have settled on Zali as her name."

"She is still Trina, as far as I know," Ben replied and shot me a hard look.

"Uhmm… yes, but research over the last couple of days leans heavily towards Zali being her real name," I said, trying to avoid Ben's eyes although I could feel them boring into me.

"Look, I can't give you any more than that on the attempted break-in. That's all I got from Mitch. And, as my team is busy right now, I won't be attempting to quiz anyone about it until tomorrow at the earliest." With that, Emily marched over to the bottle of port to refill her glass.

Silence blanketed the room again until Nick sat up, stretched and groaned. "Does anyone intend going to bed tonight? I just thought I should check and find out where I might be expected to sleep for what's left of the night."

"Go home to your own bed, Nick. I'll stay here tonight," Ben announced. "Emily, you had better stay here as well."

"No, Ben. If it's all the same to you, I'm staying here tonight as well," Nick told him.

I almost went into a meltdown. Where the hell were we all supposed to sleep? Emily's quick thinking prevented it.

"Sonny, shall we retrieve the trundle from under Ben's bed and make it up?" she asked quite casually, while all I could think about was yet another set of bedclothes to wash.

Nick elected to give Emily a hand to retrieve the trundle and left her to make it up before going for a shower. Ben and I spent a few moments of blissful silence alone in the lounge room before a thought ended the peaceful moment for me.

"Do you expect further trouble again tonight?" I asked. It seemed a reasonable question, given he seemed happy to have everyone corralled in the same place tonight. "Do you think there are more of Christos' men still at large out there?"

"Dunno… Everything feels a bit too tidy at the moment. For me, it's a bit like waiting for the other shoe to drop. It might be a case of being over-cautious, but I'm happy to go with my gut on this one."

"Any ideas about what they might have been looking for at the forensics building today? I realise Zali didn't have whatever they wanted with her when she was killed, and it appears they didn't find it at her house either, or they wouldn't have tried to break into the forensics building."

"Sonny, I'm as much in the dark as you are on this one." I went to argue with him. But he held his hand up to stop me. "All right… I believe Zali knew something about that mob's operations that could have significant consequences for them. Now, whether she had evidence to support what she knew and that's what the mob were after, or what else it might be, remains a mystery to me."

"There's another possibility," I mused. "What if Zali did have something, but it wasn't a physical piece of evidence? What if she recorded something she knew, and the only physical evidence is that recording?"

"What, like a voice recording on her phone or a recorder of some sort?"

"Possible… But what if she transferred whatever she knew to some other medium altogether? What if she had incriminating photos? She might save and store those photos digitally somewhere safe and then delete them from the phone or camera she used to take them. Or, what if she had witnessed something to do with their operations and documented everything about it?"

Ben nodded slowly as he considered my comments before responding. "In your latter scenario, Zali might have created a 'report' of whatever she knew and saved that in digital form somewhere. I suppose that's possible, but it would have to be in the cloud or somewhere like that, and not just as a hidden file on her computer."

"Here's another 'what if' for you. What if Zali didn't know something first-hand, but someone gave her vital information?

There probably wouldn't be photos or any form of physical evidence, but she might have recorded in some way the story she was given."

"Ye-es… but again, it would be some form of record, either a digital voice recording of someone passing on information, or a written record of the information gained. But, we are still talking about it possibly being stored in the cloud … or, maybe, on a memory stick or something of that nature."

"All of this is sound thinking, but it comes with a truckload of questions, the main one being how to locate whatever 'it' is."

Our discussions took a different tack when Nick returned to the lounge room after his shower and Emily announced she was going for a shower and asked to borrow a Tee shirt and knickers to sleep in. About half an hour later, Ben and I were the only two people not in bed. A few minutes later, Ben said he also would have a shower and turn in for the night, and he asked if I were in a hurry to go to bed and wanted to shower first.

My mind was still working at warp speed after we discussed 'what if' scenarios. There was no point in my hurrying to bed. Sleep would be a long time coming tonight. Then Ben stuck his head around the corner and softly called 'goodnight' before he disappeared into his bedroom. I knew I would be functioning way below par tomorrow if I didn't go to bed soon. So, after a shower, I set various alarm systems, fetched my Glock from my bag, and took myself off to bed. At last, the house was silent tonight, and I envied Emily sound asleep on the trundle in the corner of my bedroom.

Sleep came sooner than expected but was short-lived. My eyes snapped open at a strange sound from somewhere outside. I reached out and rested my hand on my Glock on the bedside table. The little voice in my head told me to relax and suggested it couldn't be anything to worry about because none of the alarms had gone off. There was a moment of indecision. Should I listen to logic, or should I go and check everything was okay?

A blazing light ended the indecision. I was out of bed and on my way to check the security cameras to see what had triggered the security lights monitoring the front yard. I had barely set foot outside my bedroom when the intruder alarm howled its warning. I detoured into Ben's bedroom and went to shake him.

He was awake and whispered, "Where is it this time?"

"Back deck again… came up the driveway and activated the front lights before setting off everything out the back," I murmured economically.

When Ben sprang out of bed, he already held his firearm. Barefooted, we padded out into the hallway and almost collided with Nick sneaking along it with his weapon at the ready.

"Do you want to repeat last night's game plan?' he whispered.

I looked at Ben as I felt sure he would want to take charge. He nodded and asked what he and Nick should do. For a moment, I was completely wrong-footed. What was I supposed to do while the blokes were taking care of things? After giving Ben instructions on how things were to happen and telling them both to set their phones to vibration only, I headed for my office to monitor feed from the security cameras at various locations around the property.

"Shit… there's two of them," I hissed.

The camera picked up one intruder crouched behind the back deck, and another one over near the righthand fence who was inching his way towards the house. Suddenly, that second bloke broke into a gallop and would soon reach the house. I woke up my phone and keyed both Ben's and Nick's numbers.

"Incoming behind you, Nick. He's armed. Ben, one crouched down beside the stairs to the back deck."

Neither man replied, but I hadn't expected they would. I was so focused on monitoring the cameras, I jumped and let out a strangled yelp when a voice in the room beside me asked, "What's all the noise? What's happening."

"Nothing to worry about, Emily. I suggest you go back to bed," I told her, and I hoped I sounded convincing. I didn't feel it.

She chose to ignore my suggestion and flopped down on a chair across from me. That's when the sound of sirens racing along my street competed with the sound of my intruder alarm.

"No point in going back to bed with all that racket going on," Emily told me. "The whole neighbourhood will be wide awake now." She sounded a bit put out, and I don't suppose I could blame her.

Soon, my front yard was lit up again as a couple of police vehicles arrived. The cameras picked up a scuffle happening near the front corner of the house as police wrestled one of the intruders to the ground. Another camera picked a figure racing towards the street along the right side fence.

"Escapee along the northern boundary fence," I yelled into my phone. A shot rang out as I did so.

I watched the figure arch up, then stumble and fall. Then Nick was running towards the man on the ground. Others were there first. Three bodies in dark uniforms swarmed on the intruder, hauled him to his feet and dragged him to a police vehicle. A few moments later, two officers frogmarched the other intruder along the other side of the house and into another vehicle. Ben trailed them out and spoke to one of the officers before both police vehicles drove off.

Chapter 23

Having disarmed all the security systems to save the neighbours any further lost sleep, I opened the front door for Nick and Ben.

"What do we do now?" Emily asked as she joined us in the lounge room. "It's just a bit after three o'clock. Do we go back to bed or stay awake for the remainder of the night?"

"Another few hours sleep for me," Nick announced. "See you all in the morning."

"Me too," Emily added.

Again, Ben and I found ourselves alone in the lounge room. "I don't suppose you would refuse a single malt about now," I asked as I headed to the kitchen for glasses and ice cubes.

It didn't feel as though we had stayed up long after the other two returned to bed, but the sun seemed to make an appearance not long after I climbed back into bed.

"Good morning," Emily mumbled. "I suppose we have to go out to face the day. No doubt, Ben will want to hold a debriefing session this morning."

"So far, the rest of the household appears to be still asleep. You're right, though. When they finally surface, we should look as though we are firing on all four and ready to face the day." To emphasise my point, I swung my legs over the side of the bed and sat up.

Emily groaned as she did likewise. "I ache all over. All I want to do now is to go home, have a shower, and fall into bed for the rest of the morning."

The coffee machine was already doing its thing when Ben, followed closely by Nick, joined us in the kitchen. Emily took charge of the toaster while I dealt with the coffees – and the two men slumped at the kitchen table. Coffee and toast appeared to bring Ben to life, even if the rest of us remained like death warmed up.

Ben's debriefing session occurred as expected. As soon as it was over, he asked what my plans were for the day.

"Probably go into my city office sometime this morning after I take Emily home," I replied offhandedly, as I had no idea about what I might do today.

"I'll drop Emily wherever she wants to go… if you will be right to go in a few minutes, Emily," Ben volunteered.

"What about me?" Nick asked. "Am I back in uniform today, or am I still on special assignment."

"Argh, for God's sake, Ben, put him back in uniform," I snapped. "I don't need a babysitter and he is just going to be bored to tears."

"Okay… It seems you are relieved of special duties, Nick. Take the rest of today off, and we'll see you back at work tomorrow." Ben gave a satisfied nod as he finished speaking and then added, "Right, Emily, you have five minutes before we leave."

Nick was last to leave. I watched him all the way down the driveway before heaving a sigh of relief and going inside. I knew the hardest thing I had to do this morning was to overcome the temptation to go back and fall into bed.

It felt as though normalcy was returning as I drove myself into the city and let myself into my office.

Right, I'm here. Now, what am I going to do? I asked myself as I sat drumming my fingers on my desk. Everything you would normally do first thing in the morning, the little voice in my head counselled me. So, I did. After dealing with a couple of messages that had come in, I read my emails and sent off brochures and other information in response where necessary. But then, my usual admin tasks were complete, apart from making coffee and visiting the bakery for something to have with it. On a 'normal' day, I would start work on my current case. No current case meant today wasn't normal… but I could make coffee and visit the bakery.

Unable to decide what I wanted to have with my coffee, I returned from the bakery with a box of assorted sweet treats. While the coffee machine did its thing, I stood peering at the contents of the box. I had almost reached a decision when my phone played its tune.

"Where are you?" Ben demanded.

"My city office…."

"Right; I'll be there in about five minutes. A coffee would be good."

True to his word, it was only about five minutes later he banged on my door. He had no trouble deciding what he wanted to have with his coffee, and we were soon sitting at my desk with cakes and coffee.

"Is there a particular reason for your visit this morning," I asked a bit tentatively, as I wasn't entirely sure I wanted to know the reason.

"Well, yes. I thought you would want to know straight away. We've been applying pressure to Greta Lomax in a bid to get her to talk to us. It wasn't having much success until this morning. I observed a session with her yesterday. It was obvious to me she was too terrified to tell us anything. Given everything that happened last night and the number of bad guys we now have in custody, I thought it was worth another attempt today… after I had acquainted her with all that happened last night."

"With special emphasis on Christos's being in custody along with many, if not all, of his gang…?" I asked unnecessarily.

"Yeah, and it did the trick. It loosened her tongue no end. After Christos forced her – for whatever reason – to participate in a particularly nasty operation a couple of years ago, he has kept her on a leash ever since."

"What about her 'best friend', Zali? What did she have to say about what happened to her?"

"It all ties back to Zali's younger brother. Apparently, Xavier has spent the last few years overseas and somehow became involved with Christos' operations. Lomax thinks Xavier fell foul of the authorities overseas. His future looked bleak until

Christos stepped in, pulled some strings or whatever, and made it all go away."

"But, that left Xavier deeply indebted to Christos and Christos, being such a magnanimous person, allowed him to work off the debt. So, what was Xavier's role?"

"Xavier was a 'procurement officer'. He 'procured' young girls who, willingly or otherwise, were shipped to various other parts of the world, mostly to work as sex slaves."

"And Zali knew about this and condoned it? How could she not report it to the authorities?"

"Life is not so simple in that murky world of kidnap and people trafficking. Anyway, Lomax thinks that about six months ago, Xavier saw the light, experienced an epiphany or some other form of enlightenment and disappeared from Christos' radar. Christos' business suffered a major financial meltdown. With Xavier missing and uncontactable, no girls were acquired for shipment, and no drugs were coming into the country either."

"So, the well had dried up for Christos. I understand that, Ben, but how did Zali get involved?... Or, was she always involved?"

"Lomax thinks Xavier contacted his sister for help in some way to enable him to disappear. She doesn't know whether Zali did help him, but she thinks that as some token of good faith, Xavier passed on certain information to Zali. Somehow, Christos knew, or suspected, what had happened, and Zali became expendable. Lomax thinks the mob found Xavier and probably eliminated him before coming after Zali. Christos does not like loose ends that could come back to bite him." At that point, Ben decided he needed another cake and would probably need another coffee to wash it down.

My mind was anywhere but on the coffee as I made us both another cup. No wonder Zali was terrified when she visited my office. She would have known what was in store for her. A major question slammed in from left field as I carried the coffees back to my desk.

"Ben, why would Zali come to see me and not the police? What did she think I could do for her – or her brother?"

"Good question, but one I can't answer, not with any certainty anyway, but Lomax thinks increased pressure was applied to Zali for her to tell them Xavier's whereabouts. Regardless of whether she did or not, there was only one outcome for Zali. Lomax thinks it's possible Christos' mob discovered where Xavier was in hiding overseas and dealt with him sometime in the week leading up to Zali's death."

"Are you saying that, once Xavier was no longer a problem, they set about devising a plan to kill Zali here? It had to be well planned. It required too much precision timing to be successful. All right, I suppose I can sort of understand their perceived need to eliminate Zali, but what were they looking for in her handbag, her shopping, her house…? And, I suppose the other big question is, did they find it?" Ben gave me a long, hard look, but didn't reply for what seemed like an eternity.

"Uhmm… Yeah… Good question. Sonny, do you think it's possible Zali intended to give you something but chickened out or thought better of it at the last minute?"

"Like what? What might she pass on to me that she wouldn't give to the police?"

"As I wasn't here at the time, how the hell would I know if you don't have any clues? Tell me what happened while she was here. I've listened to the recording of her time with you, but I didn't see it. Give me a blow-by-blow description of how it went down, but focus on her physical behaviour and not so much on her words," Ben requested.

"Well, Ben, there wasn't anything about her physical performance worth reporting. It was on a par with her verbal performance. Together, they suggested to me she was terrified, and in the end, she decided she shouldn't have come to see me at all. She got up and left."

"Sonny, sit back in your chair and relax. Close your eyes and picture Trina here in your office." I did as he suggested but was sceptical of its outcome. "Right… Relax… Good. Now tell me where Trina was sitting while you spoke to her."

"She sat here at my desk, just like you are now."

"No, there are two chairs on this side of your desk. Which one did Trina use, and was it located then as it is now?"

"Yes, she sat in the same chair as you are sitting in now. Uhmm… but it was squared up with the desk and pulled in closer."

Ben pulled his chair around so it was square to my desk. "Like this…?" he asked.

"Not quite… Move it in closer as if you need it to be close enough to write on a pad on the desk." He dragged the chair closer. "Yep, that's how it was."

"Describe Trina coming to the desk and taking her seat here. Obviously, the chair wouldn't have been pulled in close like this?"

"After a few words to her when she came in, I realised the interview would be better conducted at my desk, rather than in my interview corner. So, I ushered her over to here and indicated for her to take a seat. She chose that chair you're sitting on and dragged it around to the same position as it is in now."

"Previously, you had commented on her handbag. Was that the same bag as later was handed to Lomax at the crime scene?" His shifting the focus from the chair to the handbag threw me for a moment.

I pictured the bag slung over Trina's shoulder when she first arrived at my office. "Yeah, it was the same bag, a brown leather, swanky, expensive number."

"You said the chair was positioned close enough for her to write on something on the desk. Did she pull out a notebook or something as though she might take notes?"

"It wasn't her intention to take notes. I just used that description to give you a clearer idea of how she was seated."

"What about that handbag?... What did she do with that when she sat down?"

"The handbag…. Let me think… Oh, yeah, as soon as she had positioned her chair like yours is now, she dropped the handbag onto the floor beside her chair."

"Did she take anything out of it, look in it, or do anything else with it before she put it on the floor?"

"Nah, not then… Later, I knew she was getting ready to bolt when she picked up the bag and sat it on her lap. I think she might have opened it then… Yeah, she opened the bag, dug around in it for a moment, and came out with a tissue in her hand. After that, I don't remember her opening the bag again. It just sat on her lap until she stood up and left."

"You never gained the impression she might give you something from that bag?" I shook my head.

Ben's question was almost laughable. "Trina wouldn't even take anything I tried to give her, let alone give me anything."

"Okay, so how did she sit?" I obviously looked confused, so he rushed to rephrase the question. "Did she sit back on her chair like this? Was she stiff and upright with her hands in her lap?"

"None of those. She leaned forward towards me. Her hands were on the desk. Towards the end of the interview, when she was becoming really agitated, she was running her hands along the edge of the desk."

"Sorry, I don't understand the bit about the edge of the desk."

I demonstrated. "Like this," I said, running my hands along the desk. "It was as though she was checking how smoothly the desktop had been finished."

"Like this…?" Ben asked, raising his eyebrows at me as he slid his hands along the desk.

"Yep, that's how I remember it… Although, for the life of me, I can't image why it might be an important detail. I…."

Suddenly, Ben froze. For a moment, he just sat there as though someone had hit his PAUSE button. Then, I watched him gingerly run his fingers along under the edge of the desk. I was about to ask what the hell he was doing, when he shoved his chair back and dropped to his knees. I was on my feet on the other side of the desk and jumped when his chair crashed to the floor. With my pulse racing and my breathing almost non-existent, I started to go around to the other side of the desk.

"Stay there... Don't move… Just give me a moment." Then, it was my turn to freeze.

Although I didn't know what Ben was doing, whatever was happening on the other side of my desk terrified me. As I stood there willing myself to breathe, I saw Ben's head slide up from below the desk. I couldn't read the look on his face. The suspense was killing me – literally, if I didn't get my pulse and breathing under control.

"How long do I have to wait to know what's going on?" I demanded in a voice that didn't sound like mine. I cleared my throat and tried again, this time without the croak. "Ben, talk to me."

Slowly, he eased himself up off his knees and carefully placed something on the desk. He fished in his pocket and brought out a Swiss Army knife. After pulling up the main blade, he took a couple of deep breaths.

The thing he had placed on the desk was a small parcel. It was wrapped in black plastic and with a length of black double-sided tape running along one side of it.

"My assumption is that you have never seen this before, am I right?" he asked.

"Never… where did you find it?" I demanded.

"We can talk about that later. Right now, I want you to leave this office. Go down and wait in your vehicle until I come down to you."

"Don't be ridiculous. I'm not going anywhere. If that thing is likely to go bang, it's not big enough to do much damage. And, if you really thought for one minute it might explode, you wouldn't have handled it. You would have simply called the appropriate team to come and deal with it. Now, instead of standing there wasting time, slit the plastic so we can see what's inside … Or, if you would prefer, I could come and do it."

Ben wiped his hands on his trousers, picked up the knife, and delicately slit through the length of the parcel. Nothing went bang… nothing else happened either, except the two of us stood motionless and with our eyes glued to the parcel. The tension got the better of me.

"Unwrap it, or at least open it up so we can see what's in it," I demanded. "There is nothing to be gained from the two of us standing here like statues. If you have a problem with revealing its contents, I'll do it."

"Right… Stand back…," Ben said as he eased the plastic back with the blade of the knife.

"Oh, for Christ's sake, get out of the way and let me do it," I said as I reached down and snatched up the parcel.

It was a fit of bravado that almost deserted me the moment I held the parcel. But, still nothing had gone bang, I told myself, and started easing the black plastic wrapping away from what felt like something small and hard inside.

"Safe as houses… It was never going to go bang or do anything else," I laughingly said as I held the parcel's contents out to Ben.

"A memory stick… Is that all that was in the parcel?

"That's all. I've only held it by the plastic, so I won't have stuffed up any fingerprints that were on the stick before it was unwrapped," I said.

He had been holding out his hand for me to give him the stick, but quickly withdrew it at my mention of fingerprints, opting instead to produce a plastic bag from one of his pockets.

"Drop it in here, thanks, Sonny. We'll get forensics to lift any prints on it. You don't feel like a drive around to Emily's office, do you?"

"I wasn't planning to go there. Anyway, why can't you drop it off on your way back to your office?"

"No vehicle… I walked here. So, do you think you might see your way clear to drive me and this stick to Emily's office and then drive me back to mine?"

"Huh… I don't suppose I have a lot of choice. The sooner someone lifts those prints, the sooner we might find out what Trina was so desperate to leave with me." I picked up my bag and, moments later, I keyed in the code to let us out the building's back door.

Emily wasn't in her office, but Mitch saw us and came to see if he could help. Ben stressed how urgent it was to be able to identify any fingerprints on the memory stick. Mitch laughed and said he would do it straight away while we waited. Emily returned and came in search of us while we waited outside Mitch's part of the lab.

"Should I be anxious about this unscheduled visit?" she quipped as she joined us. I let Ben explain our presence.

"Let's go and see how Mitch is getting on with the stick," Emily suggested. We followed her into the lab.

"I just asked the computer for a match," Mitch said as we marched in. "Of course, there's always a chance they won't appear on any database, and they might not be much help to you."

Mitch was right. There was no match for the prints, but I thought there would be a match, but with prints not yet on any database.

"There is something else you might check, please, Mitch. Check them against the prints of the woman run down on the street in front of my office building," I suggested.

"You think they are Trina's?" Emily asked.

"Well, I'm reasonably sure some of them will match hers, but I'm curious about whether there are any others on there as well."

A few moments later, Mitch cleared his throat and looked a bit sheepish. "There is a match with the dead woman's prints. We were waiting to see if there was a definite identification before we put them up on the database… But they are not all her prints. Others that I haven't matched are on the stick as well. There is a fair bit of 'layering' of the prints. Some of the unidentified prints are partially obscured by the dead woman's prints over them."

"Well, that gives us something else to speculate about now, doesn't it?" I suggested to Ben. "Who is your best bet for the owner of those rogue prints?"

"I'll let you know when I think of someone."

He didn't sound too pleased, so I didn't mention them again. About five minutes later, I was driving him back to his office, after first having established there would be three for dinner. As I dropped him at the police precinct, I thought I might do my good deed for the day.

"As I don't have much else to do in my office, I thought I might leave early and cook something for tonight's dinner. Does that fit okay with your plans?" I asked almost as an afterthought.

After buying a salad for lunch, the first thing I did when I returned to my office was to check every inch of my desk for any other hidden 'surprises'. Although I found none, this morning's surprise package left me unsettled for the rest of the day. For a few minutes, a couple of enquiries helped take my mind off what that memory stick might contain, but I left the office early to go home via the supermarket.

Soon after six o'clock, my next surprise of the day was Nick's arrival. He looked well-rested after his day off. I felt the red mist start to descend.

"Has Ben reinstated your special assignment and put you back on childminding duties?"

"What? Oh, no. No, I think I left a notebook in your office. Well, I hope I did, or I've lost it somewhere."

"Come through, and let's see if we can find it."

"By the way, apologies for arriving unannounced like this, but I wanted to come early so as not to interrupt your dinner with whoever might be eating here tonight. Hope you have a bit quieter night than your last couple."

"It should be, and Ben assures me it will be. Is that book over there the one you are looking for?" He grabbed it and clasped it to his chest as though it was the world's greatest treasure.

"It contains all my notes and a rough draft of the thing I have to submit by the end of the week," he said, waving the book at me. "I was just about ready to go into meltdown when it wasn't in my bag this afternoon."

"Now you're here, would you like to share a drink with me?… To help settle your nerves after thinking you had lost your book – and by way of thanks for the last few days."

We took long glasses of iced tea out onto the back deck. I again took the opportunity to thank him for what must have been a tumultuous few days for him.

"Don't apologise. You can't imagine how much I gained from my time on that assignment. I experienced situations I might never have experienced in my entire career if I hadn't been given that assignment. It also helped me focus on what I want my future to look like."

Chapter 24

"I hope you're not going to tell me you're abandoning the police service in favour of something safer and less demanding. I really would feel guilty if that were the case."

"No fear of that. I'm going to see if I can be accepted onto the 'fast track to detective' program the service has running. That's what I want to be. I looked up a few things today and discovered that, as a forensic psychologist, working as a detective will give me the best of both worlds."

"Any precinct you're posted to will score very well indeed. By the way, now you're here, would you care to join us for dinner this evening?"

"If that beautiful smell is coming from what's on tonight's menu, yes, please. I was going to have either fish and chips or avocado on toast."

Ben arrived earlier than usual and Emily came a few minutes later. It felt wonderful for the four of us just to sit and have a quiet, relaxed drink before getting stuck into a roast dinner. Nevertheless, we stuck to our well-established tradition of no 'shop' talk until after dinner. As soon as we had eaten and cleared the table, I was dishing up bowls of fruit salad when Nick sidled up to me.

"Thanks, Sonny, but don't do one of those for me. I really should go. I've intruded long enough… and I'm sure you and Ben have things to discuss."

"Nonsense… we wouldn't be discussing anything you shouldn't know about," I replied. Ben heard me and came to investigate.

"What's the problem here?" he demanded.

"Nick doesn't want dessert because he says he is going home?" I answered to save Nick having to, but I didn't manage to save him.

"Going home…?" Ben echoed. "Why? Have we upset you, or do you find our company boring when there is no other action happening?" I watched Nick squirm at Ben's comments.

"Don't be mean to him," I admonished Ben. "He's trying to do the right thing and not intrude in his boss's private life. He's concerned we might want to discuss things he's not entitled to hear."

"Oh, I see. In that case, here's your dessert," Ben said as he handed Nick one of the bowls of fruit salad I had already dished out. "I don't think Sonny has anything personal or top secret she wants to discuss, and if she does, she will soon send you all packing so she can get on with it. Now, go and find yourself a seat in the lounge… and not that one," Ben added, pointing to his favourite chair. "It's mine."

That's when the 'shop talk' began. Emily initiated by asking about the memory stick Mitch had lifted the fingerprints from. At that point, I suspected there was no chance of an early night, and I hoped Nick didn't have anything important he wanted to take care of tonight. But, I thought I might be proved wrong when Ben's phone demanded his attention.

"Argh, no, not tonight," Emily cried. "I'm on call tonight, and I'd like a quiet one, thanks."

I'm sure we all expected the call would be about some major crime in Millhaven that would keep Ben and probably Emily, too, occupied for most of the night. I watched Ben drag his phone out of his pocket and check the caller ID. I heard him murmur *Neil* as he strode out onto the back deck to answer the call.

As Ben strode out to the back deck, Emily and I exchanged a look. Nick saw it and realised he was odd-man-out when it came to knowing what it was about. He raised his eyebrows in question at us.

"Neil…?" he asked. "What's that all about? Judging by the way you pair reacted, I'm guessing it isn't just a call from a mate."

"You're right, Nick. Neil is Ben's brother, who just happens to be one of the big brass in the Federal Police. It could be Neil has something he wants to share with Ben, but it is more likely Ben wants to talk to him about the Zali Standish case."

"Has something new developed since last night? If he is chasing more information on Zali and her family, Ben could contact his opposite number in the New South Wales police service. Why does he need to involve the Feds in this?"

"Uhmm… there was a development of sorts this morning. I can't tell you too much about it. I hoped it would be the main topic of conversation tonight so I would learn more about it," I told Nick. "But, I can give you some background on what happened and what I think that call might be about."

My report on this morning's 'find' in my office took up the next few minutes. Emily helped out with some of the details and, by the time we had shared all we knew, Nick was sitting slack-jawed and staring at us.

"She didn't even tell you about it… just secretly hid it under your desk? Why would she do that? Why didn't she take it to us – the police?"

I was about to try formulating an answer that might satisfy Nick when I realised there was a better way to handle his confusion.

"Nick, you're the psychologist…."

"Not quite yet… Sorry, what were you going to say?"

"You're the psychologist. What does your training tell you about Zali's actions? Why might she think I was her best option? Remember, I thought she looked terrified when she came to see me."

"Oh, yeah…Hmm, she was killed only a couple of hours or so after she left your office. So, maybe somehow, she knew her future looked a bit bleak. No, more than that… Maybe she knew whatever was going to happen was imminent. But how would she know that? I mean, how would she know with any degree of certainty?" Nick, who had stared off into the distance as he considered Zali's actions, now looked from Emily to me.

"Good; yes, I agree she probably knew her days were numbered," I confirmed.

"There is one thing that bothers me about that," Nick, deep in thought, said. "Why go shopping if you think you're about to die? The stuff from the bakery doesn't interest me so much as her purchases at *Bianca's*. It's unlikely she would buy new clothes or jewellery if she knew she would be dead before she could wear them."

"Right... I don't think we have any argument with your analysis of the situation so far. Do we, Emily?" Emily shook her head and held her hands out, palms up, to indicate she had nothing to offer. I continued, "So, Nick, why might Ben consider it necessary to talk to the Feds and not one of the other states' police services?"

"Perhaps, if the investigation was going to involve a number of states... or needed to look overseas. There was something about her brother being overseas, wasn't there? Was what happened to Zali a result of something the brother did – or didn't do?"

Ben strolled back in before I had a chance to answer Nick's last question... And saved me from having to admit I didn't have a clue. I searched Ben's face for any clues about how his conversation with his brother had gone but found nothing helpful there. The hope was that, as soon as Ben had reunited with his favourite chair, he would tell us what had transpired during the phone call. But, he seemed oblivious to the fact all eyes were on him and casually drained his glass of port before announcing he might help himself to another.

Emily sprang out of her chair. "I'll get it for you," she said as she grabbed his empty glass.

Then, on her way past me to refill his glass, she directed an almost imperceptible jerk of her head in Ben's direction. It was meant as an encouragement for me to initiate a conversation about what Ben and Neil had discussed. Bugger! It could be difficult, but I did want to know. So, I plastered on my sweetest smile and set forth.

"How is Neil? I haven't heard anything about him for a while. Is he still with the Feds?"

"Yeah, they'll have to carry him out in a box to get rid of him. I thought it might be worthwhile having a chat with him about our current case. I'll send him some stuff tomorrow and see what he makes of it." Ben didn't look as though he was going to say anymore, so I encouraged him.

"What sort of stuff are you sending him? Do you need any of those recordings of mine or their transcripts? I don't think I have anything else that might be of interest to him. Do we need to look for anything else to send?"

"Nah, I think I have all I need for the moment. I'll send him copies of your transcripts, the fingerprints we lifted today, and the files on that memory stick. There's nothing else he needs to start his investigation. I want him to focus on Xavier Standish (or whatever name he goes by now) so we have some current intel on where he is and what he is up to if...."

When Ben didn't finish the sentence, I thought I'd help him out and finish it for him. "...*if he is still alive*. Is that what you were going to say? Ben, what was on that memory stick, and when am I going to see it?"

"You won't be seeing it, I'm afraid. The material on the stick will not go outside the investigation. All I will say is that the stick appears to have been created by someone overseas and that it took a while to reach Zali."

"So, Xavier, Zali's brother, sent her the stick?"

"We don't know that. Perhaps, after Neil's men look into it, we might know something definite. At this stage, it's as well not to speculate too much. Suffice to say, the investigation will now be centred away from Millhaven."

I know when I'm beaten, and the tone of Ben's voice warned me against any further probing. There were a million questions I wanted to ask, but I knew better than to do so... And I also knew one quick look at the contents of that memory stick would answer most of them. I settled for one last risky throw-away line before I let the matter drop.

"Little enough material was gathered locally throughout our investigation. It will not give Neil's team an easy starting point for their investigation."

The only response from Ben was a sly smile, but it was enough to tell me he knew a lot more than he had shared with me. But Ben's phone played its tune, and this time, he did have to go. About a minute later, Emily's phone did likewise. At the end of her brief call, She gave us a wry smile, picked up her bag, and left.

"It's probably time I wasn't here as well," Nick said as we watched Emily let herself out the front door. "Will you be all right here on your own if I also leave?"

"Of course, I'll be all right... But, if you could hang around for another couple of minutes, there's something I want to run past you."

Nick sat down again and said, "Fire away."

"Don't feel pressured in any way by what I'm about to say. Please remember you are under no obligation even to hear me out." Again, he told me to 'fire away'. "Okay, I have a few thoughts about that memory stick, mainly about how Zali came to have it. If the material on it is such that Ben won't even let me see it, I'm intrigued by how it managed to arrive safely in Millhaven and ended up in the possession of its intended recipient."

"Are you questioning whether Zali was the intended recipient or someone who, by whatever means, managed to get hold of it?"

"Good question.... But, no, I don't think Zali had it by chance. In that case, how did it arrive safely? The mob we are dealing with in this investigation, the mob that had her killed, would stop at nothing to protect themselves and their operations."

"If they knew the memory stick existed, and if they knew the stick was destined for Zali," Nick added. "So, Sonny, what devious plan have you hatched, and what is my role in it?"

"I want to find the box or the wrapping paper the stick was in when it arrived in Millhaven."

"Wasn't that the plastic it was wrapped in when it was found under your desk? The plastic Ben cut through to expose it."

"No. It was wrapped in that black plastic specifically for its final destination, my desk. I'm not sure why I think that, or how it might have been achieved, but I suspect that stick took a long and meandering route to Millhaven."

"Right… So, how do we find out more about that? Sonny, you've lost me a bit on this one. Try explaining what your thinking is so I can try to understand what's possible."

"Okay, I'll try, but I'm not sure even I understand what my thinking is yet. Here goes. Sending something as small as that memory stick from, say, somewhere in Europe requires it to be packed in such a way as to create a parcel big enough not to get lost along the way. It might have been surrounded by loads of packing material and placed in a smallish box or some other container."

"Yeah, I go along with that idea, but what's this 'meandering route' thing that you mentioned?"

"Instinct suggests that, if I had something small that contained significant information that others would want to destroy, I wouldn't simply address it to the final recipient. I might send it to someone in another city. When they opened it, they would find a note telling them to remove the outer wrapping and send the parcel to the address then shown on what's left of the parcel. That first recipient complies and sends it on to another country (England perhaps), where the recipient then goes through the same procedure. There might be a few or many iterations of that process before the package finally arrives at its intended final destination."

"Oh, that is clever. It's a bit like a dangerous game of *Pass the Parcel*, with the parcel to be passed on to the address on the next layer of wrapping."

"Good analogue… And, when the final recipient unwraps the parcel, she finds a package gift wrapped as a birthday or Christmas present."

"The thrill of the chase has a hold on me. What are we going to do, and how soon do we start?"

I eyed Nick cautiously. He oozed excitement. For a moment, I wondered whether his enthusiasm was a good thing or if it could prove a liability. But I understood how he felt. The thrill of the chase was something I was familiar with, and it was something I was experiencing right now. But, how to go about proving my theory? A wild thought slammed in from nowhere.

"Nick, I think we need to go over Zali's house with a proverbial fine toothcomb."

"What do you hope to find? And, are we likely to find anything? After all, the cops and the forensic guys have been all over that place." I saw Nick's earlier excitement slipping away.

"Here's something to think about, Nick. The cops didn't know what they were looking for when they and the forensic team went over the place."

"Do you know what we might be looking for? I admit I don't. And, why do you think we might find whatever it is when they didn't?"

Yep, he was definitely losing interest, I told myself, and I needed to reignite his enthusiasm. "I'll tell you something that might be handy to remember if you become a detective. People involved in a search look for what they expect to find. They have possible targets in mind. We don't know what we will be looking for or where we might find it. That can result in a significant difference in the outcome.

There is one other problem we haven't discussed and it might be insurmountable: how do we access Zali's house? After last night's raid on the place, I'm confident your mob will have it sealed off as a significant crime scene."

"Hmm… That's true. We won't be able just to drive up and let ourselves in. Do we need Ben onside for this exercise?"

"God, no. The last thing we want is for Ben to know about it. If he finds out about it, we will both probably be strung up. No, the first thing we need to know is whether it is being guarded around the clock or not."

"Not a problem, I can do that. When do you think we might action this plan – if it's possible at all?"

"The sooner, the better. Tomorrow would be good, but you will be at work. I'll have to think about when to do it after we find out whether it's possible or not."

"Well, here's my suggestion for what it's worth. I will go now. On my way home, I'll call at the precinct to check whether Zali's house will be guarded tomorrow. If it's not, we'll go in tomorrow morning… Say, sometime after nine o'clock when most people on that street will have gone to work. How's that sound?"

"How are you going to be involved if you are supposed to be at work? Or are you planning not to be involved?" Nick gave me a wicked grin in response to my question.

"I've taken a few days off – to study and recover from last night. So, should we tentatively plan for tomorrow?"

"Nick, you don't seem as though you need time off. Why are you taking leave?"

"This case is a long way from wrapped up… And I wanted to be available and involved in whatever your next moves are."

What I wouldn't give for a full night of sound sleep…. After Nick left last night, I knew sleep would be a long time coming, and it was. I suppose the frisson of excitement running up and down my spine didn't help, but my mind was working at warp speed as I tried to put together some semblance of a plan for what we might do if Nick found that Zali's house was not being kept under guard.

We didn't arrange how or when he would let me know about the house, and I think I slept with one ear on my phone all night. "Damn! It's already nine o'clock, and he still hasn't contacted me," I told the universe.

Should I call Nick? Maybe he's waiting for me to contact him… No, I can't do that. What if my call compromises him in some way? This is what comes of working alone. You never have to rely on anyone else. You just get on with the job on your own and in your own time.

After having become increasingly frustrated as I sat dawdling over my second mug of coffee after breakfast, I wandered into my office. "Why am I in here?" I asked the empty office. It was a valid question. I had nothing to do – nothing I could do to progress my investigation. I flopped down behind my desk and absentmindedly flipped open my Trina Blewett file. There was nothing in it I hadn't already read at least three times, but what else did I have to do? The answer arrived a couple of moments later.

"Sonny, Zali's house is not being guarded, but it is locked. The keys were logged, but I couldn't find them anywhere. Maybe they are in Ben's office. Sorry, but it looks like we have to shelve our plan." Nick sounded so upset and apologetic, I felt for the lad.

"Nonsense, Nick. That's really good news. Now, when suits you for us to kick this thing off, and how do you want to play it?

"You're going ahead with it! Maybe you should tell me how it's going to happen, because I don't have a clue."

"Are you at home now?" Nick confirmed he was. "Okay, kick-off is in half an hour. Do you want me to collect you on my way over to the north side?" It suited me to have only one car close to the site, so I was pleased when he agreed to my suggestion.

I parked where I had parked two nights ago, next to the little park at the back of Zali's house. After entering the street from the northern end, I drove the length of it to check for any activity in the street that might prove a problem. There wasn't a person or vehicle moving anywhere along the length of it, so I drove out of the street and around to the rear of the park.

"Now, how does this next bit play out?" Nick asked as we set out through the park on foot.

"Follow me, but stay close. You won't need to do anything until we are in the house."

"How is that going to happen? I still don't have the keys… And I would prefer we didn't batter down the door."

"Nothing so uncouth will be required. All you have to do, Nick, is to trust the expert in such matters – me – and look the other way when you are told to do so. In the meantime, keep your eyes and ears peeled for anything out of the ordinary or unexpected."

We aimed for a nonchalant stroll across the park, only stepping up our pace through the final strip of bush before we reached that house. No dogs barked… No one yelled at us… Nothing delayed us, and we were soon at Zali's back door. Police tape across the doorway stirred gently in the light breeze. I checked the lock.

"Good," I murmured, more to myself than Nick, and then I was ready to go to work. "Right, Nick, now you need to turn around and keep an eye on the backyard and the parkland for anyone who might be interested in us."

He turned his back to me but couldn't help himself. He had to ask what I was doing.

"Just do as you were told and keep watch," I hissed at him.

"Yeah, but what do we do now we are here? How are we supposed to get inside?"

"Through this door… Are you coming inside, or would you prefer to stay out here to keep watch?"

"What?" he demanded as he spun around again. "How did you open it?"

"That's for me to know and you to wonder about. Now, stop wasting time and come inside so I can shut this door."

Chapter 25

Nick looked as nervous as a kitten when I turned back to him after shutting the door. "Our first job is to check the layout of the place. There are bound to be places we need to search and others we might search as a last resort."

With Nick following close behind, I set off along a hallway running between two bedrooms. A smaller third bedroom (possibly originally intended as a nursery) had been used as an office. We passed a bathroom area and a small laundry before exiting the hallway into a combined kitchen and dining room. Through an archway at the northern end of the dining room was a lounge room and a small entrance area inside the front door.

"It's not a big place," Nick commented as he continued to follow me around. "What are we looking for, and where do we start?" he asked.

"Let's start with that office," I said as I led him back to the small room. "It's not a big space, but don't let that fool you. If you look around, you'll see it was set up with plenty of storage space.'

"I'm sure the cops would have turned over everything in here. I doubt we will find anything," Nick whined.

After checking the wastepaper bin, I started on the desk. "Nick, you check the drawers on that end of the desk. I'll deal with the ones on this side." He yanked the top drawer about half open and scratched around in it."

"No, nothing in this one except pens and pencils, clips, scissors, adhesive tape, and a broken ruler."

"Well, there might be, but you won't know for sure if you don't take the drawer right out of the desk and check through it thoroughly."

As an example of what I meant for him to do, I indicated the drawer I had taken out of my side of the desk and that now lay on the desktop. Although I returned my attention to my drawer, I watched Nick out of the corner of my eye. He went through the contents of the drawer thoroughly and then went to insert back into the desk.

"No… You need to check the drawer itself, underneath it and around all the sides, before putting it back where it belongs."

Reasonably confident he now knew what was required, I let him get on with it while I worked through my side of the room. Apart from the occasional grunt, we worked in silence. After the small room, we attacked the kitchen and dining area. Again, I had to remind Nick to check under the seats of all the chairs. We had still come up empty by the time we moved to the lounge room. It was sparsely furnished with an ancient plush lounge suite, a reasonably new TV set on a small TV unit, a side table beside one of the chairs, a floor lamp, and a fairly well-stocked bookcase along one wall. I allocated the rest of the room to Nick while I concentrated on the bookshelf and its contents. At the end of our search of the lounge room, we were still empty-handed. I sent Nick to start on what appeared to be the spare bedroom while I tackled the main bedroom.

Reasonably contemporary bedside cupboards accompanied an older style bedroom suite, and there was a cheap rug on the floor on one side of the bed. As with the other room, everything was clean and tidy. The bedhead was a hutch-like arrangement that held a couple of trinkets, a dogeared novel with a bookmark sticking out of it, a small packet of tissues, and a reading light was precariously clipped to the top of it.

While, like the rest of the house, there wasn't much to search, somehow, I felt this room might yield results. Ten minutes later, I let out a quiet yelp and called Nick. When he joined me in the bedroom, I pointed to the book, now back in its place on the shelf in the bedhead. After photographing everything *in situ*, I picked up the book and opened it to show Nick the small cavity carved out of the pages.

"Just big enough to hold a memory stick," I quipped as he stared at the book.

"What do we do now?" Nick gasped as he continued to stare at the book. "Do we call Ben to tell him what we have found?"

"Christ, no… This has to be handled much more deviously than that. And, just so you know how it will play out, you know nothing about this book, this house, or our visit here. That's how it must be."

"So, what happens next? Do we go home now?"

"No, there's one more thing I want to explore."

"Okay, but I think we've explored every inch of this place."

"What did you notice about the bins in the various rooms when we checked them?"

"There wasn't much in any of them – and for which I was most grateful. I might have baulked at the kitchen bin if it had more in it. Come on, what have the bins got to do with anything?"

"I don't know when rubbish collection day is in this part of the city, but I'm hoping the rubbish was collected just before Zali received that book. According to Lomax, Zali had not been herself for a couple of days before she came to see me. If my hunch is right, that was after she received that book. If that was only two or three days before she was killed, and there is nothing much in any of her bins now, there could be something interesting still in her wheelie bins. Shall we look?"

We found one bin under a tree a little way off the side of the house. A couple of plastic bags of rubbish were in the bottom of it. I stood back from the bin and looked around.

"What now? What….?" Nick demanded.

"This is the general waste bin. Where is her recycle bin? I expected them to be here together."

"Ah… Earlier, I noticed the recycle bin parked beside the wall of the garage. Maybe she chose to keep kitchen waste, which can be a bit smelly by the end of the week, well away from the house."

"Sometimes we are lucky. Let's hope our luck holds and we find what I'm looking for in the recycle bin. If we don't, and in the interests of thoroughness, we will have to go through the contents of those bags of rubbish in the general waste bin."

"Whoo-hoo…," I chirped in nothing much above a whisper as I reached in and pulled out the top layer of material. "There it is, Nick. The missing piece of the puzzle."

Carefully, I spread out on the grass a couple of sheets of sturdy brown paper. The address and postmarks remained clear on one sheet. Of most interest was the clear shape left by the object it had been wrapped tightly around.

"This was wrapped around that book we found in the bedroom," I told Nick as I pointed out the still visible creasing.

"How does that help us, Sonny? All it tells us is that 'a book' – not necessarily 'that book' – addressed to Trina Blewett was wrapped in this paper. Although it gives this address, it doesn't even mention Zali. Is that a New Zealand postmark on it?"

"Good point… but look at what else I removed from the bin, Nick," I said as I eased open and flattened out a balled-up piece of brightly coloured gift wrapping paper. The paper screamed *Happy Birthday* all over it and, as I unravelled it, two lengths of bright ribbon and a couple of other things fluttered down onto the grass. I picked up and threw the ribbon over on top of the brown paper before picking up the other objects.

One was a small birthday card that had Zali's name on it. The other object was a sheet torn from a notepad. It had been folded in half and then screwed up tightly. I eased it open and ran my gloved hand across it to flatten it out. It was a handwritten note, and its message was clearly meant for Zali. Brief, it urged Zali to remember the Trina Blewett connection from their teenage years. The remainder of the note, although concise, told me all I needed to know: *Although I hate burdening you with this, keep it safe and use it as you see fit. Stay safe and make a good life for yourself.*

The note was signed with a single letter: *X*. Of course, it could be assumed that the writer had simply signed the note with a kiss, but I believed it was more significant and would have meant the world to Zali. I believed the X stood for Xavier.

"Right, Nick, now we have everything we came for, we can go home," I whispered. "I'll just close up again, and then we can be off."

As I drove him back to his place, we discussed our morning's outing and its outcome. I noticed something subdued about Nick. I decided to wait to see if an explanation might be forthcoming. It wasn't, and we were almost at his place. It was time to ask some questions. It meant that, after I parked on his driveway, we spent a while sitting out front in my car as the discussion continued.

"Come on, Nick, what's bothering you? Did I say or do something to upset you? …Or, perhaps it was everything about this morning's operation that concerns you?"

"No… Well, yes… No, I'm not being critical, not of you, anyway. This morning has been an eye-opener for me, a major learning experience. You knew exactly what you were doing. Why you were there and what you were looking for. I didn't have a clue. I guess it showed me just how much I don't know about how to look for evidence – how to investigate a crime. I had this grand ambition to become a detective, and now I see how ridiculous such an idea is."

"You sell yourself short, Nick. No one knows how to be a detective until they *learn* how to investigate a crime. It's a bit like becoming a baker or a motor mechanic. You don't know how to bake bread or service a car until someone teaches you how to do it. Investigating a crime is no different. Becoming a detective involves learning what you need to know to do the job."

"I know you've been a private investigator for some time, but it seems to me you know instinctively what to do, where to look, and for what. You can't teach someone instinct. It's an inherent characteristic. Hey, I'm the psychologist, remember? I know about these things… And I also know I haven't a clue about how to go about investigating a crime scene."

"Perhaps I do operate by instinct to some degree, but that instinct – if that's what it is – was acquired through training and constant application of that training. And that's exactly how it is for coppers when they have the chance to become detectives. Stop beating yourself up. You will be fine as a detective and better than that, given your psychology training. Look, I know that from a copper's perspective, just about everything we did this morning was not aboveboard – not strictly legal. I understand that might now bother you. In hindsight, perhaps it was unfair of me to involve you."

"Christ, don't think that. Even if you hadn't involved me, if I knew what you were going to do, I would have been there with you whether you liked it or not. I'm grateful for this morning… Even if I haven't given you that impression. My problem lies with the realisation of how inexperienced I am and how little I know. There is one thing, though. I would like to know how you're going to play this with Ben."

"Ah, well, I can sum that up in two words: *carefully* and *deviously*. Oh, he will not be impressed with my actions this morning, but if I manage the next stage carefully, what we discovered this morning will allow him to overlook how it came to be found. My advice to you – and I mean this quite seriously – is not to give any hints to anyone that you knew about it, let alone that you were involved."

At last, Nick seemed reassured and scrambled out of the car, and I was on my way home… And wondering what 'carefully' and 'deviously' meant in terms of telling Ben about this morning.

As it turned out, I had plenty of time to think about it. I didn't see Ben for the next two evenings as a result of a new crime spree that erupted in Millhaven. But, the prospect of the evidence I found being left at the crime scene for too long bothered me. Two days after I found it, and ignoring 'carefully and deviously', I sent Ben the photos I'd taken of the evidence at Zali's house.

They scored me an immediate reply: *see you at your office in 15*. Oh, well, it had to happen sometime.

The fallout from my trawl through Zali's house for evidence was relatively mild and short-lived. Perhaps the fact that it cemented Ben's case against Christos and his mob was an important factor in that.

It was a bit over a week later before I was aware of any further developments in the investigation into Zali's death. It happened when Ben arrived unannounced at my city office one morning at about coffee time. I was on edge from the moment Ben opted to sit at my desk with our coffee and cake, rather than settling ourselves in my interview corner. Half my mug of coffee had been dispatched before he revealed the reason for his visit.

"Neil called me last night and sent through a whole heap of stuff this morning. He has been working with Interpol and whoever else overseas to learn more about Xavier Standish. To cut a long story short, we now know both of the Standish offspring are dead. Xavier's story is interesting – and colourful, I suppose, depending on your point of view."

"Are the Standish parents aware of what has happened? I suppose I should have asked if they are still around to be told about their offspring." I said as sympathy for them flooded through me.

"Yeah, Neil's team had the honour of sharing the news with them. It appears the consensus is that Xavier's death, while tragic and sad, wasn't exactly unexpected. Although they would not elaborate, it's believed they were aware Xavier had turned to the dark side of life some time ago. On the other hand, Zali's brutal death knocked them about a bit. It seems she was the apple of her father's eye, and she had always been close to her mother. They became worried and suspected something was wrong when they hadn't heard from Zali in the week leading up to her death."

"Ben, that memory stick Xavier sent to Zali – and more precisely, its contents – do we know why he did that? Okay, I get it that he knew he might not be around for too much longer, but what was the intent behind sending that stuff to Zali? What was she supposed to do with it?"

"That's the part of the story that remains a bit sketchy. As far as everyone can make out, Xavier had some sort of epiphany. Whatever it was, it appears to have made him reassess his life and make a sharp detour along another track.

What's been established so far is that Xavier had developed a strong relationship with a Croatian family and their young daughter. There is no evidence that the girl or her family were part of the world Xavier previously had inhabited. But, because of their connection with Xavier, they encountered that world through a tragic event. At some point, the fourteen year old daughter and her mate, as teenagers often do, were thumbing their noses at the traditional Croatian way of life for young girls. They were sneaking out and kicking up their heels at night. And on one such night, the two girls were abducted by Xavier's cronies from his previous life.

Somehow, soon after they were abducted, the girl Xavier was close to made a foolhardy attempt to break away from her captors. Her bravado resulted in her being brutally killed."

"So, that was Xavier's epiphany, was it?"

"Who knows? But so it would seem. Afterwards, the girl's family helped Xavier escape and find a safe refuge while he prepared to track down the other young girl. During the time he was on the run, he worked covertly with authorities, resulting in a number of members of the mob either being locked away for a long time or permanently 'neutralised'. It appears that apart from all the other fun things the mob was involved in over there, one of their main operations was human trafficking."

"It's not hard to see why Xavier detoured to the path he did. I suppose it might come as some comfort to his parents to know that, in the end, his life wasn't wasted. Do we know if he was successful in tracking down the other missing girl?"

"The abduction of young girls for the sex trade was a key aspect of the mob's human trafficking. There is some suggestion that Xavier discovered the girl he was searching for had been shipped to Australia. How he gathered that information is a mystery, but it is believed he passed on that information to Zali.

Details of exactly what played out after that remain unclear. What has been established is that Zali became instrumental in the girl's escape from where she was being held somewhere in the Sydney area. Using information provided at some time by Xavier, Zali obtained a false passport for the girl under the name Trina Blewett. The girl is now living with an immigrant Croatian family in New Zealand."

"Her interference in the operations most likely put Zali on the mob's 'most wanted' list. While Xavier's final good deeds probably earned him some atonement for his earlier life, they might have resulted in the end of Zali's life." Although I struggled to deal with the emotion the story created, one question still niggled me. "Does anyone know what that Trina Blewett supposedly from their teenage years was all about?" I asked.

Ben shrugged and shook his head. "Nah, not really. All we know is that Zali's middle name was Katrina. When they were younger, teenagers probably, Zali often was in trouble with her parents for various misdemeanours or misbehaviour – for which she would be 'grounded' for various lengths of time. It is believed she explained such situations to Xavier by telling him *Trina blew it again*. Over time, that reduced to a two-word take on the original phrase – *Trina Blewett*.

Over the next day or so, it became obvious nothing more relating to Zali Standish would be forthcoming. My one goal was to resurrect a 'normal' life.

Chapter 26

"Well, that's about it. Another case file all but closed." Ben announced as we sat sipping a pre-dinner drink. "Zali's case is being wrapped up here, but most of the mob we have here, including Christos, have a whole lot of questions to answer in other states and overseas. But, the fallout from Zali's death will keep Neil and his team busy for a while yet."

"Changing the topic, how has Nick settled back into life in uniform?"

"You know he was studying to be a forensic psychologist?" I nodded, and Ben continued. "He has today received unofficial word that his thesis has been accepted. Once it becomes official, Nick will have completed his postgraduate studies. The other bit of news about Nick is that he has applied to join the Service's fast-track program to become a detective. Any thoughts on that?"

"Only that he will make a good detective. He is young and still has a bit to learn, I suspect, but he is no fool and will probably learn fast." I tried for a positive reply that didn't divulge anything Nick and I had discussed.

"Yep, that also seems to be the consensus among those who run that program. And, as a forensics psychologist, I want him in my detective team."

That was about the last I heard regarding Nick until about a month later when he called me. It was an unmistakably excited young man who told me that not only had he been accepted into the program, but he had been assigned to the Millhaven detective squad. His thanks for what I had done for him were profuse, not to mention embarrassing. Now, a week after that phone call, I'm still trying to work out what he thought I had done to merit his thanks.

Whittington Investigations has resumed normal operations. It felt like forever since I had last sat in my city office interviewing prospective clients, but my 'holiday' has resulted in a mountain of new clients and new cases to investigate. The memory of that interview with 'Trina Blewett' and all that followed still haunts the place, and unexpected strange sounds still make me twitchy. But, with each passing day, everything associated with the Trina Blewett case retreats further into the back of my mind. It might never go away completely, but in the meantime, it will remain firmly under lock and key in one of the dark corners of my mind.

Life outside the office also has returned to normal. I'm busy with what I do, as are Ben and Emily, but most evenings, we continue to gather at my place for dinner and to unwind in a safe space.

The End

Other Books by the Author

Sonoma Whittington series:
An Ancient Solution
A Public Service
Missing!
Connections
A Different Obsession
Shattered Illusions
After The Ball
Unholy Secrets
Fateful Reunion
A Dark Place
Layers of Deception

Merivale Retirement Village series:
Close to Home
Growing Pains
One Thing After Another

About the Author

Neive Denis is the creator of the series featuring the Private Investigator, Sonoma (Sonny) Whittington. Neive Denis is the pen name of a writer who was lured from her usual genre to focus on the mystery and excitement that are a part of Sonoma Whittington's world. She came into being specifically for this series and, for the moment at least, intends focusing mainly on stories from Sonny's case files.

This series tells of the intrigue and scrapes – some on occasion life threatening – that are part of the life of Sonoma Whittington, an Australian Private Investigator, based in a Central Queensland coastal city. However, Sonny doesn't confine her escapades to Australia, and that provides Neive with an opportunity to weave some of her other areas of interest into Sonny's hair-raising adventures on occasion.

See more about Neive Denis and her work at

www.eaglemountbooks.com.au/neivedenis

or contact her at

admin@eaglemountbooks.com.au

Thanks

Thank you for reading my book. I hope you enjoyed it. If you did, please consider taking a moment to leave a review at your favourite bookstore or retailer's website.

Thanks

Neive Denis